ALPHA FOXTROT

TRACEY WARD

SHANE LOWRY
SCOUTING REPORT

Position: Offensive Guard
Height: 6-5 **Weight**: 296 **Age**: 25
Born: Everett, WA
College: Nebraska
High School: Cascade High School
Draft Declaration: December 16th

Awards
SENIOR YEAR:
Joe Moore Award - Nebraska Offensive Line
First Team All-American
JUNIOR YEAR:
First Team All-Big10
First Team All-American
SOPHOMORE YEAR:
First Team All-Big-10 Selection
FRESHMAN YEAR:
College Football News First Team
All-American

CHAPTER ONE

SHANE

April 26th
McGinty's Pub
Everett, WA

"When I say 'Shane', you say 'Lowry'! Shane!"

"*Lowry*!" the bar shouts back.

"Shane!"

"*Lowry*!"

I laugh, the thunder of my baritone covering the crowd. They stare up at me where I'm stationed on top of the bar. They have smiles on their faces and stars in their eyes. I'm a god here tonight. I'm Zeus. I'm a legend. I'm a Super Bowl champion come home to let the huddled masses gleefully kiss the ring.

"DJ!" I shout to the scrawny guy with the hipster glasses by the jukebox. "Spin that shit!"

He nods obediently before punching in the numbers I gave him. I know them by heart. This is my jam. It has been since I was seventeen and first started sneaking into this place to hit on women way out of my league and get buzzed on watered down rum and Cokes.

Timbaland's *Throw It On Me* comes bursting out over the speakers throughout the bar. Terry has turned it up for me. It has to be louder than usual to be heard over the crowd gathered around me. I stand tall, my head nearly touching the ceiling, a beer in one hand and the crowd held securely in the palm of the other.

I rap to the song that I know by heart. It's terrible. *I'm* terrible because I'm a white boy and I don't have an ounce of gangster in my big-ass body, but I don't give a shit. I'm not up here to be praised. I'm here to have fun, drink beer, and flirt with every woman in a ten mile radius.

Living in L.A., I don't get this kind of attention. The place is flooded with celebrities, and a football player is less likely to be noticed than, say, Leonardo DiCaprio or Zac-fuckin-Efron. But Everett, Washington is something else. I'm not just a celebrity here. I'm their *everything*. I get recognized at the Costco. The Dari Mart down the street. I can't go into the post office without getting swarmed. Hell, there's been a framed picture of me on the wall in McGinty's Pub since before I started coming here.

Because in Everett, *I'm* the Efron.

When the song ends, I throw my arms wide to embrace the people and the vibe that's bouncing off the walls, ceiling, floor, and cleavage of every sexy slice of pretty peppered through the room. I feel it in my chest. It rumbles under my feet as they applaud and scream, cheering me on. Begging for more.

"Who do you love?!" I demand.

"*Lowry!*"

"Who do you love?!?!"

"*Lowry!*"

I smile, pointing my beer at all of them. "That's what I like to hear. Terry!" I swirl my finger through the air. "I'm covering everyone's tab tonight."

"*Whoo!*"

Terry, an old veteran with long white hair and one big green eye, nods curtly. He's locked down tight. I'm not sure he even has emotions, but the look on his face is as close to joy as I've ever seen. He'll make a killing tonight. It'll probably be the first time since the last time I was here. It's the reason I came to McGinty's tonight and every night I'm in town. Terry's been good to me since before I was me. I owe him the same show of respect. The best way I can manage that right now is with the Black Amex I gave him when I kicked off the party that's now raging through his bar.

I wave at the roaring swarm of people at my feet. "Clear a hole!"

They part like the seas for Moses so I can jump down to the ground in one smooth move. Hands slap me on the back. People bump against me, shouting things I can't quite hear, but I nod and smile. Whatever it is, it's good. That's all I need to know.

Out of the throng surrounding me, a brunette with a high ponytail and flushed cheeks launches herself against me. Her legs go around my waist, her arms around my neck. Her mouth seals solidly over mine.

I don't fight it. I go with it, holding her to my body with both arms around her waist and my tongue sliding home inside her mouth. She tastes like Pabst and kisses about the same; sloppy. She's a warm, wet mess that I need to get away from sooner than later, but for now, just for a second more, I lean into the moment because that's my mantra. It's the way I live every moment of every second of my life. I lean in. I give everything one hundred. Three hundred and sixty-five.

When her kisses get a little too greedy and her hips start to grind against mine, I untangle myself easily from her arms. I set her down gently, giving her a smooth smile to soften the blow. I keep hold of her narrow hips until I see her friends clustered to my right. It's easy to spot them by the collection of cell phones recording every moment of the kiss. That's the girl's bragging rights for the year. She briefly made out with Shane Lowry – Los Angeles Kodiak's left tackle, Everett legend, and *Hustle* magazine's Beefcake of the Year Award winner.

I gently nudge the girl into their general direction. She stumbles safely into their collective arms.

"Get her home safe, okay?" I tell them with a smile.

They giggle and nod. No one forms a coherent sentence in reply.

"Shane! Shane! Hey, man! Can we get a picture?"

I stop to pose for a picture with my DJ and his friends. That one picture turns into ten as more people step up to replace them once the first round disappears. It goes on and on until I'm nearly blind from the flashes.

"Time out, guys!" I shout to the next group of people moving in for their chance at a picture. "I've gotta take a piss. I'll be right back."

My exit is followed by groans of disappointment and proclamations of love. I catch the standard plea from one woman to put a baby in her. Tempting as that offers sounds, I make my move toward the bathroom without looking back.

I don't actually need to pee. I need a break. As much as I love this shit, it gets to you after a while. It's creeping on one in the morning, meaning I've been here for four hours. I've only finished one beer but I've kept that bottle in my hand to keep people from offering to buy me more. Celebrity is a drug. It can feel amazing but it can also screw you. Alcohol makes me stupid and being stupid can get me in a lot of trouble. More than I'm already in. I can't get in a fight tonight, and it's been my experience that the key ingredients for fights are alcohol and testosterone. This bar is drowning in both.

Once I'm in the men's room, I put a guard down on the toilet seat and park my fully clothed ass on it. I pull out my phone to cruise ESPN. Tonight was the Draft and I'm curious who we picked up. I should be in L.A. at the stadium watching with the team, but I needed time away. It's been a crazy couple of months for me.

Before I can find the list of Draft picks for the night, I come across an article about Tom Berg, the quarterback for the Giants. The headline is shouting scandal but I can't believe it. The guy is straight edge as they come.

"You're hiding."

I jolt, nearly dropping my phone in the toilet. "Jesus Christ!"

"Calm down, Sally," Clint drones from the stall next door.

I glare at the mint green wall between us. "How the hell did you know it was me in here?"

"Your shoes. They're stupid. Only an L.A. asshole like you would wear shoes like that."

"Sorry we can't all wear the same Chucks we've had since high school."

"Who are you hiding from?" my brother asks.

"Everyone. I was going flash blind out there."

"Poor baby," he grunts. The toilet flushes loudly as he unlocks his stall. He comes around to stand in front of me with his pants still undone and his shirt covered in what I fuckin' hope is water. His curly brown hair looks wet too. So does his beard. "You know if you didn't rile 'em up," he burps with worried eyes before continuing, "they wouldn't swarm you."

"Have you been drinking from the toilet bowl again?"

"No. I've been vomiting in the toilet bowl again."

"Is that puke on your shirt?"

He glances down at it, swaying on his feet a little. "No. That's a drink. I spilled a drink."

"In your hair?"

Clint touches his head gingerly. He laughs when he

feels the wet locks on his forehead. "That's funny."

"Is it? 'Cause you're the only one laughing."

"I'm the only one with a sense of humor. Dick."

"Button your pants."

"Button your… face."

"Good one."

"Fuck off," he mumbles.

At the sink, he watches himself zip up his pants in the mirror with great determination. Like he's splitting atoms, not putting his penis away.

"You fuck anyone yet?" he asks me absently.

"No," I chuckle.

"Isn't that why you came out tonight? To get your dick wet?"

"No. I came out to have fun."

"Sex is fun.

"How would you know?"

"Ha!" he laughs loud and false. "You're funny."

"You're shit-faced."

"And I'm still funnier than you are."

"A dildo says what?" I ask rapidly.

He frowns at his own face. "Huh?"

"Close enough."

"You know what I hate about you?" he asks the faucet as he washes his hands. "You take the easy route. You always have."

"I'm in the NFL!" I cry indignantly. "How can I have taken the easy route?"

"You were good at it so you did it. Woopty shit! Have you ever tried doing something you're *not* good at? It's hard. But you'd never know that because you don't do things like that. You only do what's easy. Try talking to a girl who doesn't give a shit who you are and see how easy it is to get with her then."

"Dude, I do that in L.A. all the time. That's my life there."

"Then why are you here in Everett?"

I frown at his stupid face in the mirror. "Fuck you, that's why."

"You're here because it's hard to win a girl over with personality instead of fame. You know, like normal guys have to do."

I snort. "Thank God I'm not a normal guy."

"I'd like you better if you were." He wipes his hands on a shredded piece of paper towel before tossing it at the base of the garbage bin, though he didn't mean to. I'm pretty sure he meant to bank it but he has no skill. Sober or sloshed. "But, nope! You're Shane Lowry. You're a nutsack."

"Thanks."

"Nutsack Sally!" he sings in falsetto.

"Alright, buddy, that's enough," I groan, rising from my toilet. I put my hand under his arm to lead him toward the door. "Let's get you home to the basement, you little troll."

He leans on me hard. It should be tough to carry half his weight considering what a chubby shit he his, but I'm stone against him. I work out six days a week, six hours a day. I could carry him out of here princess style if I wanted to.

"Don't you have to get back to your adoring fans?" he slurs thickly.

I steer him toward the back exit, away from the crowd that's waiting to swallow me whole. Clint doesn't need the mob right now. He doesn't need a Super Bowl champ. He needs his big brother. He needs his bedroom, a bucket, and a glass of water on the nightstand, so that's what I'm going to get him. "Nah, man, I'm good for tonight."

He hiccups roughly. "Don't tell Mom I was drinking, okay?"

"Dude, you're twenty-one. She doesn't care."

"Don't tell her!" he panics.

"Whatever," I laugh. "Yeah. I won't tell her."

"Can we get Taco Bell on the way home?"

"Yes."

"Will you buy me a burrito?"

"I'll buy you two, bro."

"Thanks, nutsack."

CHAPTER TWO

SUTTON

April 27th
KBC Studios
Los Angeles, CA

I hate these meetings. Eric always calls them at the oddest hours, as though we're expected to be awake and functioning at any time because that's the way he is. But no one else in the world is like Eric Croft. No one should be. Especially at five-thirty A.M..

"Cocaine." Eric drops the newspaper down on the conference table with a theatrical *thump*. "Tom Berg was caught buying a shitload of it. He's out of the NFL. He's probably going to jail, so needless to say, he's off the show. We can't use him in the special."

"Damn," I mutter under my breath. The cover of the paper stares up at me, mocking me. Crushing my dreams into powder as fine as the dust Tom was planning to snort up his nose.

To my right, Clara rubs my arm consolingly. Over the years, she's become sort of a stand-in mother for me here on the show. She gives good advice that I rarely take, but it's nice to know someone cares enough to try.

"How much is a 'shitload' of coke?" McKay asks Eric curiously.

"I don't know, McKay. A lot."

"But where did you get the measurement of a 'shitload'?"

Eric sighs. He pushes his hand through the thick, black hair hanging down over his forehead. It's graying lightly around the temples. He won't bother covering it because as handsome as he is, Eric isn't vain. He's driven and it's his drive that's made him start to gray at only thirty-six. His face is covered in a meticulous layer of scruff, the sides of his head shaved nearly bald, making the deep blue of his eyes glow like neon. "The paper said it was 'copious amounts'. I took license and translated that to roughly a shitload. Okay?"

It is not okay. McKay doesn't deal in abstracts like 'copious amounts' and 'a shitload'. He likes facts and figures, but he can see that Eric isn't supplying those this morning so he nods in acceptance of the nothing he's been given.

Eric takes a step back from the table to address the entire room. There's a select few of us present at this early hour. Eric, of course, our executive producer. Taj, his underling. Our choreographer and my Mother Hen, Clara. Two lawyers named Bill and Bob, though which is which, I can never remember. The show's talent scout, Becky. McKay, our director. And me, a professional dancer. I'm only here because this Tom news affects me the most. Up until this morning, he was my partner on *Dance the Night Away* as well as one of the most feared quarterbacks in the NFL.

Now he's just some cokehead rotting away in a jail cell.

"The head of the network has already spoken to the Chairman of the NFL," Eric continues. "They both agreed that the best thing for everyone is to find a replacement for Tom as soon as possible. After this meeting, none of you have ever heard of Tom Berg. If you're asked about him, you have no comment. We want to distance ourselves and the show as far from him as possible."

"Who are they going to give us to replace him?" I

ask.

"No one. It's up to us to find someone."

"They're not even going to help?"

"We had enough trouble signing the men we have now," Clara complains. Her wild brown curls dance around her face in agitation. Those curls are a clear indication of her mood. They flow like flowers in the wind when she's laying out our choreography, but they spring like iron coils when she's angry. The way they're doing right now. "They expect us to find a replacement for Tom with only a week to go before the show?"

"Do I even get to meet my partner before the first episode?" I demand.

Eric holds up his hands at us like he's warding off a pack of wild dogs. "Easy, ladies. We'll sort it out."

"How?"

"When?" Clara demands.

"Today. No one leaves this room until we've got the slot filled."

He pushes up the sleeves of his expensive, dark gray sweater. It exposes the tan skin of his arms covered in black tattoos from his younger, wilder days. Days when he drank Bud Light instead of chardonnay and threw his hat into the ring of every singing competition on television. He never won but it got him interested in the business. Now here he is ten years later producing one of the hottest reality shows on the air.

At least, it used to be.

DNA is in a rut. We have been for the past two seasons. Even last year when I won with Jace Ryker, America's favorite rockstar turned Broadway actor, we didn't pull in the ratings the studio was hoping for. Not even close. Viewership is down, voting is down, and, if we don't pull out of this nosedive soon, the whole damn show is going down. That's why we're doing this special season with NFL players. The studio partnered with the NFL to raise money for the Ronald McDonald House Charities through donations from the audience. Each dancer/player pair will advance to the next level in the show based on the judges' votes and the donations made in their name. I thought Tom Berg was going to be a perfect fit. He's handsome, talented, well-known. But after last night's arrest, you can add unemployed to that list.

It might not be long before you can add it to my list of accolades as well.

"You want me to find a replacement in twenty-four hours?" Becky asks Eric warily.

"We're all going to help you. I promise."

Becky doesn't look convinced, and with good reason. No one helped her when she was setting up this special season of the show, calling every NFL player in the book to try and secure enough contestants to even get us off the ground. It's their time off. Most of them want to spend it with their families to make up for all of that time they normally spend on the road or in the gym. Others are worried about getting injured. It's not uncommon for people to pull muscles or even break bones on our show. We've had to replace our share of celebrity contestants in the fifteen years we've been on the air. I've only been one of the dancers for four years and I've seen two replacements happen. Never to me, though. Not until today.

"We need a Kodiak," Taj tells us decisively. "They just won the Super Bowl. Everyone in L.A. knows who they are. They're the kind of name recognition we need to get the viewers excited and they're more likely to participate because they live here. No travel needed."

"I want Colt Avery," I throw in, and not for the first time. This has been my demand since they pitched this charity season with NFL players. Colt Avery is a big-name player with a history of working with children's charities. He's also gorgeous and charismatic. With Colt's good looks and both our fame coming off wins, we're a lock. We'd take the stage by storm every night.

But...

"Colt Avery still says he won't participate," Becky replies sadly. "His fiancé doesn't like the spotlight. He dropped out of his Dairy Queen ads last year and he's only doing charity appearances in closed settings at hospitals. This is the exact opposite of the kind of work he wants to do."

"The opposite of the kind of work *she* wants him to do," I mutter, annoyed.

Clara looks at me with meaning. "After what happened last season, I'm sure Jace Ryker's girlfriend feels the same way."

I roll my eyes. "It was harmless flirting that only went on in front of the cameras. The audience ate it up with a spoon."

"It almost broke them up."

"That's not my fault. That girl is insecure. And it takes two to tango. He flirted with me too. I don't know why I'm the villain."

"I thought you called him a prude because he *refused* to flirt back," Clara points out.

I glare at her, not grateful for the reminder that Jace refused to play ball.

"What other Kodiaks can we talk to?" Eric steps in, redirecting the conversation. He has his own opinions about how I worked the audience to win last season, but I'm glad he's not voicing them today. I don't want to hear them. Not again.

"Trey Domata," Taj suggests.

Becky shakes her head. "He's a hard no. He's the quarterback. He can't get hurt."

"Tom Berg was going to do it and he's a quarterback."

"Yeah, and now we know why. He's snorted almost all of his money up his nose. Did you read the article? He's broke. He said yes to us because he's desperate for money."

"Shit, okay," Taj mutters, thinking. "Kurtis Matthews."

"If you can get him on the phone, you're welcome to ask him."

"Tyus Anthony," Clara suggests, sounding unsure. She and I are in the same boat; we don't know much about football except what we see floating by on the internet. "He and Colt are close, aren't they? He could be good. And he was just in the headlines for something around Christmas, I think."

"Yeah, he had a brain tumor removed," Taj informs her heavily. "He's not on the team anymore."

"He's coaching," McKay corrects.

Eric's brow draws into a tight V. "We don't want a coach. The other names we've managed to sign up are Bs at best. With Tom gone, we don't have an A-Lister in the group. We can't start scraping around for coaching staff. What we need is to find someone people know, for whatever reason. What have we got as far as scandals? Who's in the doghouse with the NFL?"

"I don't know," Taj drones irritably. "Tom Berg?"

The rest of the room chuckles, but Eric's scowl only deepens. "Tom Berg isn't in the doghouse. He's going to jail. Think less salacious than a cocaine bust."

"A player for the Steelers got a DUI last month," McKay offers.

"Get his name."

"Oh, good," I laugh sarcastically. "I'm trading in my junky for a drunk."

"I've got you covered. Don't worry about it."

"I never worry."

"Worrying is all you do."

"Someone in here has to or nothing would ever get done."

"I have ulcers older than you, sweetheart. Leave it to the professionals." He addresses the room with arms wide open. "Come on, people. What else have we got? Who else has bitten the hand that feeds recently?"

Taj snaps his fingers excitedly. "Shane Lowry!"

"Why do I know that name? Who does he play for?"

"He's a Kodiak. He got ejected from the Super Bowl game and he was in a fight in a bar on Valentine's Day about a week later."

"Pass," I declare firmly.

Eric ignores me. "Why was he ejected?"

"There was a quarterback blitz," McKay rattles off mechanically. "A Patriot put a late hit on Domata and talked trash in his face. The guy spit on Domata before Lowry pulled him off and punched him. Lowry broke the Patriot's nose and a tooth before he was ejected. He was fined thirty-thousand dollars for the infraction."

Becky smiles at him in amazement. "How do you know all of that off the top of your head?"

"Because McKay knows everything about everything," Eric answers briskly.

He's getting excited. He sees salvation and he's about to lunge for it, but I'm not so sure it's the right move. Who the hell is this Lowry? Is he some three-hundred-pound doorstop with no coordination and no hope of learning everything I need him to know? Or worse, is he ugly? Fans are shallow. They loved me and Jace last season because we're both very, very pretty. Fans don't vote for ugly, not unless it's a pity thing. And I hate pity.

"What's he like?" I ask McKay. "As a person, what would we be getting ourselves into?"

"He's nice."

Clara scoffs. "He's nice? The guy who got in two fights in two weeks is *nice*?"

McKay shrugs, as if to say, *What do you want from me?*

"I don't care if he's the Pope," I tell the room, but I'm really talking to Eric. "I need someone who can dance. And take orders. And not punch me in the face if I look at him wrong."

"That's a tall order," Becky snickers.

"Is that a jab at football players for being violent or are you saying I have a punchable face?"

"*Punchable face*," Taj and Clara answer together.

I laugh, falling back in my seat. "Well, screw you all. I'm not working with a criminal."

"He's not a criminal," Bill/Bob corrects me, reading from his phone. "He was arrested and charged with Assault for the scuffle on February fourteenth, but the charges were dropped the next day."

"Did he pay the guy to drop them?"

Bill/Bob shrugs his slouching, aged shoulders. "It's unclear. There's no record of it so I can't say for certain."

"But odds are that's what happened," his partner fills in.

"And more than likely, it was a very tidy sum,

considering Mr. Lowry's net worth."

"I'd take a hit from Shane Lowry for that kind of money," Taj mutters into his coffee.

Becky laughs at him. "When you woke up from the coma, you'd have no idea how to spend it."

"He's not that big."

"He's big."

"How big?" I ask nervously.

McKay types quickly on his tablet. I can see the reflection of a website in his glasses. He stops on the blurry image of a guy in a yellow uniform. "Really big."

"Give me a gauge. Are we talking Andre the Giant?"

"The Rock. They're the same height but Shane is a few pounds heavier than Dwayne Johnson."

Eric snaps his fingers sharply at him. "Get me a picture of him. Get me his stats."

McKay types at his tablet for a second before sending the image to the projector overhead. It beams down an image onto the blank wall behind Eric. For a second, another man is superimposed over his face. He's wearing a uniform, a big, boisterous smile, and about a hundred extra pounds of bone and muscle. Eric is dwarfed inside the man until he moves to the side and they're separated. Both of their faces immediately become clear again; absolute opposites in every way. Both shockingly handsome in their own right.

I'm immediately sucked in by Shane's eyes. They're big and blue, almost electric in their intensity, but it's softened by his smile. Everything is. His energy, his girth, the intimidating breadth of his chest and canon-sized curve of his arms is all muted and made bearable by the genuine light of his smile. He wasn't posing when they took this picture. He was laughing, and I think that kind of charisma could work on the dance floor. And the female viewers will go crazy for his face; square, strong, and sexy.

Despite the possibilities, I have to admit that his size scares me. A man that large as my partner could be awkward at best and dangerous at worst. It would be easy for him to hurt me in a hundred different ways without even trying. My stomach churns uneasily at the thought.

"Damn," Taj mutters. His eyes scan the script under the picture, his lips murmuring softly. "Six-foot-five. Two-hundred-ninety-six pounds."

"Sutton is five-foot-three," Clara reminds Eric. "She weighs almost two hundred pounds less than he does. It's not a good pairing."

"We can make it work."

I shake my head sharply. "No way."

"Sutton," Eric coos soothingly.

"Don't even try, Eric. He's violent *and* he's a mountain. I can't work with him."

"If we can get him, you're going to have to."

"Let me swap with someone else. I'll take one of the other players that's not out on bail."

"He's not out on bail," Bill/Bob reminds me.

"He may as well be!" I cry. "He's an animal."

"He was ejected from one game," Eric reasons. His voice is thick with calm, but it's a lie. An illusion. Underneath the act, I can hear how paper thin his patience is on this issue. "He got in one fight at a bar. It happens. It's not like he's a murderer."

"And if he was, you'd still pair me with him if it meant it'd save your precious show."

"Enough," he growls quietly. "Stop being a child. He's a football player. They get into fights. It's what they're paid for. We'll do a background check on him before we sign him. Bill will get to the bottom of the incidents and if he doesn't see any red flags, we're going ahead with Lowry. End of story."

"Two of the other players we have in the competition have priors," Taj tells me calmly. "There's a DUI and a Drunk and Disorderly. They've both been perfect gentleman to their partners so far."

Eric smiles down at me. "You hear that, Sutton? He'll be a perfect gentleman. You have nothing to worry about."

I shake my head angrily, growling at Eric, "You're making a mistake and I'm going to be the one to pay for it."

"We'll see, won't we?"

"I can't believe you're going to do this. You're going to shackle me with some alpha male asshole and the weight of him will sink me by the second episode. I'll go from the champion to a loser."

"That's the risk that everyone runs, and if you can't handle that, you're welcome to quit. We can replace you just as easily as we're replacing Tom today."

His words sting. They hurt like jellyfish kisses across my skin and I rub my arm unconsciously to console myself. But I don't look away. I meet the challenge of his stare head on, and I don't flinch. I don't falter. My mother taught me better than that.

Never let a man hurt you, little darling. They're not worth the salt they're made of.

McKay clears his throat loudly, adjusting his big Clark Kent glasses on his nose. "According to his Twitter, Shane Lowry is in Washington visiting family."

"We have to move fast," Taj adds warily.

The room is watching Eric and I face off. But as quickly as the argument escalated, it deflates. He looks away to the picture of the man glowing on the wall behind him. He crosses his arms pensively, giving the impression that he's deep in thought, but his decision has already been made. Whether I like it or not.

"Get him here by tomorrow morning."

CHAPTER THREE

SHANE

McGinty's Pub
Everett, WA

I come to a slow stop from my run, breathing heavily. It was five miles from my parents' farmhouse to McGinty's Pub on the edge of Everett. The place is as familiar to me as my own home but it looks a million years older. The old gray paint is chipping. Two windows are cracked and held together by duct tape and the stubbornness of the man who placed it. The sign over the front is crooked since one of the screws let go three years ago. Terry still hasn't fixed it. It's a lawsuit waiting to happen because it's only a matter of time before the other screws go too and someone is crushed by the damn thing.

I just hope it's not me. I'm not going out like that.

I yank open the door, surprised to find it unlocked at this hour. It's after noon but the bar doesn't open until four. Still, there's Terry behind the chipped oak barrier between him and the world. He's got a half empty glass of soda and a plate full of cold cuts sitting in front of him. The old, grainy TV set in the corner is playing an episode of *Modern Family* at a murmuring volume.

I hitch my thumb at it. "Can you even hear that?"

"Of course I can," he answers gruffly. "I'm half blind, not half deaf."

"Fair enough."

"You're here for your card?"

"Yup."

"No shoes, no shirt, no service," he drones.

I laugh, looking down at my clothes. I'm wearing running shoes and athletic shorts with my T-shirt tucked into the waistband. My chest is bare. "Are you serious? We're the only ones here."

He nods to the sign by the door, popping a slice of salami into his mouth.

I know what the sign says, but I look at it anyway. *NO SHOES. NO SHIRT. NO SERVICE.*

"I ran here," I explain, yanking my shirt from my waistband. "I got hot."

"I'm sure the ladies love that story, but I'm not interested."

"Are you interested in me signing a receipt for last night?"

"Are you interested in seeing that fancy black card again?"

I grin as I pull my shirt down over my head. It fights me, sticking to the sweat that's running down my tan chest, stomach, and back. California has been great for my body. I'm in the best shape of my life, cut like I've never been before because of all that healthy living they do out there. I open my arms to him, exposing myself for inspection. "Shoes. Shirt. Service?"

"We're closed."

I drop my arms with a sharp *clap!* of my hands against my thighs. "Damn, Terry. You're extra surly today. What's crawled up your butt?"

He looks at me with his one remaining eye. "Is that a gay joke?"

"No."

"It sounded like one."

I gesture to the TV behind me. "You've been watching too much *Modern Family*. After a few hours of that show, everything sounds like a gay joke."

"Hmmm," he grunts in mild agreement. He reaches down under the counter to pull out a lock box. It takes a couple tries to get the right key in the lock, but when he does he pulls out a stack of receipts with my card rubber banded to the top. "People took advantage last night."

I take a seat on the stool across from him, leaning my arms on the bar. "I knew they would," I reply mildly.

"Someone tried to buy the entire top shelf on your dime."

"Did you let them?"

"No."

"You should have."

"You shouldn't be throwing your money away like you do," he scolds disapprovingly.

I smile wide. "I'm not worried about it, Terry. Where do you need me to sign?"

"You don't want to know the total?"

"I don't know. Do I?"

He snorts, nearly smiling. "I doubt you'd care either way."

"I love how well you know me."

Terry hands over the final receipt. The sum of the stack attached to my card. I glance at the total before adding a five hundred dollar tip and signing my name with a flourish. Terry shakes his head. More disapproval.

"You shouldn't do that," he tells me about the tip.

I click the pen closed, sliding it to him across the bar. "Yeah, and you shouldn't have served me when I was only seventeen, but you did."

"No. I didn't."

"Okay. Cool. And I didn't tip you just now."

He gives me a meaningful look that I don't actually

understand, but he drops it. My receipt goes into the register, my card goes into my pocket, and Terry goes back to watching *Modern Family*. He doesn't invite me to stay, but he fills a glass with ice water and puts it halfway between us on the bar. I smile, drinking it slowly while I finish the episode with him in silence. He snickers a few times but otherwise I can't tell if he's awake, asleep, or dead. Terry isn't much of a people person. I think he actually kind of hates people, but their vices are how he makes a living, so he suffers them without complaint. He suffers me longer than most, a badge I wear with pride.

When the credits roll, I smack the bar with satisfaction. "It was good to see you, man. Until next time?"

"Hmmm," he grunts, uninterested.

"So surly. I love it."

As I'm standing to leave, Terry surprises me by offering me his hand over the bar. I hesitate, suppressing a smile as I take it. We shake firmly with our eyes locked before he lets go abruptly.

"Take care of yourself, son," he tells me quietly.

As quickly as he released me, he leaves me. He disappears into the office. I'm left alone with the quiet squeak of the sign struggling in the wind outside and a plate of warm meat sitting neglected on the bar. It's a lonely feeling. It's quintessentially Terry, like I'm living a moment in another man's shoes, and I'm a little ashamed at how uncomfortable it makes me. I'm quick to head for the door and the sunlight waiting outside.

Once I'm out, I pop my shirt back off. I'm not sweating anymore, but I will be. It's a long run on country roads back to my parents' place and the day is just starting to heat up. It's nothing compared to the heat in Los Angeles, but the rain on the road is starting to steam, rising in low waves that wrap around my ankles eagerly.

As I stand on the side of the road stretching, mentally prepping for the last leg of my workout, an old black Jetta rolls by slowly. Girls who can't be older than high school age lean out the window to whistle at me.

"Hey, sexy!"

"Wooo!"

"Take it *all* off!"

I stand up straight to smile as they pass. I flex my chest, making my pecs dance for them. They laugh and squeal, ducking back inside the car as the driver speeds them away.

It's a stroke that my ego doesn't need, but I'm not complaining. I'd never say no to a good stroking.

Back home, I sneak into the house without anyone seeing me. It's not an easy thing to do with these old floorboards that try to rat you out with every step, but I mastered that shit when I was fifteen and first started sneaking out. Sneaking in is a hell of a lot easier.

I check my phone before I jump in the shower. I have texts from Colt, Sam, a girl named Miranda who I think was at the bar last night but I don't remember giving her my number, and Chris, my agent. I check his first, hoping for good news.

He doesn't disappoint.

New contract came in. It's final. You're locked in with the soon-to-be Las Vegas Kodiaks for six years and $56 million.

"Holy shit," I whisper to myself. "Holy fucking shit."

Where does that put me? I text him with shaking fingers.

Chris is quick to answer. Like all good agents, he's

never far from his phone.

You're now the second highest paid offensive guard in the NFL.

"Yes! Suck it, Kelechi Osemele!" I punch my fist at the sky, brimming with energy I can't expel fast enough. "Yeah!"

"Quit shouting!" Dad bellows from downstairs.

I close my mouth but I jump up and down on the floor, dancing through the room erratically with a smile so big it makes my skin scream. "Fucking yeah," I chant quietly. "Fucking yeah. Fucking yeah."

"Quit stomping!"

My phone pings in my fist. *There's more.*

I laugh, typing quickly, *More money? I'll take it!*

This one's not about the money. It's the exposure.

Playgirl finally called to get me on the cover?

No. Dancing the Night Away called. They want you to take Tom Berg's place as a contestant this season.

What happened to Tom?

My phone rings. It's Chris calling. He's sick of typing.

"Talk to me," I answer briskly.

"Don't you read? This Tom shit is everywhere right now."

"I've been working out all morning. I haven't had a chance to sit down and scroll."

"He was busted for cocaine last night," he tells me solemnly. "He's out of everything. The competition, the NFL, his damn mind. I heard he punched a cop. He's toast, Shane."

"That's crazy. What the hell happened to him?"

"Cocaine," he repeats forcefully. "He was high out of his mind when he was busted. He's probably still sobering up as we speak. He's going to find a whole lot of ugly when his brain starts working again."

"So what the hell? *DNA* wants me? Why?"

"This season is packed with NFL players."

"Yeah, I heard. It's a charity thing for the Ronald McDonald House Charity, right? The houses around hospitals for sick kids' families to stay in."

"Right. Tom was partnered with last year's winner, Sutton Roe. But now that he's out, they want you to come in and fill his shoes. With your status as a Super Bowl champion and Sutton coming back as last year's winner, you guys are practically a lock to win again this year."

"Yeah, assuming I can dance."

"Can you?"

"I have no idea," I laugh. "I can hold my own at the bar but they do ballroom shit, don't they?"

"You don't watch the show?"

"No. My mom loves it, though."

"Sit down and watch some episodes with her. Actually, no, don't," he corrects himself quickly. I can hear him typing at his computer rapidly. "If you're down to do it, we need to get you back in L.A. by tonight. They want you to start shooting reel for the first episode tomorrow morning."

"Why the rush?"

"They start dance rehearsals on Thursday. Ideally, you would have met your partner and gotten the rundown on the show by now, but we're late to the party. We're playing catch up."

I run my hand over my mouth. I taste salt on my lips that burns like the fire in my muscles screaming from the beating I've given them today. "Do they know about the fights?" I ask reluctantly.

Chris is quiet for a second. He doesn't even touch his keyboard, which is crazy for him. "Yeah, man, they know. But they're willing to work around them. They asked me a lot of questions about your volatility but I played it off. I told them you're cool as ice."

"My volatility?" I repeat slowly.

"It means—"

"I know what it means, Chris. I clear my throat, choking down that word. "What would I have to do to be on the show? Will they teach me anything or do I go out there and make an ass of myself?"

"Sutton is a professional. She'll teach you everything you need to know. You should look her up," he tells me encouragingly. "She's hot. You'll love her. Plus, she's good. She's a retired Broadway star."

"Retired? How old is this chick?"

"She's young. Dancers are like football players – they retire early."

"You seem pretty pro-*DNA*. Should I even think about it?"

"No," he answers honestly. "This will be good for you. It will help erase some of that negative press we've been getting and it could change the new owner's perception of you and that ejection."

I frown at my feet. "My contract is in. I thought that wasn't an issue."

"You're going to be with them for six years, Shane. They could make it an issue any time they want."

I feel anxiety rush through my veins. It's a strange feeling for me. I don't worry about much, especially not out on the field. I'm one of the best guards in the NFL. I'm bigger than almost any man they face me off with, and if I'm not bigger, I'm stronger. No one gets by me. I earn my paycheck every second of every day – no question. No worries.

But then came the ejection at the Super Bowl and a

scrap in a bar too soon after, and that put me under a microscope. Everybody started talking about whether or not I'm too reckless. Too 'volatile'. I hate that word. I read it next to my name a lot these days and I'm getting tired of it. It's just something people say when they want to judge instead of understand.

"I'll do it," I tell him firmly. "Get me a flight out as soon as you can. I'll be ready to go."

"It's a good move, man. You won't regret it."

"I never regret anything."

"I'll send you your flight info as soon as I have it."

"Thanks, Chris."

"And Google the girl. Seriously." I can hear the smile in his voice when he adds, "You'll love her."

When Chris and I say goodbye, I hang up my phone and toss it onto my unmade bed. My room is a mess. Once I got home a month ago, my suitcase exploded over the small space. I've covered every surface with my shit and I have to make sure to get it spotless before I leave tonight. My mom would never complain to me about it, but I'd feel like an asshole if I left it for her. She has better things to do than clean up my natural disaster zone.

I yank off my clothes, tossing them onto the already massive pile on the floor. I'm getting that sticky feeling you find when you sit for too long and the sweat from your workout starts to dry on your skin like you've spent a day at the beach. Only instead of swimming and drinking in the sun, I've been running, lifting, and squatting since the sun came up. I can't stand the idea of not working out, especially when I know the team is back in L.A. training without me. I feel separated from that side of my life in a way that's almost painful. It's weird to feel homesick when you're home. That's the curse of growing up. You leave your parents' house when you go out to start your own life and you assume it will always be there for you when you need it again. And it is, but it's never the same because you're not the same. You never will be again.

When I go back to L.A., I'll still feel homesick. It will just be reversed. I'll miss my parents and my stupid brother instead of my teammates. I'll miss the lumpy bed in my old room and the lavender smell of the laundry detergent instead of my long leather sofa and marble soaker tub. It's like there are two halves to my life. I love them equally but they don't always mesh, meaning I'll never feel completely whole.

It's a thought I try not to dwell on too much. It's depressing as shit.

Just as I'm stepping out of the shower, Mom bellows up the stairs, "Shane! Clint! Lunch!"

"Coming!" Clint yells.

"Wash your hands! Both of you!"

"I just took a shower!" I shout back.

"I don't care! You're both disgusting animals and you need to wash your hands!"

"Listen to your mother!" Dad yells in support.

"Fine! I'm doing it!"

"Stop shouting!" Mom practically screams.

Last year, I spent Easter Sunday at Colt's house with his family. His stepsister wore too much lipstick and smiled at me the entire time. I felt like a pedophile without ever touching her, but that wasn't the weirdest part of the trip. The part that threw me was how quiet the house was. If someone was in another room, you went to that room to talk to them. When they ate dinner, they sat down at the table together. No TV. Just people looking at each other over ham, rolls, and matching silverware that looked like it came from QVC. No one swore. Not once. Not even Colt who usually has a mouth like a dumpster behind a sex shop. It was so far from my family, I didn't know what to do with myself. In the end, I drank heavily and didn't shit the entire time I was there.

When I get downstairs, Mom is in the kitchen filling plates with sandwiches and chips from an off-brand bag that's dangerously toeing the line of copyright infringement. I'm sure Ruffles wouldn't be too pleased about the teal and tan look of Fluffles.

She smiles at me over her shoulder when she hears me come in. "You're the first one in. You get your pick."

"What are my options?"

"Ham or turkey."

"Ham."

She nods to a plate at the end of the new marble countertop. I had it installed for her this Christmas when I paid for a total remodel of the farmhouse. It's still in progress in other parts of the house, but the kitchen was the first thing to change. Mom loves it so much she joked about bringing her bed down to sleep in here. "There you go."

"Thanks." I pick up the plate without touching the food on it.

Mom notices right away. She pauses, her hand full of Fluffles hovering over the next plate. "What's the matter, Shane?"

"I have great news, good news, and bad news. Which do you—"

"Bad news first," she interrupts quickly.

"I'm leaving in a few hours. I'm going back to L.A."

"Why? What happened?"

"The good news." I smile proudly, my heart

thumping rapidly in anticipation of her reaction. "Chris got a call from *Dance the Night Away*. They want me to take Tom Berg's place on the show this season."

Mom, a fifty-year-old woman, bounces up and down excitedly like a kid on the playground. "Are you kidding me?!"

"No joke," I laugh.

She hugs me hard, her small body like a ghost against mine. "Shane, that's amazing! I can't believe it! Oh Shane. I've never been more proud of you."

"Thanks for that," I laugh halfheartedly.

Mom steps back to look up at me with apology in her eyes. "I'm sorry. I've been prouder. I've just never been so excited. That's what I meant to say."

"I know, Mom."

"Sorry, baby," she repeats seriously.

I give her a smile that tells her it's fine. "Don't sweat it, Mom. I know what you meant."

"This is so fast. The new season starts in less than two weeks."

"I know. That's why I'm leaving tonight. I have to meet my partner tomorrow morning."

She rises up on her toes eagerly. "Who are you getting?"

"Sutton Roe?"

Mom's blue eyes go wide. "She won last year."

"That's what I hear."

"Oh my God. So this was the great news, right? What's the good news?"

"*DNA* is the good news." I cock my eyebrow at her. "Can you handle the great news?"

She laughs shakily. Her hand goes to her heart like she's not sure her body can hold it inside. "I don't know. Try me."

"My new contract with the Kodiaks is in. Six years. Fifty-six million."

"Holy shit," she breathes raggedly.

Mom doesn't swear. Not unless somebody died. That's the last time I heard her do it – when grandma passed away and she was so heartbroken she couldn't find the emotions to deal so she looked for words instead. She let lose one single, agonized curse that I can still hear like she's whispering it in my ear. It was leaden with loss and pain that I never want to see her suffer through again.

"Shane," she whispers.

I put my hand out to her to steady her, but she bypasses it quickly. She hugs me again, this time softer and somehow harder. It's tighter than before. There's a disbelieving desperation to the way she's holding onto me, like she's not sure I'm real.

"I'm gonna need it," I joke, looking for a way to lighten the feel of her. "Clint's tuition went up this year and I just paid a small fortune to Terry for the party last night."

Mom steps back to look up into my eyes. Hers are brimming with tears that make mine feel like I'm walking through smoke. "You're a good man, Shane. I knew it when you were just a kid giving hugs to strangers who you thought looked sad."

"Were they mostly women?"

"You're a good man," she repeats. She's not letting me joke my way around this. She's holding me steady with her gaze and her small hands on my arms. "And I'm incredibly proud of you."

"I know, Mom."

"I really hope you do, baby."

CHAPTER FOUR

SUTTON

Carmichael Condominiums
Los Angeles, CA

I miss New York. There are days when I feel like I'm okay in L.A., but most of the time I miss the East Coast so bad I can taste the sour sorrow in the back of my throat. It rises like bile, choking me. Suffocating me. I feel like crying but I can't because that will give me puffy eyes and I can't look tired. My mom taught me that. She taught me how to do my hair. My makeup. She taught me how to sing and how to dance. She taught me how to eat right, then eat less, then how to eat next to nothing at all without fainting. It's a science. An artform known only to the few dedicated enough to their craft to manage it.

And I am dedication personified.

It's probably my own fault that I'm so small. My diet has never given much to my body for growing. It was in my genetic code to be bigger than I am. My dad is tall. Over six foot. My mom is only a few inches shorter, and my grandparents on her side were large, round people with full, smiling cheeks. They're the reason Mom doesn't like to eat. They're also the reason she doesn't smile too much. It gives you lines, she says. Emotions age you; good or bad. Worry, anger, frustration, happiness, sadness, hate, love. If you don't feel them, you don't write them on your skin. You can't wear them on your sleeve, and that means you'll always be pretty and you'll never get hurt, and that's the trick. That's the magic my mother taught me.

The art of nothing.
Feeling it. Being it.
Knock, knock, knock.
Attracting it.

Three rapid, decisive knocks. I know who it is on the other side of my door before I open it, and that knowledge gives me pause. It should give me power, but it makes me feel weak. He has that effect on me. On everyone.

I open the door with a carefully blank expression. "Eric."

He smiles and my insides are melted butter that boils until it nearly burns. I can't name this feeling inside me; the feeling I get whenever I look at him. I feel excited and afraid. Angry and anxious. Aroused and revolted. How does he do it? More to the point, *why* does he do it? Because, make no mistake, everything that Eric Croft does is intentional.

His smile is casual, like he doesn't know about the mess I am inside. "I came to apologize."

I eye the emerald green bottle in his hand. I can't read the label but I can tell by the thickness of the gold foil over the cork that it's expensive. Eric will want me to notice that. Spending money is how he shows he cares.

"What are you apologizing for?" I ask. "Forcing Shane Lowry on me? Telling me I'm expendable?"

"Which would make you the happiest?"

"Both of them, and more."

"Everything, Sutton. I'm here to apologize for everything."

It's bullshit but it sounds pretty, so I let him in. I open the door wide enough for him to pass by me into my nearly empty apartment, but the space won't feel any fuller with him in it. That's not why he's here. In fact, he's not here at all. He's a ghost who will float through my world and leave without a trace.

Eric's smile widens as he walks through the door. He pauses to kiss my left temple softly, making the scarcest of sounds against my skin.

It makes me flinch.

It's late. He should be at the office or at home. He shouldn't be here. He should never be here, but suddenly there he stands in my small kitchen. An unwelcome intruder that I invited in. He opens and closes cupboards rapidly, rummaging through the unfamiliarity until he finds my glassware. There are no champagne flutes. He lets his disappointment show in the set of his shoulders before reaching for two wine glasses instead.

I follow him with my eyes, carefully putting the small island between us.

"You seem nervous, Sutton," he comments without looking at me.

I shrug, smoothing my warm palms over the cold granite countertop. "I'm worried about the show."

"You're going to be fine."

"You don't know that."

"Would I ever let anything bad happen to you?"

I laugh at how ridiculous that question is.

He lets himself happen to me. He is the baddest of bad things.

Eric doesn't acknowledge it. "I got him."

"Colt Avery?"

He turns, smiling as he expertly spins the cage around the cork. "Shane Lowry agreed. He's flying back from Washington tonight."

My body sags with disappointment. "I don't want

him."

"You're not honestly afraid of him."

"What if I am? Will you get rid of him?"

"No, because I don't believe it. You're not afraid of anything. You're definitely not afraid of this guy."

"I'm afraid of losing."

"So is everyone else on that stage. It doesn't make you any different or special."

"What an incredibly sweet thing to say," I reply sarcastically.

"Do you need your ego rubbed? Is that the problem?"

"The problem is I don't want to work with him."

"I heard you, but you know you can't always get what you want, Sutton. Sometimes you have to be satisfied with what you have."

A quick maneuver of his hands and the cork pops free. He doesn't spill a drop. The effervescent gold spills into one wine glass, then the next. He's generous. Too generous. I don't plan on drinking half of what he's giving me. He hasn't even asked if I want it, and that is so deeply Eric that I can barely stand it.

He watches me closely as he slides my glass across the island. He's respecting the boundary I've put between us. He knows what I'm doing, and I know what he's doing, and seeing as we're working at odds with each other, I'm curious to see how the night plays out. There's not much of it left. Whatever is going to happen, it will happen quickly. It always does with us.

"Are you angry with me?" he asks, his voice subdued.

"No," I lie, but it's alright. Neither of us believes me.

"I know he's not what you were hoping for."

"Not even close."

"Shane will be a good partner and you're still the favorite. You have a good chance of winning again this year. You'll rise to the occasion. You always do."

"You don't know that."

"Yes. I do. Because I know you."

I shake my head defiantly. "You don't know anything about me."

"I know more than most," he argues gently. Deeply.

I wish he wouldn't talk like that; like we're so familiar with each other. I wish we didn't know each other at all. I wish a lot of things weren't what they are, but wishing is like loving. It's idiotic.

"When do I meet him?" I ask briskly.

Eric takes a slow drink of his champagne, tempting me to do the same. "Tomorrow morning. Sanderson Park."

"Why not his stadium?"

"We couldn't get clearance to film there in time. The team has new owners this year. They're instituting new rules with a lot of red tape. You'll meet him at Sanderson where the team practices during the offseason. The cameras will be there. He'll show you how to throw a football, you'll show him how to Foxtrot, and we'll be back on track before you know it."

"What time?"

"Eight. On the dot."

I glance at the clock on the stove behind him. It's eleven now. "It's late. You should go."

He laughs quietly into his glass in reply. I watch a strand of dark hair wrestle loose from the gel trying to contain it. It slips glossy and black over his brow in the most impossibly tantalizing way. I want to brush it aside. I want to feel it slip cold between my fingers as his skin burns against mine. I want to feel that breathless excitement I get when he looks me dead in the eyes with all the seriousness in the world and stirs something devilish inside of me.

I want what I should not, *will not*, have.

Temptation; that's what this visit is. He came here tonight because he wants me and he's tempting me. I can taste it in the air buzzing with champagne bubbles and the rich, heady scent of Eric's cologne.

This is Eric being sweet. Smiling and giving gifts. Waiting patiently. But there's another side to him. A greedy side that takes what it wants without thought or apology. I'm afraid of that side of him, but the sick thing – the part that makes me hate myself every single time – is that I'm attracted to it too. I never tell him to leave. I never ask him to go slower or softer. I want him but I hate him. I hate me when I'm with him. Still, I never tell him no because I'm lonely. It's pathetic but it's true. That's my fault. It's my failing.

And Eric knows it.

"What are you thinking about?" he asks me.

I take a thin breath. "You."

"Good thoughts or bad thoughts?"

"Both."

He grins. He puts down his glass. "Tell me a good thought."

"I'm glad you apologized."

"Good." He steps around the side of the island. "Tell me a bad thought."

My hand tightens on the stem of my glass. "You're an asshole."

"You always say that."

"You always live up to the title."

"I'm trying to make up for that."

"Why tonight?"

"Why not tonight?"

I don't have an answer for that, but the fact that he answered my question with a question tells me that he does. He knows why he's here. Something sent him here. Something I said or did or didn't say. Didn't do. Something in the way his coffee smelled this morning or the sound his change made when hitting the top of his desk when he emptied his pockets for the night. Something, nothing, everything brought us here to this moment, and there was no stopping it. No telling what would set us off.

"Tell me another good thought," he commands.

I lick my lips, watching his. He has perfect teeth hiding behind them. Straight and pearl white against the pink of his tongue that tastes like lemon drops. "I don't have one."

"That's cruel."

"So are you."

He steps in close to me. Only inches separate us but they feel too far to cross. "We're perfect for each other."

"You shouldn't be here."

"But I am. Because you want me to be."

He's right. I was hoping and dreading that he'd come here. I wanted his dead eyes and his hard body wrapped in a cashmere sweater that I can peel off him like paper from a present under the Christmas tree. I'll hate us both in an hour, but for now, this is what I need. It's what I want in the sickest, ugliest part of myself that my mother made for me. She did it to keep me safe, to distance me from a life that is designed to kill young women from the inside out, but she went too far. She poisoned me too deeply trying to inoculate me and now I'm just a husk. A shell of a person with base desires that fly in the face of good and decent society.

Eric leans in until he's hovering over me, his lips nearly touching mine as he whispers, "Tell me a very bad thing. Tell me one dirty, dark, wicked thing."

I lean my head back, trying to find air. He follows me. He chases me, and suddenly I'm dizzy with anticipation of what we both know is coming. The hard stone of the island digs into my back as he leans me over it, trapping me. Caging me with the push of his body until I'm desperate and panting. Wanting.

"I fucking hate you," I breathe against his mouth.

"I know you do." He kisses me once, chastely. "But I fucking love you, Roe."

How can you love something you hate? How can you want someone you despise?

It's easier than you'd think.

Eric crashes his mouth on mine, his tongue diving inside to taste my own, and it's as easy as air. It feels as right as it is wrong, but the ugly won't come until later. We're both beasts fully capable of compartmentalizing our lives. This feels good, so this is good. When it feels bad, when the guilt hits afterward, then it will be bad. But in the moment, all we know is that it's what we want and neither of us is any good at denying ourselves.

Eric's hands take hold of my waist, hoisting me up onto the island like I weigh nothing. Like I'm a doll he's playing with because, in his mind, that's probably exactly what I am. A plaything. The action makes me anxious. My hands go to cover his as though I'll keep them still and patient, but I can't. He shakes me off and takes hold of what he wants without apology or permission.

I tangle my hands in his hair. I thread my fingers through the stiff locks that taunted me all day and I breathe a small sigh of relief at the feeling. It's only a matter of seconds before my top is off. My bra is gone. He strips me down to nearly nothing, inside and out, but he is left whole. Wholly dressed. Wholly in control.

Eric pulls a condom from his pocket. It's not in his wallet. He doesn't fumble for it as though he's unsure he has one. He probably put it there while he was out in his car getting ready to come up here because he knew he'd need it. He'll take it with him when he leaves along with the empty champagne bottle and my goddamn dignity. All he'll leave behind is the wetness between my thighs, the faint smell of his cologne, and the self-loathing I'll suffer for days after. Because, make no mistake, I hate this. I hate him. But most of all, I hate myself, so when he slides the condom on and roughly pushes my panties aside, I don't complain. I don't care. I let him do what he wants to me because that's the only way I know. I open my legs wide and I take him into the most hallowed part of me, aching in the hollow empty of my chest even as I gasp in delight.

He takes hold of the back of my head, forcing my mouth against his. His hips thrust hard against mine, driving him deeper inside me where it almost hurts. Eric isn't a big man, but I'm a small woman. His body pushes me to my limits and a little further, merging pain with pleasure in a way that leaves me breathless.

I'm mewling against his mouth, struggling to breathe through my nose that's pressed against his face. I'm not getting enough air. I'm desperate for a deep, solid breath, but he won't let me have it. He keeps his lips sealed over mine as he pushes me to the edge, dragging me with him, and then, just as I feel like I'll faint or scream or kill him to get air, his forehead falls against mine, and I'm free.

"Ahhh!" I gasp and scream, inhaling sharply only to exhale almost immediately on a wave of pleasure that roars through me like an ocean in a storm. I'm clawing at him but my fingers can't find purchase. I only get soft cashmere and frustration. Agony and ecstasy.

Eric grunts mutedly, thrusting into me twice more before going rigid. He shudders once, softly, before sighing.

Then he's gone. He's withdrawing and I'm left cold and shattered in the semi-darkness of my empty little apartment.

I close my legs slowly, cupping my hand over my throbbing core as I ride out the last of my pleasure. It already feels like it's gone. As though trying to hold onto it is like trying to capture sunlight in your hand.

Eric rips a paper towel off the roll behind me. He gingerly takes the condom off and wraps it inside, stuffing the small parcel in his pocket. When he's done, when his dick is back in his pants and his hair is perfectly mussed again, he looks at me with a wolfish grin.

"I missed you."

I shake my head, my eyes already starting to sting. "I hate you."

"So you keep saying." He kisses me without fear. Without regret. "But this is where we always end up. This is where we'll always be, Sutton. Right here, like this. Together."

"No."

"Yes."

"I'll tell your wife," I spit bitterly.

Eric doesn't flinch. I've made that threat before but I've never followed through, no matter how badly I wanted to. "We both know that's a lie."

"*This* is a lie," I choke out, feeling angry and so

frustrated I can't see straight. "We're a lie. I don't want you and you don't love me."

"I do love you. More than you know."

"Then leave me alone."

Eric shakes his head sadly. He grabs the half-empty bottle of champagne off the counter, letting it hang heavily at his side, as though the meager weight is too much for him to carry.

"I can't," he vows, his eyes holding mine steadily. "And you don't want me to."

"I want this to stop," I protest weakly.

"If that were true, it wouldn't keep happening."

"This was the last time."

"I know, baby." He kisses my cheek softly. "Every time is the last time."

CHAPTER FIVE

SHANE

April 28th
Sanderson Park
Los Angeles, CA

Today is a trip. I flew into town last night only to find out I was due at the park at seven in the morning. It's a rough turnaround but I've done worse. I've played against the Packers with zero sleep and a hangover, and I still didn't let anything slip. I can do a day in the park with a pretty girl any day of the week.

If she shows up.

The rest of the crew was here when I drove into the parking lot. Two cameras, a small food table, and a crowd of people easily twenty strong were waiting on me. I learned a lot of names and remember about a third of them, but one of the guys was definitely a lawyer. He was here for ten minutes to make sure the contracts he sent over last night were signed and in order. Once I convinced him they were, he was gone. He took a donut off the table and disappeared behind the deep, black windows of a gold BMW. I snagged a maple glazed for myself and parked on a bench warming in the sun. That's where I've been for the last half hour. Waiting.

The crew is making themselves busy. They run in and out of the dappled sunlight under the trees, looking for the best lighting. The best angles. They have me stand in a spot out on the field for about five minutes to make sure they've got my framing right, but then I'm sent back to my bench with an Evian and a promise that things will be rolling soon.

They aren't.

Twenty minutes later and we're still sitting around with our thumbs up our asses. By then, the crew looks as bored as I feel. People start milling around and chatting. I learn names again, this time making sure to repeat them so they stick. I sign a few autographs for fans that approach me. I spend ten minutes playing a quick but furious game of touch football with a group of eight year olds. It's a mix of girls and boys, and there's one spry little beauty that's got serious moves. She legit skirts by me to score a touchdown at the end of the game. It wasn't a mercy. I seriously couldn't get my hands on her. I sign the ball for her and tell her to call me in ten years when she's looking to go pro. I promise to hook her up with my agent.

"Cute kids," Deb comments when I come back to the shade where the crew is waiting.

I nod, running my hand through my hair to cool my scalp. The day is heating up and sprinting in jeans has never been my favorite feeling. "Yeah, they're pretty cool."

"Do you have any?"

"God, no," I laugh. "I'm not done being a kid yet. I can't have any. Do you?"

"Three. All girls."

"I have two," Jared, a guy with sideburns and a glaring Hawaiian shirt, chimes in. "A boy and a girl. The boy is hell of a lot easier than the girl."

"That's what I hear," Deb says sullenly. She doesn't sound depressed, not exactly. More like someone who ordered their food only to find out moments later that there was something way better on the menu. You'll eat what you got and you'll like it, but part of you is left wondering what if…

"What celebrities have you slept with?" Jared asks me suddenly. He says it like he's asking what kind of car I drive or what insurance I have on my house. It's so casual, I wonder for a second if I heard him right.

"What?" I chuckle reflexively.

"Jesus, Jared," Deb groans. "Do you have to ask everyone that?"

"It's interesting."

"To you. It's insulting to the people you ask."

"Whatever."

Jared looks at me expectantly.

I stare back blankly, giving him nothing. And not only because there's nothing to give, but because Deb is right. That's an irritating question.

The truth is, I haven't slept with any celebrities. Colt has but Colt used to be a slut, so apples and oranges, I guess. I'll make out with just about any girl who's willing, but I've been a lot more cautious with who I go to bed with. It's not a religious or moral thing. I just don't do it for the hell of it. For me, it feels better when you're connected with the person. It feels good even if you're not, and if I'm hard-up enough I'll fuck a bagel, but it's better when you feel something for the person. And there's only so much emotion you can muster for a cinnamon/raisin with extra Schmeer.

Suddenly, everyone's walkies come alive.

"*Sutton has arrived,*" a man's voice says briskly.

Jared gives me a consoling look. "She's here."

"Oh, she made it, huh?" I ask dryly.

"Looks like it. We need you over on the field ASAP for the first meeting."

"Well, we better hurry then."

I take my time heading over to the trash can next to

me to toss my empty Evian bottle inside. I slowly wipe my hands on my jeans to dislodge the remnants of sugar from my donut, carefully wiping my mouth when I'm done with my hands.

Blake, a skinny guy with a clipboard and anxious eyes, hops from foot to foot next to me. "Mr. Lowry."

"Yep," I answer, heading toward the field with slow, even steps.

Blake follows closely at my heels.

"I'm sure there's a good reason for the delay," he promises me.

"She's almost an hour late. That doesn't drive you guys nuts?"

"There has to be a good reason."

Whether there is or not, they'll make sure I hear one. Odds are this chick is a diva running on her own schedule, but they'll tell me she had a flat tire. She got stuck in traffic. She pulled over on the expressway to save a puppy that was running down the middle of the road. Whatever the reason, it won't be her fault.

"Where exactly do you need me?" I ask my guide. I make sure to soften my tone because it's not his fault. I shouldn't make him or anyone else pay for it by being a dick.

"This way, Mr. Lowry."

He leads me to where the cameras are set up. They've propped up big silver shields to bounce the sun where they want it. I stand in the center on the mark that they give me and listen patiently to my instructions.

Deb, the director, is the one to give them to me. She has brown hair and librarian glasses that make her full face look even bigger than it is. She's pretty, though, for an older woman. Her eyes are soft and green.

"Sutton is coming in through the parking lot over there," she explains, gesturing over her shoulder to where I can see more members of the crew swarming. "We'll be filming her reaction and yours to the first meeting. This is very important. We have to get the first time you meet down on film for the first episode."

"Got it." I roll my shoulders back, standing to my full height. "How do you want me to react to her?"

"Naturally. This is all supposed to be very organic."

"Yeah, well, organically, I'm annoyed," I chuckle. "We've been waiting for her to get here for an hour. You want me to play that for the cameras? Like I'm pissed?"

"If that's how you're feeling, yes. Everything should be natural. Like I said."

"Aren't you annoyed?"

She smiles slightly. "Mr. Lowry, if I got annoyed every time I faced a delay, I'd never feel anything else. Eventually you have to go numb."

"That's not really my style."

"Then that's what you should play to the cameras. Your style, no matter what it is."

I shrug, stuffing my hands in my pockets. "It's your show."

"When she gets here, you'll need to make conversation. Talk about how nice it is to get to meet up here at the park where you practice sometimes. Ask her if she's ever played football before."

"Has she?"

"No,"

"Then why would I—"

"We have a ball here for you." Deb glances around, frowning. "Sheila has it somewhere. We'll find it."

"I have an old one in my Jeep."

"No, no. We have one specifically for this. We want it clean. You'll throw that around with her. You don't have to say much about that. Just be laughing and fun."

"And organic?"

"Yes, exactly. Then she'll teach you to dance a few steps. Something quick. After that, we'll move on to your goodbyes. Promises to see each other at the studio. You can't wait. You're so excited to be a part of this."

I chuckle, looking around. "Is there a script I can get all of this from?"

"No. It'll will be off-the-cuff. Very casual and fun. Remember to have fun."

"I always do," I mutter under my breath.

She isn't listening. She looks at me without seeing me. Her eyes have gone vacant the way Coach's do when he's listening to his headpiece on the playing field. Suddenly, she snaps out of it. "She's coming. Be yourself, Mr. Lowry. Your fun, energetic, exciting self!"

Everyone backs away until I'm left alone under the gaze of the camera. I can see another section of the crew with the second camera coming in from the parking lot. They're following a whisper of a woman up onto the grass. She's short, even compared to some of the smaller people in the crew. She's wearing jeans and pink tennis shoes. Nearly no makeup and a yellow tank top with the Kodiak's logo printed on the front over her small chest. It looks so new I can almost smell the ink on it from here.

On my flight home last night, I Googled her like Chris told me to. I found pictures of her as a kid on Broadway. That's what she's most famous for. She was the star in *Annie* and *Matilda* for years. When she got older she did *School of Rock* and *Charlie and the Chocolate Factory*.

She played Wendy in *Peter Pan* for one year before abruptly leaving New York for L.A.

That's when the pictures changed. From one frame to the next she went from looking like a little girl to looking like a woman. A fully formed, softly molded, gently curved woman with pouty pink lips and fierce gray eyes. Her hair is long and golden, more blond than brown. In her *DNA* pics, she was wearing next to nothing. Just a glittery white bathing suit with a joke of a skirt at the bottom that did nothing to hide her legs. She's toned. Tight like an athlete. She's small but she looks strong, mostly in her eyes. In the determined set of her jaw.

"Shane Lowry," she gushes from about twenty feet away. Her smile is big and pink as her shoes. It looks genuine but so does her hair color, and something tells me she's not a natural blond.

I smile, closing the distance between us slowly so the cameras can follow. "It's good to meet you, Sutton."

"You too! I've heard so much about you."

She opens her arms to take me into a hug that feels forced and awkward. Definitely not 'organic'. She's tiny in my arms. Like a kid. Her body is impossibly narrow and her head only barely comes to my chest. I let her go quickly, worried I'll suffocate her there against my pecs.

"Thanks for meeting me here," I tell her mechanically, feeling like an idiot.

"I'm so excited to work with you."

It's a lie. I can't hear it in her voice, but I see it in her eyes. The cameras will never pick it up, meaning the audience will never know, but Sutton Roe is anything but excited to work with me.

Over the last hour of waiting for her to show up, I've started to feel the same way.

"Congratulations on the Super Bowl win," she tells me proudly. "That's such a huge deal. For the Kodiaks and the city."

"Thanks. It was one of the best days of my life."

"Of course it was. Yeah."

There's a weird pause between us. It only lasts a second, but in that second I can hear the sound of the park around us. Kids playing on a structure downfield. A dog barking through the trees. Birds above us and a warm breeze rolling up the hill and through her hair. She stares at me patiently, her smile painted on her face unfailingly.

"Oh, uh, congratulations to you, too," I fumble. "For winning the competition last year. Right? You and Jace Ryker."

"We'll edit that out," Deb shouts from the sidelines.

I glance at her where she stands next to the nearest camera. "What?"

Sutton shakes her head at me. Her face is serious, her smile gone. "Don't look at the cameras or talk to the crew."

"But what are they editing out? What'd I say?"

"'Jace Ryker'. We can't use his name this season."

"Why not?"

"You don't need to worry about it," Deb promises me brusquely. She rolls her hand impatiently. "Let's keep moving forward. You're doing great."

I blink rapidly, looking back at Sutton.

She's smiling again; big and bright as before. "Thank you. It was an amazing feeling. Are you ready to win again with me this year?"

"I'm ready to try."

"That's all anyone can do, isn't it? But before I teach you anything," she playfully pokes at my stomach before walking backwards a few steps, "I want you to teach me to throw a football. I've never done it before."

Suddenly, the crowd shifts. A football is thrust into my hands and I'm being sent toward the end of the field. I'm followed by one camera while Sutton is trailed by the other. She ignores it effortlessly, jogging a little ways downfield until we're roughly fifteen yards apart. She turns to face me with a quick pivot that's graceful in a way I didn't know a human could be, her hair flying behind her like a long, white flag. With her eyes suddenly on mine and a smile on her lips that looks genuine as the air in my lungs, I forget the cameras. I forget the football in my hand. I forget the irritation that built inside me with every minute she made us wait for her to arrive. All I can think is that she's beautiful. Brutally so.

"Is this close enough?" she calls.

I nod, not sure what she wants to be close enough for. How am I going to teach her to throw a football from fifteen yards away?

I balance the ball in my hands, thinking it feels under-inflated. That's probably for her sake. Her hands are easily half the size of mine. She won't be able to hold it if it's at full volume.

"Are you ready?" I ask her.

She puts her hands out in front of her, nodding. "Ready!"

I resist the urge to look at the director. I want to know how hard I should throw this thing. Do I treat Sutton like an adult or a kid, because that's what she looks like to me. She's so small, I'm worried I'll knock her on her ass if I throw it full force.

"Shane," she laughs breathily. "Come on!"

I pull my arm back, raising my eyebrows at her with

a smile that feels real. "You ready?"

"I've been ready! Throw it!"

I lob it high, giving her plenty of time to get under it. She doesn't, though. She waits for it to come to her and it falls between her hands without contact. She laughs when it hits the ground at her feet, slowly rolling away.

"Ah! I'm terrible!" she cries.

I chuckle as I watch her chase after the ball. Finally, she gets it in her hands and stands up straight. Her hair immediately attacks her face in the wind. She spits and sputters dramatically to push it away.

"You need some help?" I ask her.

"I've got it! I've got it!" Sutton squares her stance, setting her feet wide apart. She holds the ball in both hands and asks, "How do I do it?"

"Fingers over the laces. Hold it in one hand, if you can."

"Ha ha," she chuckles wryly.

I smile, showing her my own hand in the air. "Like this. Then you pull it back and throw it with the right side of your body. Use more than just your arm."

She does what I tell her to. Sort of. She's too focused on her footing and when she comes forward with the ball, she doesn't release it soon enough. Instead, she spikes it right into the ground. It bounces up at her face, making her shriek as she leaps away from it.

"How did I almost hit myself with it?!" she demands laughingly.

I chuckle, hurrying toward her. I'm vaguely aware of the cameras following me, but I focus on her. On the light sound of her laughter and the rosy color in her cheeks pushed high with her smile. She's seriously gorgeous. Better looking than her pictures now that I'm talking to her, and I think it's because of her attitude.

She's so bright. Much more easygoing than I expected her to be.

"Here." I pick up the ball for her. She eyes me with playful suspicion before closing the space between us to take it in her tiny hands. The tips of her fingers are cold but her palm against mine is warm. Her skin is soft as silk. "It's bad luck you got me for this. You should have been learning from Tom Berg. I'm no quarterback."

Sutton's face immediately falls, her shoulders going slack. She pulls her hands away from mine.

"We'll edit!" Deb, calls.

I look quickly between the two of them. "Edit what? What'd I say now?"

"Tom Berg," Sutton tells me impatiently. Every ounce of playfulness is wiped from her face. She's looking at me with sharp, gray eyes that cut me down to nearly nothing. "You can't talk about him. Didn't anyone tell you this stuff?"

"Tell me what stuff?"

"What you're supposed to be doing here."

"I'm meeting you. Am I not doing that?" I turn to the director to get away from the ice in Sutton's stare. "How the fuck am I doing this wrong?"

Sutton groans. "Jesus, really?"

"What now?"

"You can't swear when we're filming. They'll have to edit that out."

I take a step back from her. "It's starting to sound like they'll have to edit all of me out."

"Maybe that's for the best."

I frown, taken aback by the change in her. Out of nowhere, she's a totally different girl. There's nothing fun and beautiful about her. Any attraction I felt toward her is gone in an instant because the girl I was digging, the one who was laughing and playful, is gone. That's not her. Apparently, *this* is the real her.

And Sutton Roe is a stone-cold bitch.

CHAPTER SIX

SUTTON

Shane's looking at me like I'm a monster. Like I stole something from him, but I can't imagine what it was because I never gave him anything and I don't owe him a damn thing either. This megalith came here totally unprepared and he's expecting me to coach him on the spot when we have exactly zero time to mess around. I came to work, and if he's not ready, that's not my fault. He's looking at me with those big blue eyes that probably melt women's hearts in the stands at his games, but we're not on his turf right now. We're on mine, and he can stow the handsome, good guy act.

"Okay, look," I tell him curtly. "Here's the deal. You can't talk about Jace Ryker on camera because the parent company of the studio is in a lawsuit with him over the use of one of his songs. It has nothing to do with the show or the fact that he was on it, but it means we can't say his name. Got it?"

"Got it," he answers tightly.

"And Tom Berg is just as bad. We're pretending we were never associated with him. We don't talk about him and if anyone asks you about replacing him, you redirect the conversation to how excited you are about being on the show."

"Okay."

"Good. Awesome." I turn to Debbie. "Where should we pick up? Do you want us to throw the ball again?"

"A few more times. Try to fail like you did the first time. We'll play it up like you never got the hang of it with a few blooper shots."

"Alright." I wave Shane away, tossing him the ball. "Here. Back up. We're going again."

He squeezes the ball between his hands, flexing his biceps. They test the strength of the cotton wrapped around his arms, bulging hard as stone against the thin material. He's ridiculously huge. I was actually a little afraid to take the pass from him in the first shot. He could drill it through my chest and into my heart if he wanted to. And right now, he looks like he's thinking about it.

Finally, he slowly makes his way back to his mark.

"Rolling!" Debbie shouts when he's settled.

I smile excitedly, slipping into character.

I'm a girl at the park with a man. He's big and beautiful. He's fun. I'm having fun. I love this. This is a good day. We're going to have such a great time competing together.

"I'm ready when you are!" I shout to him happily.

He hesitates, his eyes locked on mine. He's not grinning anymore. He's not frowning either. He's just looking at me with a blank expression that boils my blood.

Get it together, big guy. Cameras are watching.

Shane clears his throat before stepping back to throw the ball. I'm ready for it this time. I'm not worried he'll murder me with it, so when it sails toward me in a tight spiral, I scurry forward to catch it. It lands neatly in my open arms.

"I got it!" I shout, jumping up and down with the ball tucked in tight to my chest. "Touchdown!"

Shane chuckles mildly. He waits as I wind up to throw the ball back to him.

It goes about ten feet before nosediving into the

dirt.

"Oh my God, I'm awful," I blush, burying my face in my hands.

He jogs toward the ball, shrugging. "It takes practice."

"I'm ready to work. Throw it to me again."

He does. Ten more times. And I fail ten more times; each one more spectacular than the first. Shane laughs now and then, but he bottles it up quick as though he's catching himself. Like he forgot that this was all for show.

To be fair, there's a moment where I forget too. He's running to get the ball back, never making me retrieve it, and as he leans down, his eyes meet mine. I'm still smiling from my last fit of laughter. He smiles back, grinning crooked and genuine in a way that makes my heart twist sharply in my chest. The sun is golden behind him. It shines in his brown hair like flax in the wind. His eyes are big and blue and so, so full. So real. It's almost painful, the way he looks at me.

But then, just as quickly as it happens, the moment passes. He turns his back on me and I'm left alone with my errant thoughts. With my traitorous heart.

I won't pretend Shane Lowry isn't hot. He is. He's hot as hell. He looks like a god on the field with the ball in his hands and the wind at his back. And that hug he gave me was so surprisingly tender it made my spine shiver with delight. But this isn't *The Bachelor*. We're preparing for an intense competition that I fully intend to win, and he needs to be on board with that. I don't want to play around or flirt like I did with Jace. That shit won't fly a second time. I'll be seen as a slut who throws herself at every partner she gets.

No, things with Shane have to be different. They

have to go the way I planned for them when I was partnered with Tom. Professional. Clean. Tight. No gray areas. No hesitation. We'll win because we're the best, and I'll make Shane the best by working his ass off. He can hate me if he wants. It doesn't matter. This is my world and this is how it's done.

"That's good," Debbie shouts after the tenth bad throw. "That's great, you guys. The light is shifting and we're getting a lot of extra noise from the park filling up. Let's have you teach him the Foxtrot, Sutton, and then we'll say our goodbyes."

"Sounds good."

"Whenever you're ready."

I shake my hands out, taking a quick breath. I smile exuberantly as I slowly walk toward Shane. "Okay, I think I've been humiliated enough. It's your turn, mister."

Shane gently tosses the football to the side. "Whatever you say, Boss."

I smile like I like the nickname, but inside I cringe. I writhe.

He's calling me bossy. I hate that. Why is an assertive woman considered bossy and an assertive man is proactive? A real go-getter? Why is it implied that to be a go-getter when you have a vagina is to be a bitch?

I stop just a few feet from him, making sure we're both well framed. "How much do you know about dancing?"

He shakes his head. "Nothing. Not a single f—uh, thing. I don't know a single thing about dancing."

Decent recovery, I think, trying to stay positive. *That's a good sign.*

"That's okay. The Foxtrot is simple. We'll try the box for today. It's four-four timing. Two beats for slow. One beat for quick. Ready?"

"All of that means nothing to me, but, yeah, I'm ready. I'm watching."

"These are your steps." I point to my feet to draw his attention. "The man always starts on the left foot. Your right foot begins between my feet. And slow," I glide one long step forward, "quick, quick," one step to the right before bringing my feet together on the second beat, "slow, quick, quick, slow. Your steps should rotate you to draw a box on the ground. Got it?"

"I think so."

"Let's see how this is going to work." I giggle lightly, motioning for him to open his arms for me. "You're a foot taller than I am. It's not ideal but I think we can manage."

Shane doesn't answer. He's focused on getting his hands in the right places. I help guide him where he's supposed to be, showing him how to keep his arms tight. His hand is hot against mine. His palm on my back is like a blowtorch. I can't ignore the places where he's touching me, and I remind myself to breathe slowly to bring myself center.

"It's important to keep your form. All the way down to your fingertips," I tell him gently. My voice hushed the second we touched, the way it always does. This is my church – the space inside his arms. The music in my mind. Dancing is like praying and I treat it with a reverence that I hope he'll understand someday. "Stay tight but fluid. You want to be graceful but you don't want to be sloppy."

"Be perfect but not on purpose."

I smile up at him. It's the first time it's been real all day. "Exactly."

Shane hesitates, his eyes on my lips. My eyes.

My smile begins to falter.

He looks away, clearing his throat. "Start with my right foot."

"Your left," I correct quickly.

"Yeah, right. Sorry. Start with my left foot and put my right foot between your toes."

"And try not to step on them."

"Luckily we're on the grass. You'll hardly feel it."

"You're nearly three hundred pounds, Shane. I doubt that's true."

He nods, looking down at his Nikes next to mine.

"Eyes up," I command softly.

Shane looks up. He takes a steeling breath that I feel under my hand against his shoulder. He launches us into motion. It's jerky at first. He's counting the steps in his head. To his credit, he doesn't mouth them the way Tom did.

The cameras move next to us, in and out of my peripheral. I try to ignore them. Shane makes it easy. When they're behind him, it's like the sun in an eclipse. It's like they're gone and we're alone and we're graceful as a star skittering over the sky. I expected him to be rigid given his size, but he's surprisingly fluid.

He flexes his hand holding mine. It nearly hurts, but he stops just in time. "How am I doing?"

"Really well," I admit with a surprised chuckle.

Shane smiles, taking the compliment greedily. "My mom will be proud. She loves the show."

"Do you watch it with her?"

"No. I've never watched it before."

I feel my smile tighten with annoyance. I lick my lips to stretch it out, giving it a break. "That's fine. I've never watched a football game before."

"You're missing out."

"So are you."

He meets my eyes for a second. He lingers just a beat too long. "I can see that."

"Aaaaaaand good!" I tell him theatrically, coming to a firm stop. "That was it. You just learned the basics of the Foxtrot, Mr. Lowry. You're a bit of a natural."

He releases me with a grin. "You're a good teacher."

"I'll have to be if we're going to win."

"Do you think we have a chance?"

"Are you kidding? We're going to kill it."

I offer him my hand for a high-five. He claps his against mine firmly, careful not to leave an ounce of sting behind. In addition to being more graceful than I expected he's also more in control of his strength. It's clear he's making a conscious effort not to be too rough with me today.

"I can't wait to work with you," I gush. "I know you're an athlete, but I'm not going to go easy on you. You better bring it every day."

"I'll be there. And I'll bring whatever you tell me to. Boss."

That's a dig. He knows I hate being called Boss. He must have read it in my face the first time he said it. Now he's throwing it out to try and shake me. What he doesn't know is that it takes an earthquake of devastating magnitude to shake me, and his sweet little jab is nothing but a hiccup.

I point at him playfully. "I want a mug on Thursday with that name on it."

"You bet."

I step into another hug with him. It's the second of what will become many. We'll embrace before performances, after performances, when we survive another round, when we get a good score. When I'm teary eyed and burying my face in his shoulder because we got a bad score. When we're eliminated in the second round and I can't face the world. I'll need a place to hide, and that massive chest of his looks as good a place as any.

"How long do we do this for?" he whispers in my ear.

I start, shaking free of him. I wasn't paying attention and now I have no idea how long I held onto him. The cameras do, though. They see everything. They remember *everything.*

"Sorry," I laugh. I brush my hair away from my face, rolling my eyes. "I was in my head choreographing our first dance. I have a lot of ideas."

Shane grins slyly, higher on one side than the other. His eyes are on mine and they're full of knowing. "I can't wait to see them."

"You will. Ad nauseam."

I wave goodbye over my shoulder. One camera follows me as I walk to my car. They film me getting inside. I wave one more time through the windshield to Shane.

I drive away out of the parking lot, loop around the block down the road, and head back in. I'm gone for less than a minute but by the time I get back, the cameras are on their way to an unmarked van, along with most of the crew. As I park, I see a few people talking with Shane. No, not just talking. Laughing. Joking. I'm barely gone and they're having a grand ole time. I doubt a single person has reprimanded him for knowing absolutely nothing about how this day was supposed to be shot.

I'm out of my car and back on the field in record time. Debbie sees me coming. Her smile slips as she mutters to the rest of the group. As soon as they spot me, they disband, leaving Debbie and Shane alone.

"What happened today?" I ask Debbie, feeling exhausted. I didn't sleep well last night, for... reasons. I wasn't ready for today, but I showed up anyway only to find out that the perfect match they found for me needs a crash course in TV Production 101.

Debbie crosses her arms over her chest, shrugging. "I don't know what you mean. I think it went great."

"Me too," Shane agrees. His hands are in his pockets, the way they were when I arrived.

They way he does when he's copping attitude.

"You were totally unprofessional," I snap at him.

He laughs at me. "*I* was unprofessional? Me?"

"Yes. You."

"Maybe, but at least I showed up on time."

"What are you talking about? I was early. It's not my fault you all got here even earlier."

"You got here at seven-forty."

"Yes, and filming was set to start at eight."

"Seven," Debbie corrects.

I blink at her. "What?"

"Call time was seven. For everyone."

"No, but he told me eight."

"Who did?"

Eric, I think viciously.

Eric arranged the shoot. He made the times. He knows what they are in his sleep, and he definitely knew them at my apartment last night. But he told me eight. He did it on purpose to put me on the back foot.

I shake my head. "I don't remember."

"Well, whoever it was, they were wrong. And you're wrong. Shane did great for a newcomer. He'll get the hang of it. Right, Shane?"

"Damn straight, Deb," he agrees, his voice deep and quiet.

I scoff. "You're just renaming everybody today, aren't you?"

"It's her name."

"No. It's Debbie."

"No. It's Deb."

"No, it's not," I laugh.

Debbie frowns sympathetically. "Yeah, Sutton, it is. It always has been."

I fall back a step, stunned. "Then why have I been calling you 'Debbie'?"

"I have no idea."

I curse under my breath, looking up. Only 'up' is occupied now. 'Up' doesn't get me blue sky and clouds like it used to. Now it gets me blue eyes and a smile that makes me feel like cotton candy inside; airy and sweet.

"What about you?" I demand of him, sounding as hard as I can. "Is your name Shane or am I making that up too?"

"Nope. I will today, tomorrow, and always be Shane Lowry."

"So I'm not a complete bitch."

"Not a complete one, no."

Maybe not, but I definitely feel like an ass. Eric has made me feel this way. I blame him for everything. For Shane and how unprepared he is. For the show slowly going under, taking all of us with it like the crew on the Titanic. I blame him for how tired I am. How jaded I feel. I blame him for that sick feeling in my stomach that aches like I ate poison because I did. Being with him was like drinking arsenic. I'm lucky to survive it.

"You okay?" Shane asks gently.

The soft sound of his voice shakes me from my inner

rant. He's caught me off guard for the second time today, and the way he's looking at me scares me. It's like he sees me. For real sees me and what's happening inside me, and that thought is even more horrifying than Eric at my door.

Seriously, how observant is this guy? Am I transparent? I don't look at myself in the mirror much, but when I do, I'm pretty sure I'm not made of cellophane. I have skin and blood to cover my secrets. I have organs that shroud the pit of me where my demons lie. Where angels hide. But if that's true, how is it that every Chuck, Fuck, and Larry out and about today is able to see right through me?

I smile warmly like I don't have a care in the world. Like I have no idea what he's talking about. "I'm golden. Don't worry about me."

Shane nods slowly, but he doesn't believe me.

Deb squeezes my arm wordlessly before leaving us alone. The crew is almost packed up, meaning the day is over. We can go home now.

Then why are me and Shane standing here staring at each other in silence? He doesn't move. Neither do I. Only our shadows do. They trace across the ground together as the sun moves slowly overhead, like they're locked in a dance. Smooth and graceful. At ease with each other in a way their masters will never be.

"I wasn't talking just for the cameras," I tell him suddenly. "You were quick to pick up the steps. You're good. I think you're going to be good."

He nods once. "Thanks."

"Thanks for stepping in for Tom."

"No problem."

"It was a shock when we heard what he'd done. I didn't think he was that kind of person."

"Me either."

"I'm not a bitch," I tell him stiffly. "I know I come across as one and people on the crew are going to tell you that I am one, but I'm not."

Shane's lips twitch with a smile he keeps under wraps. "Okay."

"I'm passionate. This show means something to me and I hope it will mean something to you too. I hope we can work together toward our goal."

"Earning a buttload of money for the charity?"

I hesitate, feeling like… well, feeling like a bitch because that's not what I was thinking about. I was thinking about winning. I'm always thinking about winning.

"You're due at the studio on Thursday," I remind him, sidestepping his question. "Seven sharp."

"I'll be there."

"So will I." I grin, though I feel like growling with frustration. "On time. I promise."

"I'll see you then, Boss."

Ugh, I think angrily. But I don't let it show. I smile, wave goodbye, and head back to my car for the second and last time. I'll leave for real, go straight to the studio, and lay into Eric for making me late.

At least, that's what I want to do, but I know I won't. I can't. There's no way I can look at Eric today. Or tomorrow. I'll be lucky if I can stomach the sight of him by Thursday for the first day of rehearsal. He's a sickness in my blood. He's septic. If I could find the piece of me that he infects over and over again, I'd cut it out.

I'd gladly take a pound of my own flesh and leave it lying on the ground at his feet to be free.

CHAPTER SEVEN

SHANE

May 1ˢᵗ
Palmetto Warehouse
Los Angeles, CA

Colt Avery is a handsome son of a bitch. I'm good looking, but Colt is *great* looking. It's disgusting. I'd hate him if I didn't love him.

"Where are you taking her?" I ask him curiously.

Colt stretches his arms to expertly tug his shirt's white cuff out of the dark wool sleeve of his jacket. He's wearing a muted blue tie and shining black shoes I've never seen before. His dark hair is combed to one side and held in place by a thick coat of gel that makes him look like an extra on *Mad Men*.

Dude is dapper as hell.

"Caprice," Colt answers. "It's new. I think Tom Hanks owns it."

"What kind of food is it?"

"Big."

"Funny."

Colt smiles like a model on a runway. "I'm hilarious, man. You want me to bring you a doggy bag?"

"Nah, I'm good. I've got leftover pizza in the fridge."

"You need any beer, help yourself to my stash upstairs."

"I already have."

"I'll add the cost to your rent."

I chuckle because I know he's lying. Colt never drinks the beer that companies are constantly sending him. He's also not a miser. He's letting me live in the loft below his, the one he normally rents out to tourists, for next to nothing. I had a place of my own but a couple of months ago when we found out the team was sold and the new owners had plans to move us to Las Vegas, I put my condo on the market. The team isn't leaving L.A. until after this coming season, but I figured it'd take a while to sell the place. I was dead wrong. It sold in the first week, putting me out on my ass until Colt picked me up. Now all my shit is in storage and I'm living in a totally neutral apartment with too many pictures of the ocean on the wall. The only thing that's actually mine is the wobbly ceramic fruit bowl on the island that my mom made for me when she was going through her pottery phase. Everything else you could probably find at any department store in town.

Colt nods to the black pen drive in the middle of the coffee table. "How many episodes did they send you?"

"The letter from the network said it's all of last season and some highlights from the three seasons before."

"Ah. Sutton's run."

"Is that how long she's been on there?"

"Four seasons," Colt replies knowledgably. Lilly, his fiancé, is a huge *DNA* fan, meaning Colt has had to become at least okay with it. "This is her fifth. I bet you anything the 'highlights' are all of her."

I snort into my beer. One of the many I've stolen from him. "Double or nothing she put it together herself."

"Is she full of herself?"

I glance over at Colt where he's checking himself out in the mirror by the door. He's adjusting his hair, fitting it perfectly into place with the kind of care most people would reserve for brain surgery. "Not as much as some people.”

“Fuck you,” he deadpans, not looking away from himself. “I’m pretty but I’m not dumb. I get what you’re saying.”

“A chimp could understand what I’m saying.”

“But does a chimp look this good in a suit?”

“You know they call it a ‘monkey suit’, right?”

“A chimp and a monkey are not the same thing, dumbass.”

“What the hell is the difference?”

He turns to me, giving me his full, undivided attention. “An ape doesn’t have a tail. A monkey does.”

“I thought we were talking about chimps.”

“Chimpanzees are apes.”

I shake my head in disbelief. “That can’t be right.”

“Look it up. We’re apes too.”

“That I believe.”

Colt shakes out his hand to check his watch. “Gotta go. Lilly will be off work soon and I want to surprise her before she leaves the bakery. Enjoy your show. It sucks.”

“Can’t you just tell me what happens so I don’t have to watch?”

“It’s not that kind of show,” he laughs, grabbing a garment bag off the arm of the couch. “And if Lilly made me suffer through it, you have to suffer through it too. Those are the rules.”

I gesture to the TV with disdain. “If she loves this show so much, why aren’t you doing it? I know they asked you.”

“Of course they asked me.”

“And?”

“You know Lil. She hates celebrity shit. The paparazzi will be all over your junk when you’re on this show, and she wouldn't want anything to do with that. And I'm not looking to stay away from her for ten weeks to keep them off her back. We've got a wedding to plan. We don't have time for that shit."

"When is that going down?"

He shakes his head helplessly. "I don't know, man. Every time I talk to her about it she freaks out. I think it's overwhelming for her so I'm just trying to give her time. She knows I'm not going anywhere. I'll marry her tonight or ten years from now."

"You think she's freaking because of her dad?" I ask carefully.

"Yeah," he admits. "A lot of it is because of him."

"That's a tough situation. I'm sorry, man."

"It is what it is, you know? We'll get through it."

I nod in understanding but it's not without sympathy. Lilly's family has it rough. Her dad has been sick for years. Going to the store can be stressful for them, so planning a wedding is turning into a nightmare when it should be fun and exciting. Colt has suggested more than once that they elope in Vegas, but Lilly wants a church wedding. She wants both of their family and friends there, but that brings her back to her dad, and that's where everything falls apart for them. There's no good solution. You can't fix her dad and you can't exclude him, so what do you do?

You enter into a holding pattern, apparently.

Five minutes later, Colt is gone and I'm alone with my desire to procrastinate. I look at the coffee table where my phone and the pen drive sit side by side. I'm tempted as hell to call someone, anyone, to get out of doing this. I've got a roster. I could call a girl and get laid, but I'm not in that kind of headspace. I'm not hard up, I'm just not interested in doing homework. I could call Sam and see what he's doing. Maybe he's out at the clubs or chillin' in a bar. I could join him for a few drinks before coming back home to pass out with a good buzz and a better story than sitting here all night watching people get judged on their two-step.

The more I look at that drive, the less likely it seems like I'm doing this. And why should I? I'll give it everything I've got once I'm in the studio learning from Sutton first hand, but what good is watching a bunch of videos going to do me? Sutton is obviously a Type-A personality. She'll want to be in control of my education. I'm muddying the waters by watching anyone else. Ditching is doing her a favor. It's not selfish. It's altruistic.

It's decided. I'm ditching. For Sutton's sake.

My phone rings against my ear as I hurry down the steps away from the loft and my homework. The night is young. It's barely seven o'clock. Sam shouldn't be in for the night yet, and if he is, I'm dragging him out. We're too young and way too sexy to be kept locked up inside tonight.

"I was just about to call you," Sam laughs over the line. "How the hell do you do that?"

"It's a superpower. What are you doing?"

"Nothing. You?"

"Nothing. What do you think? The club or the bar?"

"Dinner first. Beer second. I'm starving."

"I can always eat."

"Meet me at Beast Burger on Pacific?"

"See you in ten."

I hang up as I unlock my bright red Jeep with a quick click of my keys. It's lifted with fat tires meant to climb a mountainside or tear up a beach, because that's what I do when I'm feeling frustrated. When the cement of this massive city is too dull to deal with and I miss Washington so much I can smell the rain. I can feel wet moss under my fingers and rich, dark earth under my toes. That's when my Jeep and I make it to the closest piece of nowhere we can find and I lose hours with her.

I could do that tonight. There's time. But Sam isn't big on mudding and I'm not in the mood to be alone. I'm blowing off my responsibilities; I know that. I'm not dumb. I see it. I feel it. But it doesn't stop me. It never has. Clint was at least partially right about me; I like to take the easy way. My path is the one of least resistance. I have a lot of experience taking shortcuts and it's always worked out for me. I have no reason to think this is going to end up any different.

CHAPTER EIGHT

SUTTON

The Carousel
Los Angeles, CA

"This club is weird as hell!" I shout over the music blaring from every corner of the building. Bright lights in all the colors of the rainbow swirl in dizzying patterns over the black velvet curtains hung on the walls. In the center of the room is a giant carousel. It's populated with wild colored animals smiling with big, human teeth that freak me out like I wouldn't think possible. I can't look away from them or the way they rotate slowly, rising up and down in a hypnotic dance completely out of time with the music.

Everything about this place is an offense to the senses, especially the smell – motor oil and sugary cocktails – but I seem to be the only one who minds. Everyone else is laughing and enjoying themselves. Clara is even riding one of the sheep with green eyes and purple boots on its hooves. She sips a neon drink through a crazy straw while she nods agreeably at whatever the low-budget Johnny Depp next to her is saying.

"I know!" Tina laughs loudly. "Isn't it a gas?! I love it!"

"What do you love more? The bad music or the lazy Susan nightmare?"

"All of it!"

Tina is a bombshell. She's tall and curvy with just the right amount of flirt in her smile. Everyone loves her, even the people who should hate her. People like me.

She's my biggest competition on the show. She has been for the last two years. I've tried to hate her but I can't. She's just too damn nice to hate with a clean conscience. Luckily, this season she's been partnered with a football player without an ounce of rhythm so she's not a big worry for me. She doesn't care, though. She says he's fun. She says she's having fun getting to know him.

Tina is always having fun.

I can never be Tina.

"How's the guy?!" she shouts to me across the low, glowing table.

I shake my head like I'm not sure because the truth is, I'm not. Shane is talented. He has more skill than I expected, but he's also abrasive. I'm sure he'd say the same about me.

"He's okay, I guess!" I answer vaguely.

"He's hot!"

"I know!"

"I'll trade you!"

I laugh at the hollow offer. "Not on your life!"

"Oh, keeping the hottie for yourself, huh?! That's not like you, Sutton! Are you finally going to mix business with pleasure?!"

"No! Your guy has no rhythm! If he can't get me a win, what do I want him for?!"

"Guys are good for more than winning!" Ana tells me slyly. "Didn't your mom teach you that?!"

"My mom taught me everything about men! It's why I try to avoid them!"

Kasian, a handsome dancer imported from Russia, leans in with a sad expression. "I have noticed this, *solnyshko.* It break my heart."

I smile at him affectionately. *Solnyshko* is a Russian

term of endearment that means 'little sun'. He gave it to me when we first met and he ran his fingers through my golden hair. He told me I looked like sunlight and smelled like summer. If I didn't know better, I probably would have succumbed to his charms a long time ago.

"I have to avoid you, Kaz," I tell him. "You'd be the death of me. I can see it in your eyes."

"And in your eyes, I see all of the heavens. It is beautiful."

"That's the scary thing about you. You're a flatterer."

"What is flatterer?"

"She means you're a player!" Tina laughs over the rim of her glass.

Kasian nods in somber agreement. "Yes."

Tina and I giggle at his arrogance. Kasian and I are a lot alike. We're both blunt. Both proud. Impatient. Passionate. Driven. Aggressive in our desires and stubborn when presented with anything we don't like. He's comforting to have around, but this season we'll be missing him. With all men on the celebrity side, we've been forced to recruit some women from the chorus to replace the men we don't need. It's made things tenser than ever behind the scenes. Not only are we competing against each other, now we're competing against newcomers too. Outsiders. I don't like it, but then I don't like change.

Kasian stands suddenly. He offers me his hand and a toothy grin. "This is good song. Will you dance with me, Sutton?"

I smile at his broken English and delicate hand. "I'm feeling a little off tonight. Will you go easy on me?"

"Never."

He gently pulls me to my feet. Tina slaps me playfully on the ass, making me yelp in surprise. I giggle as I lean in close to Kasian's side, following him willingly to the dance floor.

With the giant carousel in the middle of the club, the only places to dance are on its peripheral. The space is narrow and packed with bodies, forcing Kasian and I close together. The song is slow. The lights are dim and Kaz smells divine. When he puts his long arms loosely around my waist, I feel myself relax. This club is insane and annoying, but Kaz is familiar. Dancing is like breathing. The two together are so easy and comfortable, I feel like I could fall asleep right here in his arms. I'm exhausted for so many reasons, but dancing has always been a break from life. It's a chance to catch my breath when things are moving too fast to comprehend. That's what it feels like now; like I'm breathing. Like the wild dogs nipping at my heels have fallen away and all I can hear is the sound of the music and the beat of my heart finding time with it.

"You will miss me this season," Kasian tells me lightly.

I smile. "You'll still be around. You'll be in the group numbers."

"It will not be the same."

"No. It won't. I've never done a season with only women pros."

"No one has. It is strange."

"It is very strange."

"You have met your partner?"

"I have. I met him yesterday."

"He is big?"

"Yes," I laugh at the understatement. "Yes, he is very big. Too big."

"You are small. All men feel too large to you."

"Not you, Kaz. You're perfect."

"Yes."

I chuckle as he turns me, dipping me down until my long hair touches the floor. He snaps me back up again so that my arms go around his neck tightly, pressing our bodies closer together. We move slowly with the music. I'm sure from the outside it looks sensual. Like we're a couple wrapped up in each other, but that's the outside. That's what people who don't do this professionally are programmed to think. Closeness = intimacy. But they're wrong. So wrong. I've danced a hundred times with men I couldn't care less about, and even though I adore Kaz, there's nothing sexual about the way he's holding me. His hand hovers just above my ass but I trust that he won't drop it down any lower because I don't want him to. He knows that. He respects that. That's what dancing requires – respect. Trust. Faith. It takes time to earn it. It takes only a moment to lose it.

The song changes, turning to something more upbeat. It's in Spanish. Kasian immediately dives us straight into it. He's chosen the Samba. A dance like that with a man like Kasian takes skill. You have to keep up with his energy, matching his pace as he spins you around and around, nearly tossing you away before snapping you back. It's not a beginner's dance.

Luckily, I am no beginner.

"Oh, we're doing this?" I laugh at him as he paces around me with rapidly snapping feet.

"Yes, *solnyshko*. We do this."

I smile as I tie up my long rays of sunlight in a ponytail. "Alright, Kazy. Let's show 'em how it's done."

I rise up on my toes as I offer him my hand because on my toes is the only way I'll survive this dance with him. He twirls me in close, running his hands slowly down the sides of my body before launching me away. This dance is a lot of hips, ass, and sass, so that's what we give.

Everything.

I leave everything on the floor, no matter where it is. A stage on Broadway. A studio on the KBC lot. A dancefloor in a wild club in the middle of downtown L.A. Dancing is therapy and I don't care where I attend it.

We're about halfway through the song when I notice we've gathered an audience. It's not a surprise. We're pros in a sea of amateurs grinding against each other clumsily. When Kasian spins me so quickly the thin, pink skirt on my dress rises up to my hips to expose my underwear, the crowd cheers loudly. Someone wolf whistles like an animal, but I'm smiling as I come back around to face Kaz.

Kasian dips me low, bending me over his leg in a move that could snap the back of a woman without my flexibility. I hang there, breathing heavily as the crowd applauds us. That sound soothes the burns life has left on my soul. I feel calm as I listen to them. As I drink them in more deeply than the shots Tina has tried to get inside me. Alcohol has never been my friend. Adoration – that's my drug of choice. This is my high.

When Kasian brings me back to stand with him, he kisses me quickly. It's on the mouth and it's firm. It garners us more applause that he disappears into as soon as he releases me. The crowd swallows him, leaving me alone and breathless.

But not for long.

"That was incredible," Shane's voice rumbles deeply from behind me.

I spin around to find him looming over me. Even in

my heels, he's so much taller than me it's unnerving. His chest is all I can see. His cologne is all I can smell. He floods my senses in a way that sends me back a step to find myself again.

"What are you doing here?" I demand without thinking. It's a free country. He can be anywhere he wants, but it's thrown me that he's *here.*

I don't like surprises.

He chuckles, lowering his head so I can hear him better. "I'm getting an education in just how in over my head I am. You and that guy are amazing."

"Thank you."

"Boyfriend?"

"No thanks."

Shane hesitates before chuckling. "You're funny, Sutton. I didn't peg you for funny."

"And I didn't peg you for a guy who would go to a gay bar."

"Is this a gay bar?" he asks in amazement.

"It's called the Carousel and there's a guy dressed as Rainbow Bright serving drinks," I answer without inflection. "Yes, Shane. This is a gay bar."

He laughs into his fist. "No shit. That's hilarious."

"How did you not notice?"

"I don't know. I just figured it was kinda wild. I've seen a lot of dudes but I've seen a lot of women too."

"You've seen a lot of lesbians."

Shane smiles down at me. "Not all of them are lesbians."

"How do you know I'm not here with my girlfriend?"

"Are you?"

"Maybe."

"Can I meet her?"

"Sure," I answer sarcastically. "Then we can all go

back to your place and have a threesome. Sound good?"

He shakes his head, tucking his hands in the pockets of his jeans. "Nah, not really my scene. Thanks for the offer, though, Boss."

I open my mouth to ask him what his 'scene' is, but I stop myself short. Why do I care? He's probably lying anyway. What guy on the planet would turn down a threesome with two lesbian dancers? A handful of priests and Shane Lowry? Yeah, I doubt it.

The lights overhead dim to a deep purple. Shane and I are dropped into shadow that feels oddly intimate. We're surrounded by over a hundred people but he's the only one I can see clearly. Just as the feeling starts to get claustrophobic, another set of lights kicks on. They're muted and moving. They dance over us in whites and blues that make it feel like we're underwater.

The opening cords to *Landslide* start to play. When the vocals come in close after them, I'm surprised to hear Miley Cyrus instead of Stevie Nicks.

Shane looks at me with a perplexed expression. "Seriously. What the hell is this place?"

I laugh despite myself. "I really don't know."

"It's all over the place. I can't keep up."

"Maybe you should go home."

"Or," he opens his arms like an invitation, "we could just go with it."

I should say no. He's not Kasian. He's not safe. He's an unknown and there's just so damn much of him. It's intimidating to look at him with all of his strength and confidence knowing he could crush me if he wanted to. How many fights has he been in? How many arrests? How worried should I be?

"I promise not to step on your toes," he vows deeply. But that's not really what he's promising. He's telling me he won't hurt me because he sees me. He knows that I'm afraid of him.

It's shocking how angry his intuition makes me.

"Watch your hands while you're at it," I tell him sternly.

He smiles as I put my hand in his. He immediately goes into form for the Foxtrot, taking me by surprise. Of course he sees it written on my face.

"Is this song too slow for it?" he asks.

I shake my head, avoiding his eyes. "It can work."

"Will you teach me more steps?"

"No."

He waits for me to say more. I don't, making him chuckle. I see it in his chest that rumbles in front of my face. I can't see much of anything but his body and the watercolor lights that roll over it.

"How awkward is this going to be for us?" he asks.

"What do you mean?"

"With our size difference. Is it going to be hard to win?"

I like that's he talking about winning. At least he's looking in the right direction; up. I'm always looking up. I'm always looking for the next victory and I need him to be with me on that if we're going to have a ghost of a chance winning this thing together.

"It won't be easy," I admit. "Normally when teams are paired up, they're done by size and personality. I was in the room when they picked you. They didn't consider either of those things."

"What did they consider?"

"If you were in the NFL and if you were in trouble. You were both."

Shane laughs. "How am I in trouble?"

"You're violent."

He pauses mid-step. I keep going, immediately putting my foot down right over his. He doesn't flinch. His face is impossibly blank, his voice devoid of emotion when he asks, "They said I'm violent?"

I shrug, meeting his gaze head-on. "You've been in two fights this year and it's barely spring."

"Did they ask what those fights were about?"

"What does it matter? You like to fight. That's all they cared about."

"Shit," he chuckles mirthlessly. He lets go of my hands, backing away a step. "That's why you've been looking at me like you have, isn't it? You think I'm some asshole that likes to get into shit for the fun of it."

"It doesn't matter what I think."

"We're going to work together practically every day for the next ten weeks. It matters, Sutton."

He's finally using my name, but it's only because he's angry. The tone of his voice is so serious, so irritated and flat-out outraged, I feel a strange connection to him.

I'm drawn to negative emotions like an addict's needle to the vein.

"Are you saying you're not that asshole?" I ask sharply.

"Yeah. That's exactly what I'm saying."

"What am I supposed to base that on?"

"The fact that I'm standing here telling you."

"I don't know you. I definitely don't trust you and I didn't want you. I wanted Colt Avery."

Shane smirks but his eyes are hard. "Yeah, most women do."

"He ticked all of my boxes. I could have won with

him."

"And you don't think you can with me?"

I gesture violently between us. "We don't match. Not in body shape and not in personality. There's nothing here to build off of, so no, I don't think we can win and that pisses me off."

He runs his tongue over his teeth, nodding his head stiffly. "Alright, well, this was fun. It was great to see you again and I can't wait to make a total ass of myself on national television with you."

"Have a great night, Shane," I reply with equal sarcasm.

"Yeah, you too, Boss."

I turn my back on him just as the song comes to an end. I leave him standing there alone as the lights brighten. The mood in the room lifts, but inside I'm sinking. My heart is a stone trying to pump solid ice through my veins. It hurts and it's stupid.

It feels like that's the definition of my life lately.

"Sutton?" Tina calls to me in a worried tone. She's looking between me and the dance floor, her brow knitted together. "What happened? Is that who I think it is?"

"That's Shane," I mutter as I grab my purse off the table. It jostles the drink I haven't touched.

"Did you know he was going to be here?"

"No."

"What happened? You both look upset."

I shake my head hard. "Nothing. It's fine. I'm going home. I'm tired."

"Are you sure?"

"Yes. Definitely." I look up from my bag to give her a wan smile that I wish was stronger. "Have a good night, okay?"

"Yeah. Hey, do you want me to walk you out? Or should I get Kaz?"

"I'll be fine. Thanks, though."

I lean down to kiss her cheek goodbye. She smells like alcohol; rich and too sweet.

I push through the crowd toward the door. I want to get the hell out of here. I can't stay after what just happened with Shane. I'll feel him in the building no matter where he is. I'll feel like he's looking at me, hating me. Judging me. It's only fair that he would. I'd spend the rest of my night doing the same to him.

CHAPTER NINE

SHANE

May 3rd
Mad Batter Bakery
Los Angeles, CA

Once Colt stops playing ball and becomes an old man, this place is going to be the death of him. He's a sugar addict marrying a baker. His marriage certificate will be his death sentence.

"Shane, man, you have to try one of these," he tells me excitedly. He has his own apron here at Lilly's bakery. It has his name on it and everything. He even went through a course with the city to get his food handler's license so he could play here at the store without getting her shut down. Right now, he's in the middle of making a donut filled with peanut butter, topped with Captain Crunch, and drizzled in caramel. It looks disgusting.

I shake my head at him. "No way. That looks like shit."

"It looks like shit but it tastes like heaven."

"We're not selling those," Lilly tells him plainly.

"That's fine. More for me."

She smiles at him as she squeezes by with a tray of buttery croissants ready for the oven. Now *those* look good. I plan on snagging at least three before I leave here this morning.

I'm in the back of the bakery with Colt and Lilly to watch them get ready for the store to open. I'm killing time because I wake up at four every morning without fail. I'm not supposed to be at the studio until seven, but I couldn't sleep in so I'm killing time instead. I'm on the Kodiak's clock no matter what. It's how I live because football isn't just my job. It's my life.

Normally, I spring out of bed when my alarm goes off, but today I woke up slow. I stared at the ceiling with a sense of dread that I couldn't place at first. Not until Sutton's face drifted across my mind. Her eyes like lasers bore into mine angrily under the cartoonish colors in the club, instantly making me sluggish. That's the other reason I'm here – to talk to Lilly about what happened with Sutton. The girl obviously hates me and I don't know what to do about it. I want a woman's opinion, but Colt is making it hard to have a conversation.

"I'm taking these to the team tomorrow morning," he vows reverently, drizzling an extra layer of caramel over them.

"You can't bring those to practice."

"Breakfast is the most important meal of the day, Lowry. The guys have got to eat."

"If anyone eats that before practice they'll be puking on the field in the first hour. Do you think Coach is going to go easy on us the first day he gets us back on the field?"

"What are you talking about? You guys have been practicing since April," Lilly comments.

Colt shakes his head. "We haven't been practicing. Not yet. We're only allowed strength conditioning, and it's been optional. That's why this son of a bitch was allowed to live it up in Washington while the rest of us were working our asses off."

"You weren't working your asses off." I snag a plain donut from the pile Colt hasn't assaulted yet. "We're not allowed to."

"So what's the big deal about tomorrow?" Lilly asks curiously.

"Tomorrow is the first day of on-field workouts. We'll basically be running for four hours straight. Still no football. Only training. And no rookies. They have their own training they're going through."

She shakes her head, wiping a stray hair away from her eyes with the back of her flour-coated hand. "I can never keep all of this straight."

"It's easy when it's your life."

"Some days it feels like we don't take a shit unless the Commissioner tells us to," Colt mutters.

I look at him, head down over his donuts in deep concentration, and I feel sick inside. The team has been sold and the new owners are moving us to Las Vegas, but Colt has decided not to go with us. His contract is up after this year, same as mine, and he's decided not to renew. With anyone. He'll retire at just twenty-five years old. It's not uncommon. Football is a brutal game and it takes years off your body. Colt has an old knee injury from his college days that gives him trouble sometimes. Apparently more trouble than it's worth, because he says it's one of the main reasons he's quitting.

I'm lucky. I've gone my entire career nearly unscathed. I've had a few broken fingers, a concussion, and a spasm in my back that took me down for three weeks, but other than that I'm healthy. I'm rock solid and ready to roll.

It just isn't going to be the same. Not without Colt.

"Tell me again what happened with Sutton," Lilly says to me as she hoists the bread into the oven. "You saw her dancing with some guy..."

"She was dancing with a dude at Carousel—"

"The gay bar?" Colt asks with a scowl.

I drop my hands impatiently on the counter. "Does everyone but Sam and me know that place is a gay bar?"

"Yes."

"Shit."

"You should have gone to 171."

Lilly and I groan in unison.

Colt glances back and forth between us. "What? What's wrong with 171?"

"Nothing, except we *always* go there," Lilly complains.

"We don't *always* go there."

"If we're not at 171, we're at that dive you and Sloane are in love with," I argue.

Colt smiles proudly. "Beer 'N Burger. The Hotness and I found it on Yelp. It had the worst reviews in town."

"It should. It's a shithole."

"You're a shithole."

"*Anyway,*" Lilly interrupts, physically stepping between us to get my attention. She leans back against the table where Colt is working his sugar wizardry, her arms crossing over her chest. "What happened with Sutton?"

"I saw her dancing with the dude. I joined the crowd watching them because they were good. When they finished, the guy ditched her to go suck the face off a redhead with sad boobs."

"Hold on," Lilly laughs. "How can a woman have sad boobs?"

"It's a thing."

"It is," Colt agrees.

"But it's not really relevant to the story."

"Then why'd you bring it up?" Lilly demands.

"Why'd I bring up her hair color? It doesn't matter either but you're not getting hung up on that detail."

"Alright, fine, it doesn't matter, but we're circling back to this later. I want to know how a woman can have sad boobs."

"I'll draw you a picture. I promise."

"This story is taking forever," Colt complains.

I sit forward in my chair. "We're getting to the important part. The guy leaves, she's alone, so I go to say hey. I tell her she danced really well. She says thanks. *Landslide* comes on. I ask her to dance."

"Stevie Nicks or Dixie Chicks?" Colt asks.

"Who cares?"

"The guy from Kansas cares! Which was it?"

"Miley Cyrus."

He rolls his eyes. "Lame."

"Whatever. Anyway, she agreed to dance with me and we talked about the show. I asked her how hard it's going to be for us being so different in height and everything. That's when she got bitchy. She told me she didn't want me as a partner. She wanted Colt."

Colt chuckles smugly.

Lilly and I ignore him.

"Did she say why she didn't want you?" she asks.

"Yeah, she said it's because I'm violent."

Lilly laughs. "What? For real?"

"Those were her words. She said they picked me purely based on the fact that I'm in the NFL and I'm 'in trouble'."

"In trouble with who?"

"I didn't ask, but she said it was because of the fights."

"Are you in trouble for the fights?"

"No! I paid my fines. I settled the lawsuit. I'm clean."

"Huh," Lilly muses quietly. "And she got angry at you?"

"She told me she doesn't know me, she doesn't trust me, and she doesn't think we have what it takes to win. She basically shit in my face. That's when I decided to bail on the conversation. I told her to have a great night and she stormed off. She left the club."

"Wow."

"Yeah."

Colt whistles quietly. "I dodged a bullet on that one."

"You know the part that really bothers me?" I ask, feeling the frustration from last night rise up in my chest, constricting it tightly. "I think she's seriously afraid of me. She really thinks I'm one of these douchebags that goes around looking for a fight. She looks at me like I'm a grenade someone dropped into her hands and she has no idea if I'm live or not."

Lilly frowns sympathetically. "She's a small woman, Shane, and you are a very large man."

"I'd never hurt her."

"Of course you wouldn't. I know that, but that's because I know you. If I didn't, if I just met you on the street after hearing all the rumors, I might not be so sure."

"Great. What am I supposed to do about that if she's already made up her mind about me?"

Lilly stands up straight, shrugging her shoulders. "I don't have an easy solution for that."

"Well, damn," I laugh.

"You just have to go ahead with the show and prove to her that you're not a jerk. It'll be easy. You're a sweetheart."

"Why is it up to me to win her over? She's not

exactly an angel herself."

"You don't have to like each other to work together," Colt reminds me.

"But it'd be easier," Lilly adds.

"You could always speed things up."

"How?" I ask Colt.

"You aren't going to like it."

"So far, I'm not loving any of this shit."

"You have to say you're sorry."

"But I didn't do anything!"

"It doesn't matter," Colt laments. "She's upset. You apologize. It's the only way it gets better."

"Listen to the expert," Lilly recommends.

"I've apologized for all kinds of shit I didn't do."

I stare at him in amazement. "That makes no damn sense."

"It doesn't have to. But you do have to do it."

"Fuck!"

Lilly smiles at my annoyance before walking away to grab another tray of bread for the oven. They'll be opening soon. It's almost six, meaning I need to get going, but I don't know if I want to. Not if it means I'm walking into a hostile situation where my only course of action is to surrender. It's bullshit. The rules for being on this show are nothing like football. In football you kick each other's ass all day and you're friends the same night.

Football means never having to say you're sorry.

CHAPTER TEN

SUTTON

KBC Studios
Los Angeles, CA

I love being on the lot in the early morning. Next to no one is here. It's a chance to be alone without being lonely. The world is quiet and cool, blanketed in a soft gray glow that will warm with every hour until I'm fully awake and ready to face the day. But not yet. For now, it's just me, my coffee, and the lovely evening chill that still hangs in the air and to the tip of my nose. This hour is in-between. It's half in and half out, and it's all mine. It is the very best part of my day.

"Mornin', Boss."

Shane's voice doesn't startle me, but it does surprise me. He's not supposed to be here until seven. It's barely six, but here he stands in the parking lot just ten feet away in shiny yellow athletic shorts and a worn gray T-shirt with the Kodiaks bear tenuously clinging to the front. His legs are intense. Thick thighs of corded muscle covered in dark hair. His kneecaps are as large as my hand and his calves bulge like cantaloupes just under his skin. You could fit both of my legs easily inside one of his, that's how large he is. No matter how many times I meet with him, I doubt I'll ever get over his size or my lack of it. There are inches and miles between us in a million different ways, and I don't think I've ever traveled that great a distance in my life. I don't believe I can.

I squint up at him before shaking out my hand to look at my watch.

"I'm early," he confirms before I can read the exact time.

"Why?"

"To see you."

"How'd you know I'd be here this early?"

He smiles softly. "I'm a good guesser."

"You don't have to be here just because I am. Everyone else comes in at seven."

"I don't mind. I'll be up anyway. Practice is at six. I'm up before dawn almost every day."

"You can do whatever you want," I mutter without inflection.

He pauses, watching me. I can feel his eyes as sure as the sunshine on my skin. He's working up to something. Something he's unhappy about, and I know what it is he's working toward because I'd be unhappy about it too. But he's bigger than me. He says it first and he sounds more genuine than I could manage.

"I'm sorry," he says quietly, his voice rich with feeling. "I upset you the other night and I shouldn't have."

"It's fine," I answer quickly.

"It's not."

"It is if we leave it alone." I push my fingertip into the lid on my coffee. It creaks in protest, hot steam rising up into my eyes. I feel embarrassed that we're talking about this. Like I overreacted. That's what Eric would tell me. He says I'm pure drama, through and through. He says it's his least favorite thing about me – the biggest thing. And then he tells me he loves me, and I don't know north from south for all the sense it makes. "We should just forget about it."

He clears his throat, shifting on his feet. "Can I sit? Is that okay?"

I look up at him, then at the cement planter I'm sitting on. The rim is thick with plenty of room for me, but two of us will be pushing it. Still, I nod agreeably.

His bicep brushes against my shoulder as he sits. He's crowding me, but not on purpose. That's just what his body does – takes up space. All of it.

"You're scared of me," he guesses gently.

"If I was, I wouldn't have said you could sit."

"You sounded like you were the other night."

"I think I scared myself the other night." I wince, looking up at the sky to disguise it as a squint. "I do that."

"I would never hurt you, Sutton," he promises solemnly.

I nod without looking at him. "I know."

"I don't think you do. But if you give me a chance, I'll prove it to you."

"I don't have much of a choice, do I?"

"I guess you don't," he replies deeply.

The silence between us is weird. There are so many things that are being left unsaid, it makes the air thick like smog on a busy L.A. afternoon.

"Where's my mug?" I demand.

Shane looks at me cluelessly. "What mug?"

"I told you I wanted a mug with 'Boss' on it by Thursday. It's Thursday." I hold out my hand expectantly. "Where is it?"

He chuckles, air rushing out of his body like steam from a kettle. He looks looser without it. "You know what? I actually thought about bringing you one."

"And?"

"I figured you'd smash it. It felt like a waste of a good mug so I didn't do it."

"Well, you were wrong." I take a deep breath, letting

it out slowly before I lower my hand to let him off the hook. "And you don't have to be sorry."

"About the mug or the other night?"

"The other night. You should feel like absolute shit about the mug."

His eyes dance like stars winking in the sky. "I do," he promises, amused. "I feel like total shit."

"What do you smell like?" I lean in closer to him unconsciously, sniffing the air around him. It's butter and something else. Something sweet.

"A bakery."

"You got here early *and* you stopped off at a bakery first? You weren't kidding. You do get up early."

"I had to get my breakfast somewhere." He nods down the alley ahead of us. "I have fresh croissants in my car. Do you want one?"

"No, thanks. I don't eat carbs."

"Your loss. They're good."

"I'll survive. Somehow."

There's another silence between us. More weirdness. I'm fine with it but I can tell that Shane isn't. It makes him jittery. His leg starts to jump next to mine, his fingers playing with each other in his lap.

"I was in a diaper in that fight on Valentine's Day," he tells me suddenly.

I blink in surprise. "I'm sorry, what?"

Shane smiles wide. He smooths his hands over his thighs, relaxing a little. "The fight with the Patriot was a football thing. It was about loyalty. He cheap shotted my quarterback and it's my job to protect Trey. The Pat earned the punch I gave him, and it was only one. It wasn't a fight."

"That's great, but that doesn't explain the diaper."

He chuckles, lowering his head. "The Valentine's Day

thing was a real fight. I was at a bar with friends and I was dressed like Cupid. Diaper, wings, bow and arrows. The whole nine yards. It got late and I got drunk. Not wasted, but definitely buzzed. I was chatting up a girl at the bar, thinking I was getting somewhere and maybe I wasn't going home alone on V Day, when this guy comes up all pissed off at nothing, yelling that I need to get a shirt on. 'No shoes, no shirt, no service!'. He's completely blitzed and shouting at everyone, even the girl. He starts talking shit to her, calling her a skank and a gold digger. He says I'm probably impotent from the steroids. Everything. Every insult you can think of, he's hurling at me and this girl. But then he put his hands on her and that was it for me. I punched him in the face and he and his buddies jumped me. Three of them against me and there's this girl screaming in the middle of it.

"The cops got called. We all got arrested, and because I'm in the NFL and I'm bigger than all of them, I got slapped with an Assault charge. My lawyer told me it doesn't matter that three of them jumped me because I threw the first punch and I had the lesser injuries. He said any judge would say it was my fault, so I settled out of court to avoid having it on my record. The arrest is still there but the Assault charges were dropped."

"How much?"

Shane shakes his head, confused. "How much what? How much did I have to pay?"

"Yes."

"A lot."

"A lot as in I could buy a new car with the money or a new house?"

"Why?" he laughs. "You looking for a payday? I'm

not hitting you so you can upgrade your ride."

I smirk. "You can't upgrade my ride."

"It's that good, huh?"

"It's over there." I nod to the first row of spaces in front of the studio where my fire engine red Fiat sits gleaming in the sun.

Shane laughs when he sees it; a sound so full I feel it pushing against me harder than his shoulder. I taste it in the sugar in my coffee. "That's not a car. It's a Matchbox."

"No, it's not!" I cry defensively. "It's beautiful."

"How many clowns can you fit in that?"

I laugh, hugging my coffee against my chest. "Shut up. I bought that the first day I was in L.A. I've never been so excited in my life."

"A golf cart would have been cheaper. And faster."

"Alright, Vin Diesel, what do you drive?"

He gestures far down the alley between the buildings to a Jeep with the top popped off and wheels as tall as I am. "That's my baby."

"I like the color," I concede, admiring the red. "That's about it."

"Nah, that's just the outside. She's so much more inside."

"If your croissants are inside, they won't be for long. Without a roof, a bird or a squirrel is going to sneak in there and steal them."

"They can have them. They probably need them more than I do."

My smile softens as my insides start to thaw under the warming sun. It's getting close to seven. I can feel it in the air. In the way the birds are chirping overhead in the trees above us. The lot will be loud soon, but for now, just for a few minutes more, it's peaceful. Just

Shane and me and our awkwardness slowly evaporating into nothing.

It makes me uneasy, that easy feeling. I've never trusted it.

I take a short breath that tastes bitter on my tongue. "I'm sorry too."

"Sorry for what?"

"I'm sorry I went after you at the club. I shouldn't have. And I'm sorry I was late to the park. And that I blamed you for the package."

"What package?"

I try not to be irritated. Even if he'd been better briefed on the show, he still might not know what a 'package' is. I should try to be patient because he came here eating humble pie this morning. The best I can do is not throw it in his face. "It's a production term. Our meeting was a package. Our rehearsals will be packages. It's an edited series of videos that will be put together to tell a short story."

"We were interviewed for a documentary last year and I never heard that term."

"They probably never used it around you so they wouldn't have to explain it."

"I guess they weren't as good a teacher as you," he replies lightly.

I look at him sideways, not sure if he's being sarcastic or not. He stares down at me innocently and I can't tell. It's frustrating. "Anyway, it was your first time shooting a package. You didn't know the rules. Someone should have told you, the same way someone should have told me the right time."

"Did you ever figure out who gave you the wrong one?"

"Yeah," I answer heavily. "I know who it was."

"Are you going to bite their head off or forgive them?"

"I don't forgive easily."

Gently, he bumps my leg with his. "So, are we cool?"

"Yeah, we're cool." I bump his leg back, adding dryly, "For now."

"Good enough. For now."

His smile makes me warm inside. It makes me pliant in a way I shouldn't be. I hate the feeling because I like it, and I like it because it's nice. Who hates nice things?

A girl who was never allowed to have them, that's who.

I look away from Shane, turning to my drink because we have a perfect relationship; coffee and me. We are bitter and sweet with just the right amount of sugar. Just enough heat to keep me happy. Shane, on the other hand, is going to be confusing. He's going to be difficult. All sugar all the time with so much heat I can feel it in my belly before I've even taken a sip.

"You'll have to meet with wardrobe today," I tell him, getting our ship back on course. Steering us into familiar waters that I know how to navigate. "They want to get your measurements."

He nods amicably. "Just show me where to go."

"And here I was worried you wouldn't be able to take orders."

He chuckles. "I'm in the NFL, Boss. All I do is take orders."

"And hit people."

"When they tell me to."

"Does it hurt," I ask curiously.

"What? Taking a hit or doling one out?"

"Either."

He considers it for a second before shrugging. "Nah.

It did, at first, but you get used to it. It's probably like dancing in those heels you were wearing at the Carousel. They look like murder to me but I bet you can't even feel 'em on your feet."

"No, I feel them," I chuckle darkly. "And they hurt."

"Why do you wear them?"

"It's my job."

"But do you like them?"

I cast him a wary glance. "Do you like hitting people?"

"Kind of, yeah," he admits, unashamed.

I shake my head in amazement. "I can't understand that."

"And I can't understand those shoes."

"I can't exactly win going out there in flip flops."

"Winning is important to you?"

"It's not important to you?" I fire back.

He nods as though he understands. I think he actually does. We want to win at different things, but we both want it badly enough to become accustomed to pain for it. If you're willing to ache for a thing, you have to love it. It's the only kind of love I can understand.

In the distance, I hear the whir of an electric engine. My heart races and stalls, falling flat on its face inside my chest. I'm grateful I'm not so translucent today. Shane doesn't see it. All he sees is the gleaming white golf cart headed our way.

"Who's the big shot in the wheels?" he asks.

"Eric Croft," I answer evenly. "The Executive Producer."

"What's he like?"

"A producer."

"Bossy?"

"Extremely."

"Bossier than you, Boss?"

I smile mildly. "No one is bossier than me."

Eric isn't driving the golf cart. He has Taj chauffeuring him while he clicks away on his phone. He looks fresh, like he only just got up, and I wonder if he slept here last night. I wonder if he stayed home with his wife. I wonder how I feel about it if he did, but the feeling doesn't come. I reach for my reaction but all I find is empty air.

"Is that him riding shotgun?" Shane mutters to me. "The aging Adam Levine?"

I laugh into my coffee. Eric would hate to hear him say that. *The Voice* is stiff competition for us and Adam Levine is a thorn embedded deep in Eric's side.

"That's him," I whisper.

"Do we love him or hate him?"

"*We* are not a *we*."

"Sure we are, Sutton," he corrects me matter-of-fact. "We're a team, aren't we? We're in this together."

"We are, are we?"

"That's how I'm playing it."

"Then I guess that's what we are."

"So? Love him or hate him?"

Isn't that the question? Easy answer is, I hate him. But if I look a little deeper and really consider my feelings – our past, our present, and our future – well, then, I *really* fucking hate him. I hate him with every ounce of blood inside my body. I hate him with the pieces he's left inside of me, because he hasn't always been so careful and calculating as he was the other night. There have times he's been downright reckless.

"Eric loves himself enough for everyone," I tell Shane quietly.

Eric spots us. He immediately paints on his happy face.

"Shane Lowry," he calls. He steps out of the cart before Taj has it to a full stop because he thinks he's cool and busy and too much for everyone and everything.

Shane stands to meet him. He towers over Eric, sparking a strange sense of glee inside me. "That's me. It's nice to meet you, Eric."

"My reputation has preceded me again."

"Sutton has been talking about you."

"All good things, I hope."

"Sutton only ever says good things."

Eric laughs at what a lie that is. "She's our brightest star," he tells Shane as though it's an agreement. As though my talent is a testament to my character. "She has you here early. I know she likes to crack the whip, but not this hard this soon."

"I want people to take their job seriously," I explain coldly. "That doesn't seem like it should qualify me as a slave driver."

Eric grins at Shane. "See what I mean?"

"She's really passionate about the show," Shane sidesteps neatly. He glances down at me with that smile of his; the warm one that makes me vulnerable. Like a turtle without its shell.

"You're a lucky man," Eric promises. "She's our reigning champion on the show. Did she show you The Wall? It's where we have photos of all of our winners."

"I haven't seen it yet, no."

"Let's do it now. We have some time before everyone else gets here. You can have the Grand Tour."

Shane glances at me furtively, checking on me. Asking me what I want because whatever my answer is, he'll follow. I feel it without needing to ask. He's letting me lead because he's seen something I wish he wouldn't notice; Eric isn't looking at me. Eric is talking only to him, acting as though I'm not even here. What he doesn't know is that this is normal. This is what Eric and I do after we've slept together – we ignore each other.

I wish the silence could go on forever.

I want to say that Shane's concern annoys me or that I don't want his pity, but that's not what it feels like. When he looks at me, waiting for my marching orders, it feels like solidarity. Like a partner in my incredibly isolated world. And that feels absolutely amazing.

It also feels so foreign I don't know how to handle it.

"Let's get it over with so we can get to work," I agree bitingly.

Shane waits for me to fall in line behind Eric before bringing up the rear. He keeps a good distance but I can feel him at my back. His heat, his presence – it presses against me like a warm wind rushing up from the ocean.

It's a sharp contrast to the arctic chill coming off Eric.

CHAPTER ELEVEN

SHANE

May 4th
Charles Windt Stadium
Los Angeles, CA

I smell bacon. It's in the air inside the stadium. Maybe the concessions are cooking up hotdogs or maybe I'm having a stroke, but it doesn't matter why I smell it, the problem is it's making me so hungry I can hardly think straight.

We've been training all morning. Four straight hours of running, rushing, and being extra careful not to touch each other so we don't get fined, and I'm ready to collapse. But there's no time. I have to rush from here to the KBC studio for rehearsals with Sutton.

She and Eric showed me around yesterday. They introduced me to the crew and the other teams paired up for the show. I didn't know a single one of the players, a fact that surprised Sutton.

"You seriously don't know any of them?" she whispered to me when we were lined up around the stage. The choreographer, Clara, was in the middle, explaining the basics of the opening number for the first show.

I didn't understand a word of it.

I shook my head at Sutton. "There are fifty-three players on every team and thirty-four teams in the league. You do the math."

"You do it. I want to see if you can."

I cast her an amused/offended frown. "Are you calling me dumb?"

"That depends. Can you do the multiplication?"

"One thousand eight hundred and two players," I rattled off from memory, not math. "I know maybe two hundred of them by name."

"All of these guys knew your name when you walked in," she pointed out quietly.

"Because I got ejected from the Super Bowl. I doubt you knew every dancer on Broadway but if they shit their pants on stage during *Wicked*, you'd know their name."

Sutton laughed, drawing Clara's attention. We were scolded, we said we were sorry, but I don't believe for a second that either of us honestly was.

Sutton is a tough one to pin down. One minute she's sour as a lemon and the next she's light as air. She's warm as a summer breeze, and I can't figure out how to make that girl stay. She's never around for long. As far as I can tell, the default setting for Sutton Roe is annoyed. It's not always at me but I'll probably take the brunt of it while we're working together.

"Step it up, Lowry!" Coach Bailey shouts at me. "Five more minutes! Don't you dare let up now!"

I push through the burning in my legs and lungs to run at full speed when what my body wants more than anything is to collapse on the cool ground and pass out. I'm in a herd of men thumping their feet against the ground in a disordered drum beat that I feel in my heart. It's screaming. It's propelling me forward because I refuse to be the slowest beat. I've never been and never will be the weakest link on this team. I'll leave that to the fat asses on the defensive line.

When the five minutes are up and Coach Bailey blows a shrill whistle to stop us, it feels like it's been an hour. I stop slowly, pacing to keep my body moving so it doesn't cramp. Everyone around me does the same – all thirty-eight of them. We're missing rookies not allowed to train with us yet and the injured guys still healing up for the new season, but the field looks full with so many bodies on it after a long drought. It feels good to get back at it.

It feels good to be home.

"Listen up," Coach Allen commands. He doesn't raise his voice. He makes us quiet down to hear him. "You're off for the weekend. Enjoy it but don't get crazy. Remember you have four days of this to look forward to next week, so rest up and don't do anything stupid." He points at me with a small smile on his old, puckered lips. "I'm looking at you, Lowry. Remind that TV show they've got you on loan. I want you back in the same condition you're in now. No injuries."

I nod, sweat dripping down over my eyes. "Yes, sir," I huff.

"All of you go get cleaned up and then hustle back out here. We have a surprise for you."

I hurry to the locker room with the rest of the team, but I don't fight for a chance at the showers. I don't have time. If I hesitate I'll be late and there's not a chance in hell I'm evening the score with Sutton like that. Her showing up late to the park is the only upper hand I have. Judging by what I've seen of her so far, I'm going to want to hold onto that. I stink of sweat but she'll have to deal with it. All I can do is spray a cloud of deodorant and cologne to walk through, and I'm out the door. I leave men gagging on the mixture behind me.

"What the fuck, Lowry!?" Sam shouts after me.

Tyus coughs roughly, trying to wave away the scent with his hat. "My eyes are watering. Is that teargas?"

I ignore them, bolting through the door with my

duffel bag slung heavily over my shoulder. The sound of my feet thumping through the tunnels echoes like a drumbeat; the same one I was playing on the field. I don't see a soul as I make my way toward the exit, but the smell of bacon is getting stronger. My empty stomach grumbles greedily in anticipation of nothing.

When I round the corner to the backdoor, I run right into Sloane Ashford. She's in a long, loose dress that hangs like yellow flower petals to her knees. Her blond hair is tied into a smooth ponytail that shows off a pair of simple pearl earrings. She's barely wearing an ounce of makeup. Not a single piece of jewelry besides the pearls, and it hits me how soft she looks. That's unusual for her. She's beautiful, no doubt about it, but she's also tough as steel. Sloane is what my mom calls a spitfire. You don't cross her. Not unless you're looking to get burned.

She stumbles back a step, her hand coming up to press against her stomach. "Shane, you scared me," she breathes.

"Sorry." I reach out to take her elbow to steady her. "I figured people would hear me coming and get out of the way."

"I should have. I wasn't thinking."

"Are you okay?"

She waves me away, taking a step back. "I'm good. Thanks."

"Are you sure? You look kind of pale."

"Are you leaving already?" she asks, sidestepping my question.

"Yeah, I've gotta get to KBC in the next thirty minutes."

"Oh, that sucks. You'll miss the party."

"What party?"

Sloane drums her fingers gently on her stomach with a small smile. "The baby shower."

"Whose?"

"Shane," she laughs, looking down pointedly at her stomach.

"Holy hell," I mutter.

I fall back a step to look her up and down, taking in the whole picture. I feel like an idiot that I didn't notice before. I mean, I noticed that she'd put on a few pounds recently but you don't say anything about that to a woman. Not if you want to live to see tomorrow. But now that I know, I can see it in the slight bulge under her dress and the softness in her skin. She has that glow they say mothers get when they're pregnant. Coach Bailey's wife looked the same way a couple years ago when she was expecting, only she was huge. She could barely sit down without a forklift to get her back up. Sloane just looks like she's had a big meal.

"Congrats, Sly," I tell her with a smile. I tug at my shirt that's stuck to my body by a thick layer of rapidly drying sweat. "I'd hug you but I smell like shit and I don't want to drip on your dress."

"You always have been the thoughtful one," she laughs. Her hand goes back to her belly and I think it's an unconscious, protective thing.

"Sorry I'm going to miss the party. And that I don't have a present for you."

"No, it's fine. We don't want anyone to give us anything. We did it as a surprise so no one would have time to buy a gift. We just wanted to do a meal together as a family."

"Now I feel worse that I'm leaving."

Sloane smiles encouragingly. "Don't. It's good that you're doing that show."

"It's for a good cause."

"It is, but you could write a check to them any day of the week. I think it's good you're going to be a contestant."

"Why? Have you been dying to see my sweet dance moves?"

"No."

"Oh."

"I'm glad because they need a jumpstart and you're the kind of guy that could give it to them. That show has gotten too boring to watch."

I laugh. "My mom wouldn't like to hear you say that."

"Tell Lynn I'm sorry," she chuckles. "But it doesn't mean I'm wrong. They know it, too. I did my research before bringing it to Colt when they called. Their ratings are way down. People aren't watching like they used to because it's the same old shit every time. To spice it up, they tried manufacturing drama. This dancer doesn't like the other dancer. So-and-so doesn't get along with their partner. They made a big deal of injuries that were nothing. All for the ratings and none of it has been helping. It's why they're doing this charity special. If it doesn't get viewers back, the show is finished in three seasons. Maybe less."

"Damn," I mutter. "I wonder if Chris knows all of that."

"He's a good agent. I'm sure he did his homework. It's our job."

"Is all of that why Trey said no when they offered it to him?"

"No, I told Trey to do it. He'd be great PR for them. If they could get brand name faces on the screen they might be able to save themselves, but Trey was thinking about me and the baby. I'm due while you're filming and he didn't want to miss anything."

I hesitate, my eyes instinctively going to her stomach again. "You're due in under ten weeks."

"About six, actually," she confesses quietly. Her face is serious and drawn, and for a second she looks tired. Maybe even scared. It's hard to tell. I never imagined Sloane Ashford could feel fear. "He's small. Really small."

I have no clue what to say to that. A 'really small' baby doesn't sound like a good thing. It sounds dangerous, and the tightness in her shoulders tells me that it is. She's afraid, and my pity isn't going to do a damn thing about that. Nothing can. If I can't help, the least I can do is not make it worse.

"You're naming him after me, right?"

Sloane chuckles, shaking her head. "I might have to. We're having trouble agreeing on a name."

"Shane is classic. That's all I'm saying."

"I'll run it by Trey. I promise." She gestures over her shoulder toward the door. "There's a food truck outside with a roasted pig in the back. Ask them to fix you a plate to take with you before you go."

I touch her arm to lean in and kiss her cheek. "You're a saint."

"I know."

I drive like a bat out of hell to the studio with the top and doors off the Jeep. A big white to-go container of deliciousness sits pretty as anything on the seat next to me. It almost slides off and out onto the street when I take a hard left toward the KBC gates, but I grab it just in time. I'd legit cry if I lost it. The people in the truck were an older Hawaiian couple and they fed me like family. My plate is heaped with BBQ pork, fresh coleslaw, homemade sweet bread, and some kind of paste in a weird gray color that I'm scared of but excited about too. I'll try anything once.

When I spot Sutton's Fiat parked in front of the studio with an empty space next to it, I slide right in. With the two cars side by side like this, I get an even better idea of how small hers is. I'm ninety percent sure you could fit the Fiat inside the Jeep, like a mom and her baby. If the Fiat's mom was an American made badass with fatty tires and a snorkel.

I walk through the door to the studio right at noon. Inside the first door there's a guard. He checks my ID against the list on a worn-out clipboard before letting me through to the second area. It's bigger than the first but emptier. The floors, the walls, and the ceiling are all black. It feels like a giant coffin. Despite its size, I feel claustrophobic when the doors close me in. Yesterday Eric told me it's to let people in and out of the studio during filming without allowing daylight to ruin the show. Both doors are never open at the same time and they're engineered to open and close soundlessly.

I'm relieved to pass through the second door and into the main studio area. The space explodes from a black box to a massive ballroom. There's a dancefloor in the middle surrounded by a stage for an orchestra and a staircase that leads to nowhere. On every side there's seating. Tables with unlit candles in the center are closest to the dancefloor, but in front of it, where the view is the best, are rows of chairs lined up like in a theater. They rise up and up to a second floor. Then a third. Balconies all around the room are lit up with bright white lights that make it all feel more garish than I imagined. Maybe they dim them for the show. Maybe it's a trick of photography that makes it look softer on

TV. I don't know. Even after my tour yesterday and an afternoon full of explanations on the show and how it works, I don't feel like I understand all of it. I'm out of my element. That should bother me but it doesn't. It gets me excited; the feeling turning in my stomach like a living thing inside me. Or maybe that's the hunger.

Dammit, I'm starving.

I pop the top on the box in my hand to pull a piece of bread from the corner. It's warm and wet with condensation from the pork next to it. I'm tempted to dig my fingers into it to get a taste, but I satisfy myself with the bread for now. One bite destroys half of the roll and my cheeks are full with it when I turn the knob on the rehearsal room.

There's a brass bar running across a wall of mirrors on the east side. The floors are light wood, the walls red brick, and the ceilings are high and exposed. I can see every fixture and wire running wild overhead. Yesterday, Eric told me that there are offices above us. His and his assistant producer. The director. The choreographer. On this first level, behind the rehearsal rooms, is a doctor's office with someone on hand at all hours, in case of emergency. A kitchen is next door to the infirmary to make sure we're well hydrated and fed. There are green rooms for the posher contestants, but none of us NFL boys have claimed one. Eric told me to make use of any of them in my downtime to watch TV or take a nap on a couch that's barely long enough for Sutton to catch forty winks. I'd be lucky to get my torso to fit on one.

She's in the rehearsal room waiting for me. Of course. Her back is to the door but she can see me in the mirror behind the gold bar she's stretching on. Her leg is up high, reminding me how flexible she is. Her hair is pinned high on her head, exposing her serious face. Her clothes hug her body tight as a second skin in blushing pink and heather gray. She's barely showing any of her natural skin, but her clothes leave me wanting for almost nothing and everything at the same time. Her body is beautiful packaging wrapped around a sour candy, and I can't decide if I want to lick her slow or spit her out.

"You're late," she tells me in the mirror.

"Hello to you too."

"Hello," she replies drolly, adding, "You're late."

"By a minute. I was in the building on time."

"On time is late."

"Sorry, Boss."

She frowns at the box in my hand, slowly switching legs on the bar. "What is that?"

"My lunch."

Her frown deepens. "You can't eat in here."

"Is that your rule or the studio's?"

"Would it matter to you?"

"Not much." I drop down onto my ass in the middle of the floor with my legs crisscrossed in front of me. I pop the top on the box and dig out a massive sporkful of pork. It dissolves in a savory-sweet breath on my tongue. "Dammit, that's good," I mutter happily.

"It smells disgusting."

"Does that mean you don't want to share?"

"Fuck no," she replies emphatically.

I laugh, digging into the coleslaw. "Your loss."

"That's what you said about the croissants and I'm still standing."

"Let me guess. No carbs and no meat?"

"I'm a vegetarian, yes."

"So what *do* you eat, anyway?"

She bends her body flat over her leg, grunting, "Nothing, if I can help it."

"Sounds miserable."

"It has its perks."

"Like what?"

She doesn't answer me. Her forehead is pressed against her knee, her arms stretched out to curl her fingers around her foot. Her body is incredible, and I think that's her answer. That's the perk of not eating anything but lettuce. She looks good, yeah, but she could use a little extra meat on her bones. She's so thin it's almost scary.

I eat as she stretches, both of us listening to the soft classical music that fills the room.

"What song is this?" I ask her between bites.

"It's *Fantasia*," she answers, her voice muffled and small. "Mozart."

"Like the Disney movie?"

"Sure. Yes."

I smile as I try a bite of the gray pudding. It tastes like glue. "I like it."

She turns her head to look at me incredulously. "You like Mozart?"

"I definitely wasn't talking about this shit." I hold up a load of the viscous nasty for her to see. It slips off the spork and plops back into the box. "Whatever the hell it is."

"It looks disgusting."

"Tastes it too."

"And smells it." She wrinkles her nose, dropping her foot to the ground. I watch with interest as she makes her way over to me, the disgust on her face deepening. "My God, Shane. You stink. What is that? Pig flavored body spray?"

"It's BBQ pork in the box and a mix of CK One and Old Spice on my body."

"And sweat. You definitely smell of sweat."

"You weren't supposed to smell that through the CK One and Old Spice."

"Well, I do and it's awful." She turns her back to me, going to the other side of the room. "When you're finished feeding, go take a shower. There's a big one in the greenroom closest to the exit. You might fit inside."

I nod, turning back to the remains of my lunch. "I would have showered before I left the stadium but I didn't want to be late. I was sure you'd give me a hard time about it."

"So you decided to show up smelling like a frat house after a weekend bender?"

"Glad to see I was wrong about the hard time," I mutter under my breath.

"I heard that," she shouts from the corner.

I smile at her as I finish my lunch. She watches me in the shadows of the far side of the room, arms wrapped around her stomach impatiently.

"Take the box to the trash in the greenroom," she tells me when I stand. "I don't want this space stinking of poi."

"What's poi?"

"The gray shit. Get it out of here. Get cleaned up. Come back immediately so we can *finally* get to work."

"I'm on it, Boss."

"Go!"

CHAPTER TWELVE

SUTTON

I wander the room as I wait for him. Occasionally I'll leap or spin. Lunge. I try standing up on my toes the way I used to when I was a ballerina but I'm too out of practice. My feet scream in protest until I drop back down on my soles. I'm only twenty-one but I'm painfully aware that I'm not as young as I used to be. I'm not as balanced. Not as agile. I'm definitely not as innocent. What I still am is angry. I've always been angry. It's my constant companion. The only thing that changes is who or what I'm angry at.

Today it feels like everything. I'm angry with me and the show and Eric and air. I'm angry at so many things. So many people. All the time.

It's exhausting.

I wish I was back on the stage in New York. I could step outside of myself and into a character with a completely different life. I'd be someone else with a different world full of different problems that feel so much smaller than they are because they aren't really mine. Nothing in the world is as daunting as your own troubles. They can be the size of planets in your eyes while to the rest of the world they look like distant stars. I want that distance. I want anonymity from myself.

I go to the digital display on the wall that controls the speakers hidden throughout the room. I can pull any song from one of the millions in the digital library stored here in the studio, but it takes me only a second to pick the one I want. The one I need. The song will hurt like knives through my heart, making me bleed on the floor until I'm limp and listless. It's old medicine. The dangerous kind. I'll bleed myself until the sickness is out and I'm nearly spent, but I'll be better when it's over. I'll be less and I'll be me, and that's the only way I can live anymore.

I jump right into the dance. It's mournful. Painful. I glide across the room on air and sorrow, my limbs heavy with emotion that tries to drag me down. That's the way the song feels; like lead. I immerse myself in it completely. I live it as I dance it, letting it take me over. Take me away. I let it move me in broad, rich strokes across the canvas of the dancefloor. I'm painting a picture in dark grays, rich purples, and aching reds that slash at my mind with every arc of my arm. I don't have to think as I move. This dance is one I remember as clearly as my own name even though I never performed it. I thought I was meant to, but maybe I wasn't. My whole life feels like that. Like I thought I'd be one thing but I'm something else entirely. I just have no clue what that is or who I am, and maybe that's what has me so tired. The never knowing.

"I love that song."

I pause mid-step. My heart slams in my chest with surprise and exertion. I keep my eyes closed for just a second longer, just one more breath to myself, but then it's gone. I blink into the brilliant light of the studio to find Clara standing in the doorway. She's watching me curiously.

"Me too," I answer, feeling breathless and oddly out of shape. "*On my Own* is one of my favorites."

"I didn't know you were in *Les Mis.*"

"I wasn't."

"Do you just like—"

"I'm sorry if it was too loud." I cross the room to smash the STOP button on the display. The space falls into a deafening silence. "I know how much Eric hates it when I turn the music up too high."

"He's not here. You can have it as loud as you want."

I shake my head tightly. "I'm done."

She studies me closely. I feel her scrutiny down to my marrow, but that's my body. She can't see what I won't let her. I shroud the rest of me. The most precious, delicate pieces that aren't ready for the light of day.

"You look tired," she tells me quietly.

"I didn't sleep well last night."

"You should take something tonight. Get some rest. Ambien has always worked wonders for me."

I wrinkle my nose in disgust. "No. I don't like drugs."

"I wasn't suggesting you take meth or something."

"I know, but my mom made me take stuff as a kid. Tons of stuff. Uppers. Downers. Diet pills. She had me on birth control the second I turned thirteen to stop my periods because they got in the way of rehearsals." I frown down at my feet, my chest burning. "I'm not doing any of that anymore."

Clara nods, her eyes digging deeper. "Okay. I'm sorry."

"It's fine."

She glances around the room, sniffing softly. "What is that smell? Is that bacon?"

"BBQ pork."

"You ate meat?" she gasps.

"No," I laugh. "I've never. Shane brought in his lunch."

"Are you kidding me? You let him eat in here?"

"I told him he couldn't and he did it anyway. What

do you want me to do? He's like a thousand pounds. I can't stop him from doing anything."

"Where is he now?"

"Showering. He stank from football practice so I sent him to the green rooms to get cleaned up."

"He's just going to work up a sweat again."

"Yes, but this will be dance sweat. It's different."

"It's all going to smell like pork."

I feel my stomach roll; same as it did when I caught that first whiff of him. Chemicals in the deodorant. Alcohol in the cologne. Sweet BBQ sauce on the pig. I don't mind sweat. Sweat I can handle because I'm used to it. It's the mix of everything else that makes me sick to my stomach. The smell of cooked meat has always been like manure to me.

There was a brief window in my teens when I dabbled in bulimia. I had to stop because I was losing too much weight too fast, but ever since then, my gag reflex is on a hair-trigger. The littlest thing can set me off, turning my stomach to the point of total revulsion. There are certain smells that do it. Certain tastes. Certain people.

Clara comes deeper into the room. She folds her arms over her chest, getting down to business. "Maybe try to go easy on this one. We can't afford another Joey Lawrence incident. The show isn't strong enough to handle it right now."

"Joey Lawrence was not my fault."

"They never are."

"Don't take his side," I demand. "He drew first blood. He called me a raging cunt."

"After you called him a bald has-been!"

I snort, trying to contain laughter that doesn't want to be contained. I lose the battle in the end, laughing harder than I have in days. It feels good; like stretching. Like I'm pressing against my body and making it bigger than it was before.

"He might have been right," I admit, still chuckling. "Maybe I was a cunt."

Clara smiles. "You certainly weren't sweet."

"I don't do sweet."

"You could try with Shane."

"Don't start," I warn her.

"He'd be good for you."

I shake my head firmly. "Nope. He'd be perfect for some nice West Coast girl with cowboy boots and bangs."

"You could pull off cowboy boots."

"But never bangs, so let it go."

"Fine," she relents on a sigh. "What's your song choice for this week? You guys got the Charleston, right?"

I smile devilishly. "I picked *Lucky Strike*."

"Maroon 5?"

"Adam Levine himself."

"Oh honey," Clara chuckles, dropping down to sit on the floor by the mirrors. "You're going to give Eric such an aneurysm."

"I hope so."

"You might not want to poke that bear. With the show in the state it's in, he's not feeling very forgiving lately."

I cross the room to drop down next to her on the floor. She immediately takes my hand in both of hers, warming my cold fingers that never seem to be anything but icy. It's a circulation issue. My mom has it too.

"I'll stop," I lie about Eric.

That's something else I inherited from my mom; lying.

Clara reaches out to tuck a stray hair behind my ear. "You really do look tired, honey."

"I really do feel tired," I admit with a sigh.

"Have you eaten today?"

"I had a banana at breakfast."

"Nothing since?"

"I'm not hungry."

She frowns with disapproval. "Have you ever thought about having fun with the competition and enjoying it instead of pushing yourself to the brink of hospitalization every season trying to win it?"

"That was one time, and it was because we all got the flu. I threw up more than the girl on *The Exorcist*. Of course I almost went to the hospital."

"Linda Blair."

"Here we go," I mutter. "You're going to do that thing, aren't you? The one where you give me a Hollywood history lesson every time I mention a movie?"

"She was nominated for an Academy Award for that one. She didn't win it but she got a Golden Globe."

"Oh my God," I lament sarcastically. "She was robbed."

Clara smiles. "You're just jealous."

"I'm really not."

"You are. It's okay."

"I have two Tony Awards and a Grammy. I wouldn't wipe my ass with a Golden Globe."

"Jesus, I would hope not."

I laugh, leaning into her warmth. She lets me sit too close until our sides are running parallel and I can feel her breathing. This is the kind of contact I like. The easy kind. The kind where no one wants anything from me in return. Clara is like the mom I always wanted but never had. Affectionate without being cloying. Teasing without being cruel.

"Why'd you come in here today?" I ask her quietly. "You're not supposed to interact with us during our rehearsals. They'll think you're playing favorites and helping me."

"Of course I'm playing favorites. You think I want to look at Melisandre's pinched face on The Wall for the rest of eternity?"

I smile affectionately. "Cheater."

"Only if you let me help you."

"I won't," I vow, my pride rising like a balloon in my chest.

"That's because you never do anything wrong."

"That definitely doesn't feel true."

"It looks true from the outside."

"Thank you."

"Not a compliment," she promises me. "You're boring."

I laugh, jerking my hand back playfully. "And people call *me* a bitch."

"I'm serious. You should do something ugly once in a while. It's good for a girl to get some dirt under her nails."

"Why would I ever want to do that?"

"Because it's fun."

"I've never done anything just because it's fun."

"And that's your problem right there."

It's not. My problems are mountains high and oceans deep, but a lack of fun has never felt like one of them. It feels like a side effect of everything else. Like the symptom of a sickness, not the source. Men are the source of my problems. They always have been. Ever since I was just a girl.

Dread floods my body. I feel faint for half a heartbeat. Like my blood disappears from my veins before it comes rushing back at full force, nearly knocking me out of my own body. Garret's face flashes in front of my eyes before I can get a hold of him, and then he's there in the room. His fingers are in my hair, his hand under my dress, and my heart is rising in my throat where it beats the rhythm to a song I never want to hear again. I blink rapidly, trying to clear my mind, but he refuses to leave.

He never did what I wanted. Never. He's so much like Eric in that way, I almost can't tell them apart.

"Sutton?" Clara's voice calls from outside the cotton crammed in my ears.

I swallow thickly. "Yeah?"

"Are you okay?"

The door to the studio opens suddenly. Shane steps in, his head nearly brushing the top of the frame. His hair is wet from his shower. It clumps together in bright tresses that glisten like sunshine. His face is flushed, his chin cleanshaven for the first time since I met him. It makes him look younger. More my age than his. It also softens him somehow, or maybe that's me. Maybe it's the light. Maybe it's Clara. Maybe it's the way the moon is lined up with Mars — I don't know. But the change is good. As the first breath of him comes into my lungs, I smell soap and hot water. A man's musk without any assistance from cologne. He smells nice and natural, the scent instantly washing away all lingering images of Garret from my mind, and suddenly I feel good. Better than I have all morning.

He smiles when he spots us sitting together against

the wall. "Ladies. I have been detoxed."

"Give us a spin," Clara commands, twirling her finger in the air. "Let's see."

I push her hand down into her lap, shaking my head at Shane. "Don't do that. Don't listen to Clara unless you absolutely have to. She's a sexual harassment suit just waiting to happen."

Shane smiles at her. "I won't tell if she won't."

"Do not encourage her," I mumble. I stand, reaching down to help Clara up off the floor. "Besides, she was just leaving."

"She's not going to watch?" Shane asks.

"I'm not allowed to interfere or assist," Clara explains. "I only get you guys for the group numbers."

Shane opens the door for her when Clara leaves. She smiles at him, thanks him, and casts me a meaningful glance as she exits.

"Are you ready?" I bark once the door is closed.

Shane nods, bouncing up on the balls of his feet. "I'm ready."

"You ran at practice, right?"

"That's almost all we did."

"Good. We can skip the workout and jump right into the dance. We need to practice that shoulder lift. The dismount was shaky yesterday."

"I'm nervous I'm going to drop you on your head," Shane confesses bluntly.

"Me too, but the only way to get over that is to practice it until we can do it in our sleep." I motion for him to stand in front of the mirrors next to me. "Right foot to start. Ready and five-six-seven-eight."

We launch into the number from somewhere around the middle. I watch Shane in the mirror as his feet fly, sharply kicking out the steps I taught him yesterday. We do a few gestures that he describes as 'totally Chaplin' before he slides out on his knees in front of me. He pounds his palms on the ground to the beat, keeping his head low. I run at him from behind, leapfrogging over him. I stand with my feet apart and my body rigid as I wait for him to make his next move. If he does it wrong, I'll fall. If he does it right, I'll be sitting over eight feet in the air.

Shane puts his head between my legs, takes hold of my ankles, and stands effortlessly with me on his shoulders. It's dizzying how quickly he manages it. How incredibly strong he obviously is. His hands are hot on my ankles, steadying me on my perch, but he doesn't need to. I clench my thighs tightly around his neck, tickled by the thick tresses of his hair. It sends shivers down my spine. Luckily, the feeling only lasts for a second before he's supposed to bring me back down into his arms. Or two seconds. Three? *Five*?

I look at him impatiently in the mirror. "Shane?"

"I know," he replies apologetically.

"What's the problem?"

"I forgot which way you come down?"

"On your right."

"Right. Okay." His hands flex on my ankles nervously. "Are you ready?"

"Whenever you are."

Just like I taught him, he leans us to the right, toppling me off his shoulder. It's an uneasy feeling, but I keep my cool and tuck my arms in tight to my body to make myself a sleeker package. He catches me easily in his arms. He's meant to drop my upper body, holding onto my knees to swing me around his torso where he'll catch my shoulders and release my legs, only it doesn't happen. He freezes again, holding me cradled in his long arms.

I stare up at him impatiently. "What's wrong now?"

He frowns deeply. "I'm nervous I'm going to drop you."

"Am I that heavy?"

"No," he chuckles absently. "You weigh nothing. That's part of what scares me. I'm worried about flipping you around and losing hold. What if you fall?"

"I get back up and we do it again," I say sternly.

He doesn't like that answer. "Can't we put some mats down or something?"

"No."

He hesitates, his eyes on mine. He's searching for something but I won't let him find it. I won't give on this. If he can't get the confidence to do this first move, he'll never find it when we really need it later on.

"I promised I wouldn't hurt you," he reminds me quietly.

I feel my heart heave. It lurches somewhere south before rising up again, fuller than before. I can feel his own beating against my body where it's held tightly to his chest. His heart is steady and strong; just like the man it beats for. "You're not going to hurt me. But you're not going to be a coward either."

A smile plays at the corner of his mouth. "No one's ever called me a coward before."

"Don't make me do it again."

"Yes, Boss."

"Are we going to do this or are you going to stand here holding me all day?"

His fingers move against my sides, warm and wide. "I mean, I wouldn't mind," he teases, his voice deep and sultry.

"I would," I lie sharply. "Put me down. We're going

again. No hesitations."

Shane puts me down on the ground. I'm steady on my feet, but my skin is humming in warm bands around my body where his arms held me for too long. I'm burned by him. By his hands and his eyes that watch me intently as I try to wipe away the lingering feel of him.

It doesn't work and we both know it.

CHAPTER THIRTEEN

SHANE

May 10th
KBC Studios
Los Angeles, CA

Everything has been leading up to this. I've been working with Sutton non-stop for a week solid and it still feels like I'm not prepared for what's about to happen. We've been in the studio since seven this morning going through full hair, makeup, and dress rehearsals for every single element of tonight's show. It will air for an hour but it takes at least three times that to run through it in dress. We were constantly stopped for wardrobe and lighting changes. There were so many interruptions and changes, I don't actually feel like the rehearsal did me a damn bit of good, but Sutton said it's not about us. It's about making McKay, the director, and Clara, happy. It's nearly five o'clock, ten hours after I first got here, and whether anyone is happy or not, the show goes live in ten minutes.

I've got half a boner, I'm so excited.

"I want *nothing* in your mouths." Taj walks down the strict line of football players and dancers with a black trash can in his hand. "No gum. No chew. Not Tic Tacs. If you have any false teeth, make sure they're glued in securely. I don't want another Cloris Leachman incident. Our lawyers can't take it."

I lean down to whisper to Sutton, "What happened with Leachman?"

"Her teeth flew out during a dance," she answers quietly. "They hit an audience member in the face.

Three stitches."

I stifle a laugh. "Holy shit, that's awesome."

"It wasn't for them."

"Bull. That's the best story they're ever going to have in their life."

Sutton smiles, stifling a laugh. She looks tired but focused. It's comforting to see because I'm completely fried. This week has been exhausting. Half my days are spent on the field with the Kodiaks running my ass off, and the other half is spent in the rehearsal room with Sutton dancing my ass off. I go home at night completely wasted. I've fallen asleep on the couch twice because I can't keep my eyes open. When they close, I see Sutton. I hear her voice like the ringing of a beautiful bell telling me to get my shit together and at least try to remember some of the choreography from the day before. She's a hard-ass for sure, but so is Coach Allen. Taking orders from one feels pretty similar to taking orders from the other. They're yelling at me to be better than I am, and I rise to the challenge every time.

They filmed us rehearsing a few times for the 'package'. Sutton didn't like it but she pretended to. She's a good actress. Even I started to believe it after a while. But the thing is, I've noticed that I don't especially like Happy Sutton. That's the girl she is for the cameras and the fans that have started camping outside the studio the closer we get to the first episode. Seeing her be sunny for them feels weird. She smiles just a little too big. A little too tightly. It's like seeing someone put on the mask of another person's face. It's not right. It's not real. The real her — the rough, angry, irritable her — isn't a picnic but at least I feel like I'm starting to understand her. A week in and I'm starting to predict her moods. I can see it when she's about to lose her shit and I can either do my best to diffuse it or, more commonly, make it happen in a heartbeat. All I have to do is bring a Big Mac into the studio and she hits the roof.

"This is live television, people! There are no reshoots!" Taj continues. His face contorts unhappily when Brett Conners spits a long, dirty brown line of chew into his trash can. "No cursing. Please. Remember your marks and keep to the schedule. Your only chance for a bathroom break will be during another couple's performance or commercials, so make sure you go now to get it out of the way. If a camera is on you, you're smiling. With teeth."

When Taj gets to me, I open my mouth wide for inspection. He nods his thanks that it's empty before moving on. He skips over Sutton because he knows her. She wrote the rule book on this bitch. No way she's doing anything she shouldn't be.

Taj tells us to break a leg before disappearing into the dark wings of the studio. He'll be in the booth upstairs watching with Eric and the rest of the production crew. On the other side of the set, I can hear people chatting quietly as they take their seats.

There's a lottery system for picking who can be in the audience. Family members are allowed first, but then it's open to fans of the show. Some people fly in from other states to take a shot at getting seated, but it's not a guarantee. Even if you've been out there at the head of the line waiting all day to get in, if they don't like the look of you, you're out. I heard there was a woman out there crying earlier today trying to get in. She was so upset she started to hyperventilate. They had to call out the show doctor to calm her down.

"Do you remember your steps?" Sutton asks me, her voice as tight as her shoulders.

I shake my head. "No. My mind's gone blank."

A look of pure horror crosses over her pretty face, darkening it until it's almost unrecognizable.

I laugh, feeling a little like a dick for scaring her. "Sutton, chill. I remember everything you taught me. It's going to be fine."

"That's not funny," she growls.

"It was a little funny."

"Am I laughing?"

"No. But you never do."

She closes her eyes for a second. "It would be nice, Shane, if you took even a little of this seriously."

"I'll try," I promise.

She looks at me, reading me. I don't know what she finds but whatever it is, it suits her. Her face lightens a little, her brows parting in an easier expression. She glances around at the other contestants waiting with us in the wings.

"No one goes home this week," she tells me for the tenth time. I think saying it to me reassures her, so I don't stop her. "They tally the judges' votes for this week and combine them with the viewer votes and donations made in our name. All of that together can either save us or sink us next week. Someone will have to go and I'd rather it wasn't us."

"Me too. My mom would be bummed. She's coming out for one of the shows in June."

"Don't book her plane ticket yet."

I tsk sadly. "So little faith."

She looks up at me hard. The shimmering makeup around her eyes makes her face dance in the low-light. "I've never seen you on live TV. I don't know how you're going to hold up."

"Like a champion," I vow fervently. "Watch the Super Bowl game and then ask me how I hold up under pressure."

"You got kicked out of that game for punching a man in the face."

"He had it coming."

"Sweet Jesus," she pleads, her eyes going closed. "Please just do your best, okay? Promise me you'll take this as seriously as you take the Super Bowl."

I step closer to her. She feels me. Her eyes pop open with surprise but she doesn't retreat because Sutton doesn't back down from anyone or anything. I lower my voice, admitting honestly, "I can't promise that, but I promise I will not let you down. I'll make you proud out there, Sutton. I'll make those other men look like assholes and the women will wish they were you. That's the best I can do, but it's a lot. Believe me."

She licks her lips slowly, and I wonder for one fleeting, fiery second what they taste like. "I do believe you," she breathes.

She sounds as shocked to be saying it as I feel hearing it.

I grin down at her. "We cool?"

"We're cool. For now."

The lights around us flicker, then dim. The show is starting.

My heart beats hard in my chest; excited and erratic. I can't believe it, but it feels like the rhythm it drums when I'm about to head out onto the field. The energy in the studio is more subdued than the stadium during a game, but it's still electric. It's alive. I feel it in my veins when I hear the stage manager announce the start of the show.

All hands on deck. This is it.

Sutton leads the charge to our marks like a General going to war. Everyone follows her without question. We line up in front of our doors, waiting for them to open when the first number has finished and we're meant to rush out onto the stage. This first opening is a recording. We made it on the KBC lot the day before yesterday dressed in the same clothes we're in now. All black uniforms covered in silver sequins that spell our names on the back and our numbers on our chests. The girls are wearing silver cheerleading uniforms with a lot more flare than any you'd find on the field. Their sequins are black; their outfits opposites ours. Sutton shimmers in the low lights like a million stars in the night sky, and I can't escape how beautiful she looks. She's wearing too much makeup, but then again, so am I. Her hair is an unmovable force of gel and spray that I can't imagine will ever wash off, but she's still gorgeous with the determined set of her jaw and cold fire in her deep, gray eyes.

I take her hand without thinking. She jolts, but she doesn't shake me off. Her eyes rise to mine, asking questions I can't answer, so I only smile at her. She stares at me blankly for a second longer before looking away. Her hand squeezes mine once firmly.

It's the nicest thing she's ever said to me.

The opening beat to *Eye of the Tiger* blasts through the studio. The video is starting. The audience cheers immediately, excited by anything that tells them the show is about to kick off. My head is down as I listen, watching the steady rise and fall of Sutton's chest that makes the light dance off her dress in time to the beat. It's soothing to watch her be so calm.

Cheers erupt at random through the building as each

of our names are announced on the screen. I know when mine is coming. I'm the last, falling in during the final climax to the song, and I don't think I'm imagining things when I gauge my applause as the loudest. Sutton hears it too. I watch her, waiting to see if she'll smile, but she keeps her face perfectly flat. Resting Bitch Face is what Colt calls it. Sutton has it down to an art.

In the video, we were in a park playing a friendly game of touch football while the women cheered from the sidelines surrounded by children and families who have benefited from the Ronald McDonald House Charities. Toward the end of the song they joined us on the field in a massive dance that showcased a lot of the dances we'll be doing throughout the season. Sutton and I did a little Samba. It's fast and sexy. Her body molded to mine as much as it could when we rehearsed it, but we're still struggling with the size difference between us.

"In three…" Clara counts from behind us. "Two…"
One.

The doors to the stage open for us. Lights blind me immediately. Sutton's hand disappears from inside mine but she leaves the cool feel of her skin behind. I follow blindly after her as she sprints onto the stage. I remember to smile. It's chaos out here. Fans are cheering, the music is so loud it almost hurts, and the lights are brighter and closer than the ones I'm used to on the field. I wasn't ready for the heat. It's crazy hot in here under these lights with all of the bodies inside. I'm instantly sweating under my jersey and I haven't even done anything yet.

"Ladies and gentleman!" the announcer shouts over the din. "Please welcome your newest stars!"

I catch sight of the camera out of the corner of my

eye, filming us perform the Samba moves she taught me. We're the climax of the opening sequence because Sutton is the returning champion and I'm the local favorite being an L.A. Kodiak. When the last beat of the song hits, I dip Sutton deeply over my arm in perfect time to the music. Half the lights go out when it happens, but there's still a spot on us and all the other couples competing.

The crowd goes absolutely apeshit.

I lift Sutton gently to present her to the crowd. They shower us in applause that we're allowed to drink in for just a second before we're rushing off the stage. The crew has to come in during the commercial break to reset everything and get it ready for the first number. It'll be Brett and his partner, Ana. Sutton and I don't hit the stage again for another thirty minutes. The wait, she has promised me, will be grueling.

As we leave the stage, I pat Brett on the back. "Break a leg, man."

"Hey, thanks, Lowry. You too!"

He looks nervous. His face is pale. He's actually panting, his chest almost heaving with each breath. We didn't do much just now. Nothing worth breathing heavily about. It's all nerves, I think. I wonder if that's what I'll look like before I go on – like I'm about to be sick.

The rest of the teams start to slowly make their way down the hall toward our rehearsal rooms. No one will be practicing but we'll be hiding out, waiting for our turn at the stage. Most people are reluctant to go, milling around and chatting, but Sutton rushes through the crowd quickly. I follow on her heels, offering good luck to who I can along the way without losing her.

When I rush ahead to open the door for her, she

mutters a quick, "Thanks."

"You're welcome."

Once we're alone inside, she kicks off her shoes, discarding them in a shining heap on the floor. I'm jealous as shit that it's that easy for her to get out of them. The nerves in my feet have finally given up and gone dead thanks to these dress shoes, but if I free them from their prisons, they'll hurt twice as hard once they're forced to go back in.

I hate dress shoes. They're shiny bullshit.

"You don't have to stay," Sutton tells me. She paces the room slowly like she's counting out the perimeter, as if she doesn't already know it by heart. "You can go change. Or watch from the lounge. Some people like to do that. They like to be where the action is."

"But not you?"

She shakes her head. "No. Not me."

"Why not?"

"Watching someone else's performance doesn't do good things to me. I either enjoy their failure more than I should or I feel insecure because I think they're better than me."

I purse my lips together, nodding. "I get that."

"But you should go watch. It's fine. You don't really care about any of this so you're immune."

"Hey," I protest, feeling offended. "I care."

"You do, do you?"

"Yeah. I do."

"Must have missed it. Sorry."

"You keep your sarcasm game tight, you know that?"

"Thanks so much. I practice twice a week."

I watch her walking the varnish off the floor around the room. It's dizzying. I think about leaving, since I've been given permission and all, but something holds me back. Something is keeping me here with her, and it's definitely not her inviting attitude.

"It doesn't feel right to split up," I reason.

"We've been together non-stop all week. Space might not be a bad thing."

"Are you asking me to leave?"

"No."

I smile knowingly. "Are you *telling* me to leave?"

She halts her merry-go-round act long enough to look at me frankly. "If I was telling you, you'd know."

"Okay. Then I'll stay."

Sutton picks up her pacing again. "Suit yourself."

It takes five minutes. Just five minutes of silence before I'm bored out of my mind.

"You want to rehearse?" I ask her, feeling desperate.

"No. Too much practice starts to look stale. I want the number to feel fresh."

"You mind if I practice without you?"

She shrugs. Shrugs and paces. And then paces some more. "You can do whatever you want, Shane."

I chuckle at the lie, but I put my arms into form and start to run through the dance without her or the music. It's easy. I see these steps in my sleep. I can hear her voice in my head even when she's not around.

"'Straighten your arms, Shane! Shit!'" I mimic her in a high-pitched voice.

She shoots daggers at me. "Is that supposed to be me?"

"Did it sound like you?"

"Not at all."

"Bullshit," I laugh. "That's exactly what you sound like."

She watches me closely as I work through the dance without her. She doesn't say a word but her lips are pinched tightly. I know that look. I've either already disappointed her or I'm about to.

"Stop."

There it is.

"What?" I ask patiently, though my patience is starting to run a little thin. I'm tired. I'm stressed. I don't have it in me to put up with the full force of her shit right now. Not after I've eaten it every day this week and asked for seconds with a smile on my face.

"We're not doing the shoulder lift."

"Why not?" I laugh in amazement. "We spent forever getting it right."

"It's week one. We don't need it. Not yet."

"It's exciting. How do we not need exciting?"

She shakes her stubbornly. "It's a risk we don't need to take."

"What? Now *you're* worried I'll drop you? Now that I'm finally convinced I won't?"

"Just trust me."

I do and I don't. I have to because she's the expert, but it's still really irritating when she makes decisions like this without even talking to me. I was nervous about the move from the start and she drilled it into me until I was good with it, now she's yanking it. It feels like a power move and it pisses me off. I don't like being jerked around just for the hell of it.

"Whatever," I mutter, turning away from her.

"We'll do another spin in it's place. The same move you do at the start of the dance when—"

"I remember," I interrupt. "You got it."

Sutton hesitates. I can feel her watching me. I have no idea what she's thinking, but I'd bet the farm it isn't good.

"You should go watch the show," she suggests

evenly. "You've never seen anyone compete before. It'll be good for you."

I let my chin fall down against my chest. "Oh good. We're going to talk about the pen drive again."

"You should have watched at least *one* of the episodes I sent you."

I turn to face off with her. "So I could see how amazing you are at this? I don't need to see it. You make sure to remind me that you're the expert every day."

"I am the expert! You're just some jock that's doing this for laughs, but this is my career! You could treat it and me with a little more respect."

"And you could respect the fact that I am trying. I'm coming into this with no experience and I've been working my ass off all week, and all you ever do is tell me how terrible I am and how fucking amazing Jace Ryker was. I get it. He could dance. Someone get him a goddamn medal."

"It's not that he was such a good dancer. What I liked about him was that he was professional. He showed up *prepared*."

"He was also on the Disney Channel for most of his life," I argue, gesturing to the stage outside the door as though he's there now. "He grew up on TV. He knew how all this worked before he learned how to play with his own dick. You can't compare me to someone like that. You can't compare me to *you*."

"I just want you to take this seriously."

"I'm here, aren't I? Do I or do I not show up to every rehearsal?"

"You do."

"Then give me some credit, Sutton. Damn!"

"Showing up isn't the same as being invested."

"Fuck you," I growl, fed up.

She fearlessly steps up to me, pushing against me with her tiny body like she's ten miles tall. "No, Shane. Fuck you!"

Her eyes are burning. They're cold fire but they hurt just the same. Her beauty is an agony that I just can't take anymore.

I kiss her. I lean down to close that distance to her mouth and I take control of the moment as I lose control of myself. The second my lips touch hers, I brace myself for a hit. I'm going to get slapped or kicked or clawed to ribbons, but it's worth it for that one brief breath of relief. Kissing her is like breathing after being underwater. She's like air in my lungs, and when her arms come around my neck to pull me closer instead of push me away, I'm as alive as I've ever been before.

She's angry. I can taste it on her tongue. She feeds it to me until I'm angry too. I'm fighting for more of her. All of her. I want to lay her out on this hard floor and strip her down to nothing but the fierceness of her spirit that pushes me to the brink where I don't know who I am anymore. I'm an animal as I kiss her. As I fight with her. There's no difference in my mind. Everything she does is a battle, and I'll gladly let her win this one. I'll give her anything she wants, just so long as she shuts the fuck up for two seconds.

CHAPTER FOURTEEN

SUTTON

I'm a mess on opening nights. I'm insane. It's just the way I am. I never sleep well in the week leading up to it. Sometimes I throw up before going on stage. Sometimes I break out into a cold sweat that leaves me trembling for an hour after. There's no telling what I'll do before a performance. I definitely didn't see this coming.

Shane's hands are on my ass. They're in my hair. His tongue is in my mouth. He's everywhere at once, overwhelming me in a way that feels completely decadent. I feel myself letting go. I feel the tension leaving my body and pouring into his, and he drinks it up with a vigor that makes me dizzy. My mom used to dope me to get me through my jitters, but nothing she gave me comes even close to how good Shane feels. How amazing he tastes and smells. And the sound of his rough grunt as he hoists one of my legs up high, yanking my body hard against his... God, that sound could be the end of me. The feel of him is like my beginning.

Knock! Knock!

"Wardrobe needs you, Ms. Roe! Mr. Lowry!" a stagehand shouts through the crack.

Shane hesitates, his mouth hovering and panting over mine. "We're on our way!" he shouts roughly.

I'm breathless in his arms. I'm boneless and limp as a jellyfish. I'm relaxed in ways I wasn't sure I could be anymore, and it feels amazing.

But the second Shane releases his hold on me, I feel

it start to slip away.

He steps away from me slowly, running his hand through his hair. He's avoiding my eyes. "We have to get changed."

I nod loosely. "I'm ready."

We're not going to talk about what just happened. That's obvious. We don't have the time and I don't think either of us has the desire to define what the hell that was. It doesn't matter. It happened. It had to. But now it's over and we have a show to do.

Shane opens the door for me, letting me pass through his shadow before he silently follows me down the corridor to wardrobe. It's a madhouse inside. The music that's blaring from the stage takes over everything. It's in the air we breathe. It gets in my blood. In my mind. I feel the energy of the competition flood my system, and suddenly I'm buzzing. The thrill of the kiss with Shane is replaced with the thrill of the competition. I'm excited from the tips of my toes to the ends of my hair.

They strip me down until I'm nearly naked before squeezing me inside my dress. It's a short flapper style in a red color that reminds me of my car. My shoes are like stilts, they're so tall, and even with them I know I'll barely reach Shane's chest with the top of my head.

"Makeup!"

I'm pushed from the wardrobe room to hair and makeup where they pile my long locks high on my head in a mess of curls that they finish with a glittery band across my forehead. While someone sticks pins in my hair, someone else is painting red on my lips. Pink in my cheeks. I'm not a person in the chair. I'm a project. I'm a doll they're dressing up to put on display, and I sit with the perfect stillness of one while they work.

Out of the corner of my eye, I see Shane being brought to makeup as well. He's in a black tuxedo with red stitching to match my dress. I heard they had to special order it. They didn't have anything on hand nearly big enough for him. What they managed is perfect. His jacket is left unbuttoned to expose a cummerbund in the same red as my dress. His red bow tie is left undone along with the top three buttons of his stark white shirt. I can see the dark hair on his tan chest peeking through.

He winks at me when he catches me looking.

"No smiling!" the girl doing my makeup scolds.

I straighten my face immediately. I hadn't realized I moved.

When we're painted pretty and ready to go, Shane and I are ushered to the edge of the stage. We're hidden in the shadows but I can see almost the entire room from here. The show is on a commercial break as the crew moves the last set of props away and brings out ours.

"Break a leg, you two," Clara whispers from behind us.

I reach back to take her hand. She squeezes it lovingly before disappearing into the darkness. I know there are people everywhere, but suddenly it feels like me and Shane are very alone. Just the two of us in sparkling clothes, pinching shoes, and more makeup than a drag queen at Mardi Gras.

The lights on stage dim. Jerry, our announcer, goes to the center with his microphone in hand. I lead Shane out to our marks, but he finds them just fine without me.

I watch as the lights on the cameras turn red; recording.

My heart stops. It won't start again until the dance is done.

"Welcome Sutton Roe and Shane Lowry to the stage with the Charleston!" Jerry bellows.

"Are you ready?" I whisper to Shane through the shouts of the crowd.

He casts me a crooked grin that loosens every muscle in my body. It's his lips, I've decided. They're my new drug. "As I'll ever be."

Lucky Strike begins to play, sending the crowd into a frenzy. When the quick tempo starts to thump through the room, I feel it in my chest. The song is inside me when I smile with my crimson lips. I slip into character, ready to play the part of the flapper with her man at the club.

Our dance is mostly us in sync with each other. That's the Charleston. It's not a lot of flips and flying and throwing my body around like the crowd wants. That comes later. You can't start with the theatrics or you've got nowhere to go but down. This is the first week and this dance is all about quick feet and happy hands. Shane takes hold of me a total of three times in the two minutes we dance together, and I'm proud of his form every time. His body is rigid. Straight, the way I've been begging him to be for days.

He doesn't take things as seriously as I'd like during practice, but I'm relieved to see that when it comes time to perform, he's not playing around. Shane wants to win as badly as I do.

We come to a stop with him on one knee and me sitting on the other. Our arms are wrapped around each other like we're about to kiss, but we pull up short, just like we practiced a million times. It's harder tonight, though. The memory of the kiss in the rehearsal room floods my body, making me warm. Making me want. Both of our bodies are heaving, breathing hard with exertion, but I don't feel a single breath. All I can feel, hear, taste, and smell are the applause.

All I can see are Shane's eyes.

"That was perfect," I tell him breathlessly.

He nods, licking his lips. Staring at mine. "It felt good."

"You were amazing."

I hug him hard for the audience. For myself. For him. For the love of God in Heaven because I'm so proud in that moment. I'm proud of both of us.

Shane stands with me still in his arms. I dangle there against his body, my shoes hovering at least a foot over the ground. The audience chuckles lightly as they applaud and I feel myself flush with annoyance. But then he puts me down gently and I forgive him as quickly as I got angry.

"Sutton and Shane!" Jerry cries excitedly. He ushers us over from the dance floor to the judges.

We hurry hand-in-hand to the mark next to him. He gives me the customary kiss on the cheek. He shakes Shane's hand. Jerry's about forty but he looks sixty up close. The lines around his face tell a story of a short life lived hard. He used to be a singer in a band in the nineties. I guess they were huge for a while. I don't know. I was barely born in the nineties.

"Beautiful work," he gushes. "The audience definitely agrees, but let's see what the judges think. Milan?"

Milan, an ex-ballerina turned pop star in the UK, falls forward against the judges' table. "I wanted to love it so badly, Jerry! I really did, but I just couldn't."

The audience gasps and boos quietly.

Jerry holds up his hand to silence them. "Now, hold on. What was there not to love, Milan?"

"Technically, their performance was perfect, darling. It was spot on. But I didn't feel a connection between them." She looks at Shane. "You, my sweet, were lovely. I adored you. I didn't know what to expect when you came lumbering out there like Paul Bunyan, but you were graceful and energetic. The look on your face! Ah! I loved it. I loved you."

Shane smiles boyishly. "Thank you."

"You're welcome, darling. But the problem I had with the performance was how stiff the two of you felt as a couple. There was no... spark."

"I have to cut in and say I agree with you," Desmond adds in his thick New York accent that makes me homesick and just plain sick at the same time. "One hundred, Milan. You're dead on. The performance was clean but it didn't have any oomf."

"No love."

"No love," he agrees sadly.

Jerry nods in understanding. "Alright, then, so since you're both in agreement, can I get your scores together? Out of ten, what do you rate this performance?"

Milan and Desmond look at each other for one dramatic moment before lifting their score cards.

They're both sixes.

My heart crashes in my chest. I haven't seen a six since the first season I joined. The Joey Lawrence season where I made him cry and call me a cunt after I worked him too hard because I never wanted to see a six again. Now here it is. Two of them.

Shane puts his arm around my shoulders gently. He doesn't squeeze me or hug me. He just holds me loosely, like he's worried I'll float away up into the sky if I'm not grounded. And he's not wrong. I feel dizzy. Airy. Too light to be alive because we might not survive these scores. Sixes are what send people home.

Jerry cocks his head to the side, his face drawn sadly. "Oh dear. These are not what you want to see on the first night, are they, Sutton?"

I shake my head, holding back my tears.

"We can recover," Shane insists staunchly. He looks to the final judge – the worst of them. Richard 'Dick' Malone. "What have you got for us, Dick? Any love?"

I'm surprised when Richard chuckles. If I were him, I'd be worried that old withered face of his will crack if he emotes too much. He normally keeps himself propped up like an inscrutable corpse through the entire competition, doling out agony to every dancer who dares to step in front of him like it's his lifeforce. Like other people's pain is his mana.

"I'm not sure I've got much more love for your performance than the others do, Shane," he laments theatrically. "They're right. You're more talented than I expected, but your chemistry is off. I wanted to love it but…"

"The best part of the performance was Shane!" Desmond interrupts excitedly. He holds up his hand to me. "No offense."

"None taken," I lie through gritted teeth. "He's a surprise. To me more than anyone."

"You lucked out, sweetheart," Milan praises me, as though my luck in landing Shane is award enough for the night.

Jerry focuses us back on Richard. "What's it going to be? What score will you give Sutton and Shane, Richard?"

Richard stares at us for a long time. He does it for the show and also for fun. He likes to watch people sweat; especially women. He's a member of the old guard. He thinks women should be lovely and men should be strong, so Shane should tick at least a few of his boxes. Hopefully enough to get us to the next round.

Finally, he raises his card without explanation or expression.

It's an eight.

I fold in half with relief. My fingers dangle down to touch my toes while I take a deep breath to fill my lungs with something other than fear. When I stand up, my head rushes almost painfully. I feel lightheaded, and I'm actually grateful for Shane's arms around me. He pulls me into a bracing hug that leaves my feet on the ground and my face against his chest where I can feel his heart beating wildly.

"That's good, right?" he asks in my ear. "We're good?"

"We might be okay, yeah."

"I'm sorry."

I shake my head like I don't know what he's talking about, but I do. He's sorry they said he was the best part of the night for me. He's sorry his star shone brighter than mine because while Shane might not know much about me, he knows enough to see what I've never tried to hide. I need to be loved and adored by the world. I need to be the sun, the stars, and the moon in the sky, all at once. All on my own. To be stripped of it is to be flayed raw. Dissected and broken into pieces too infinitesimal to repair.

We leave the stage for our exit interview. It's quick. So quick I can't remember much of it afterward. Shane did most of the talking and I'm grateful for that. I wasn't ready to discuss what the judges said. I'm not ready to feel safe yet, either. There are still three more performances tonight and I haven't bothered to look at any of the scores we're up against. As far as I know, we're at the bottom of the heap.

"What's the score?" Shane asks Brett the second he sees him backstage. "Were we the lowest so far?"

I put my hand on his arm to ask him to stop, but it's too late. Brett is shaking his head.

"Nah, man. Tina and Vic are probably out. They got seventeen."

"What'd you get?"

He smiles proudly. "Twenty-three, baby!"

Shane gives him a half-hug where they thump each other on the back roughly. "Nice! Congrats!"

"Yeah, thanks. You too. We live to see another week, right?"

"Barely, but yeah."

"I gotta bring this water to Ana. I'll catch you later, okay?"

"Definitely."

Brett nods to me before disappearing into the lounge where the rest of the judged dancers are waiting. Shane looks to the room, then back at me expectantly.

"We going in or staying out?" he asks.

I hesitate, not sure. I don't want to go in. They saw the feed. They know what the judges said. My skin feels too paper thin to handle their scrutiny tonight.

"You go ahead and celebrate with them," I tell him as warmly as I can manage. "I'm sure Fiona and Ginger would love to get their hands on you right now. They've got a thing for sweaty man meat."

Shane scowls. "Those aren't really their names,

right? Those are stage names like Madonna and Cher."

"I'm not their mother, Shane. I have no idea."

"But if you had to guess?"

"I'd say those are the names that their parents gave them because they never expected them to be anything but dancers. On the pole or on the stage, it really doesn't matter."

"That's bleak as shit."

"You asked me," I remind him sharply.

He smiles at my bitterness. It's kind of becoming his thing and it doesn't bother me as much as it used to.

"I need a breather," I remind him, taking a step away. "I'm going to get some air."

"You sure you don't want me to go with you?"

"I'm sure." I smile brightly for him. "Go. Have fun. You earned it."

"*We* earned it," he reminds me excitedly.

I nod. "Yes. We earned it. Now, go. I'll find you before the end of the broadcast. We have to stand up on stage for the final ranks going into next week. But remember, the votes and donations from viewers will count too. We aren't safe even if we're not the lowest scored tonight."

"I know, I remember, I just…" He smiles big and bright because Shane Lowery doesn't do anything small. "I'm proud of us, Sutton. No matter what they said, we did good. We did great."

"Yes. We did." I push against his chest without effect, but it's the gesture that matters. "Go. I'll see you in a few minutes."

Shane takes a step back before pausing. His eyes are on mine, his face falling serious.

I know what he's about to say.

I shake my head hard. "Let's not talk about it

tonight, okay? We can dissect it another day. Or not at all."

"I could live with not at all."

"Even better."

He surprises me when he darts in close to kiss my cheek. The gesture is soft and unassuming. It's the perfect opposite of what happened in the rehearsal room. I feel relieved as he does it, like he's wiping the slate clean for us. This is what we are; chaste and professional. We are not and cannot be what happened before.

I smile at him when he pulls away. He waves a quick goodbye before disappearing into the lounge with the rest of the guys. I hear cheers come up from the others when he enters.

People love him. There's no denying that.

I go to the exit at the back of the studio. Most of the time I avoid it because this is where the smokers go on break. The area is empty but the scent of nicotine still lingers in the air around the ashtray strewn picnic tables. The smell makes my throat close painfully like it's shortening, vomit rising to choke me. I consider having an air freshener glued to my upper lip just to make it through the day, but that's not the real problem. My problems are in my head. In my gut.

The door to the studio opens. I look to it with a strange feeling of hope. I think maybe Shane has come out to keep me company, because, like he said, we're a team. We stick together.

My stomach clenches tight with irritation when I meet Eric's eyes.

"Go away," I tell him harshly.

He doesn't flinch and he doesn't go. "You shouldn't be out here alone."

"You shouldn't be out here at all."

"I was worried about you."

"Thanks," I tell him coldly. "I'm fine. See you later."

Eric comes closer. Just a step, to test the waters. They're icy cold but it won't stop him. It never has. "They were hard on you because you're last year's winner. Everyone expects the best and you have to admit, that wasn't your best."

"It was better than sixes."

"You're right, but so am I."

I shake my head, looking down. I stare at the grease coated cement under my shining shoes. "I'm working with what I've got."

"Shane is a solid partner. What you've got is more than most of the other girls."

"Tell it to Milan and Desmond."

"I don't speak to the judges. You know that."

"I don't give a shit what you do, Eric."

He takes another step toward me. I feel it more than see it. Like the way you feel someone invade your space in a pitch-black room. Your hair stands on end. Your fingers tremble and your stomach quivers.

"You care more than you let on," he whispers delicately. "About everything. You act like you only think about the show but you're always working on something, aren't you?"

"Go away," I warn him nervously. I wrap my arms around my stomach to protect myself. To close the cage of my body tight.

"What are you working on right now, Sutton? What's in your head?"

"Nothing."

"It's never nothing."

I close my eyes against the night and him and the

feeling he gives me. "I don't want to do this."

"Sutton."

"Stop."

"I can't," he whispers, his breath hot as fire on my face. "I never could with you."

He kisses me. I immediately compare it to the kiss that Shane and I shared, and I can't get over the difference. Shane's was passionate. It was compulsive and desperate. It lit me up like Times Square on New Year's Eve. Eric's kiss is gentle and sweet but it hurts. The sensation aches all the way down into my toes and I feel like I might vomit for the tenth time today.

It isn't healthy. None of it.

My life is literally making me sick.

I keep my arms around my body as he steps in front of me. His tongue invades my mouth. His hands tangle in my hair. He tilts my head back to open me wider for him, but I refuse. I clamp my mouth shut tight and I try to turn away, but he doesn't let me. He presses his forehead to mine, breathing heavy and needy against my lips.

"I came out here because I was worried about you," he promises.

"You came out here because you wanted to fuck me."

"I want to love you." He presses his head against mine harder. So hard it almost hurts, like he's trying to get inside my mind. "Why are you so afraid to let me love you?"

I shake free of his hold, tears blurring my eyes. "Because I don't want to. Because it's wrong. Because you're married and I can't stand you. I don't know how else to tell you so you'll hear me. I hate you, Eric."

"Sutton—"

"Go away!" I cry, unable to contain it. "Get away from me!"

"Stop shouting."

"Leave me alone!"

He holds up his hands, his face dark with anger. "Keep your voice down before someone gets the wrong idea about what's happening here."

"I will lower my voice when you start listening to me. Go. Away. Don't call me. Don't corner me. Don't you dare touch me. Do you hear me?"

Eric stands there staring at me like I'm a wild thing. Like I'm crazy and unpredictable, and that should send him running but it won't. This is all part of the cycle. We've been here before, so many times. This is the arc where the passion comes back and the trysts in dark corners begin again. This is where he can't resist me and I can't stand myself as I let him have me. Again and again and again.

For the first time, I see that this isn't only my weakness. This is Eric's too. He can't stop any more than I can. He's riding the wave, as much at its mercy as I am, but I can't anymore. I won't survive it again. Tonight I can't be inside my body if he's going to be in here too. I'm too intangible. I'll disappear forever like a wisp of smoke off a snuffed candle if he tries to take me.

"Nothing's changed," he swears to me. "We're the same as we've always been."

"I'm not," I rebel, hoping against hope that it's true.

"Maybe not yet. It's too soon. I'm sorry. I just... Roe, I just wanted to touch you. I couldn't stand to not feel you."

"Leave me alone, Eric. Please."

"I'll give you more time."

I keep my eyes closed tight as I listen to him go. He

lets the door slam shut hard behind him. The sound makes me jump. My arms tighten around my belly. I rock slowly from side to side in a soothing motion that reminds me of being a child.

"It's okay," I whisper softly to the night. "I'm okay."

CHAPTER FIFTEEN

SHANE

May 29th
Palmetto Warehouse
Los Angeles, CA

My feet hurt. It should be from cleats and days spent on the field, but it's not. It's so, so, so much worse.

Sutton has started making me wear the dress shoes to rehearse in. Six hours a day. Six days a week. It's brutal. I don't know how she does it in heels, but she's in them every day. I rarely see her wearing anything else. Her feet are red when she takes them off, but they're intact. Mine are covered in blisters and callouses trying to form before being rubbed right off by the next wave of rehearsals. I soak them in Epsom salts every night, and every day they get ravaged again.

When I stumble home from a grueling day of practice and then rehearsals, I wonder why I'm doing this. For the kids, sure, yeah, but Sloane was right – I could just write them a check. What's the real reason I'm putting up with this? It's a question I've been careful not to ask because the answer is confusing as fuck. I know it has something to do with gray eyes and a blood boiling kiss that still keeps me up at night when I'm trying to go blank and pass out. I see her in the dark. I can feel her. In my mind, we've gone so far beyond that kiss, it's indecent.

I feel like a perv for using her like that but it's my imagination. I can't control it and the girl keeps feeding it like she's creating a monster to destroy me. Our first two styles were the Charleston and the Jive, but then last week we did the Paso Doble. This week is the Tango to the Demi Lovato song *Sorry Not Sorry* and I come home with blue balls every night. The dances are getting sexy. The girl is even sexier. There's a point in the song where I lift her to spin her around and make her black dress fly away from her body like a set of dark wings, and it's the best moment of my day. She's light in my hands and heavy in my eyes. Every time I do it, she gives me this look that's not like anything she's ever given me before.

She looks at me like she trusts me. Why that's so sexy, I can't put into words, but it's true. I feel it now just thinking about it.

I'm also thinking about ditching rehearsal. It's been almost a month since I started pulling double duty between football and *DNA*, and it's catching up to me. It's not just my feet that hurt. It's my entire body, including my brain. I need a break but no one is giving any. This morning off from practice is the first one I've had in four weeks. I've spent it sitting in Colt's living room with him and Tyus watching bad martial arts movies and dreading the time when I have to go to the KBC studio.

"When is dance class?" Tyus asks me from the other end of the couch.

I glance at the clock above the TV. The time makes me wince. "In an hour."

"That sucks."

"Yeah. No shit."

"I thought you liked being on the show," Colt says.

"I do. I'm just tired, that's all."

"Don't you get days off?"

"On Friday, the day after we film, but even then Sutton wants to get together to watch the tape and talk about all the ways I screwed up while it's still fresh in my head."

"How does that work for the other guys competing? They have mandatory practice with their teams now, same as you, right?"

"They do a lot of flying. Brett told me he flies out here the day before the show, stays until Friday morning, and then he and his partner Ana fly back to Dallas together. She works with him after his practices there, same as Sutton and me."

"So you're not the only one being tortured?"

"I don't know, man," I admit tiredly. "From the sound of it, Ana isn't half as hard on Conners as Sutton is on me."

Tyus grunts unhappily. "She sounds like a real bitch."

"Nah, she's not a bitch. She's just complicated."

"Complicated is a nice way of saying she's a bitch."

"Our boy is a nice guy," Colt points out.

"Too nice. He should have told her to dance by herself three weeks ago when she went at him in the park. She's running around acting like he owes her something when he's the celebrity doing the show a favor."

"I'm getting paid," I point out. "And it's for charity."

"You're getting paid less than our Super Bowl bonus and they're doing this charity gig to try and save their own asses 'cause their ratings are shit." Tyus points at me. "They *need* you. Don't let this girl treat you like a chump when you're there to help her keep her job."

"I don't look at it like that."

"Maybe you should," Colt suggests with unexpected seriousness.

"Sutton's not that bad. She could be better, but I poke the bear sometimes."

"You piss her off on purpose?"

I shrug, smiling. "It's petty, but it's fun."

Tyus snorts. "If she's gonna treat you like you ain't shit, it's not petty. It's deserved."

"Come on, man. Are you going to sit there and act like Mila doesn't bust your balls left and right?"

"When Mila does it, it's sexy. It's foreplay. She's riling me up for something good. Are you getting off fighting with this girl?"

"No," I admit glumly.

"Then you're not doin' it right."

"You're saying I should hate fuck her?"

"Some of the best sex I've ever had was with someone I hated."

"Truth!" Colt shouts at the ceiling.

I chuckle, shaking my head. Trying to dislodge the memory of the kiss I had with Sutton. But it's useless. It's etched on my brain like a brand. "It's not like that with her. We're dance partners. That's it."

"That's a wasted opportunity."

"Whatever." I lift my foot out of the salt bath I've been soaking it in, inspecting my blisters. They're smaller than they were before but they still suck. I'll wear flip flops to the studio and I don't give a shit what Sutton says about them. She'll be lucky I showed up. "What's up with Sloane?" I ask, slowly lowering my foot. "I thought she was due this month. Where's that baby?"

Tyus scowls at me. "Dude, you don't know?"

"Know what?"

"That's right. You've been bailing right after practice every day. You didn't hear."

"Hear what? What happened to her?"

"She's fine," Colt assures me. "She's on bed rest in the hospital, though."

"What does that mean?"

"It means she's being kept at the hospital until she has the baby," Tyus explains calmly. "And they're trying to keep her from going into labor for as long as they can. Just in case."

"In case of what?"

"The baby didn't grow like it was supposed to. They're worried he'll need help when he comes out."

"What? Like breathing tubes and shit?"

"Most likely."

I fall back into the couch with a frown. "Fuck. That's gotta be killing Trey."

"Trey is Trey. He's cool as ice."

"It's probably for Sloane's sake," Colt guesses. "He's holding it together but he's gotta be freaking out on the inside."

"I sure as hell would be," I agree heavily.

"Hey, they'll be fine," Tyus tells us like it's fact. Like he's got it on the low from God himself that it's all going to work out. "She's at UCLA Med Center. It's a good hospital."

I nod, not saying a word because I'm not sure what to say. I'm worried about Sloane and the kid, but I'm also looking at Tyus with a scar the size of the California coastline running across his skull from where they took out that tumor earlier this year. They did it at UCLA Med. They saved his life, so I have some faith in the joint. Still, I remind myself to go in and see Sloane this weekend. I'll bring her magazines and flowers and shit. Anything to help keep her busy.

An hour later, I'm out the door from Colt's apartment and headed to rehearsals. My head is foggy. I'm exhausted. I'm not looking forward to breathing, let alone rehearsing. And if Sutton is in one of her moods, I don't know what I'll do. Most of the time I can take it. I don't let her bother me because her anger isn't about me. It's about something else I can't see. Or someone else that she tries not to see. I'm convinced she and Eric have something going on, and whatever it is, it isn't good. We don't see him very often around the studio but when we do, it's awkward as fuck. They barely look at each other. They don't speak directly to one another. And I've noticed that for all her anger, Sutton doesn't talk shit about anybody but Eric. Either they're hooking up or they were or she wants to be or he wants to be – I can't pin it down, but there's something there. Something ugly.

When I open the door to the rehearsal room, she's at the bar. Or 'barre' as she so vehemently corrected me last week. Her face is blank but once her eyes meet mine, she smiles brightly. "You made it."

I hesitate inside the door. For a split second, I feel like I'm in the wrong room. The energy is off. Her face is weird. She looks *happy.* She sounds it too, and that's so far from the norm, I'm convinced I've stepped into another dimension.

"I did," I reply hesitantly.

"Good timing. I have some awesome news for you."

I glance around the room, looking for cameras. This is how she is when they're filming our rehearsals. To the outside world, Sutton is sunshine and rainbows. Meanwhile, when they're not looking, she's a storm cloud hovering low overhead.

But we're alone and she's still standing there like pure daylight.

"What the hell's happening?" I ask her bluntly.

She laughs, giving me a quizzical look. "What do you mean?"

"You're being weird."

"*You're* being weird."

"Not as weird as you."

Sutton rolls her eyes. "Don't be annoying. You'll ruin my good mood and I'll make you work for an extra hour."

I drop my duffel down on the floor with a heavy *whump.* I watch her closely as I come into the room with cautiously slow steps. "I wouldn't want that."

"What are you doing?"

"I'm treading lightly. Literally."

"Well, stop it," she commands forcefully. "It's annoying."

I smile as I take up my regular stride. "What's got you in a good mood? Is it something I can bottle and save for a rainy day?"

"No, but you are part of it."

"That can't be true."

She casts me a cryptic smile before handing me a piece of paper she plucks from the seat of a chair. "The donation and voting results so far."

I snatch the paper from her excitedly. In small, simple font are the names of each team in the competition, along with columns of numbers. One is for the judges' votes, another for donations, the third is the viewer votes, and the fourth is our total.

"We're in the lead," Sutton tells me eagerly. She's standing on her toes to see the paper in my hand, even though I'm pretty sure she's memorized it. The edges are creased and worn from where she's held it over and over again. "We got one of the lowest scores from the judges that first week but we've been on the upswing ever since. They're into us, Shane. And the viewer votes and donations have kept lifting us up more and more every week. We're killing this thing."

I frown at her. "Are we supposed to know this?"

"No."

"Then where did you get this?"

She smiles that mysterious, secretive smile again. "I have my sources."

Eric, I think, and the thought irritates me in a way I didn't expect.

I hand the sheet back to her. "That's cool."

"'That's cool'?" she echoes incredulously. "That's all you have to say? We're dominating and you think 'that's cool'?"

"What do you want me to say?"

"I want you to be excited!"

"I am," I laugh at her irritation. "That's exciting. Those donations are legit. I'm proud of people for chipping in like that for the kids."

"I'm talking about the competition."

"The competition is about the kids."

She narrows her eyes at me. "I know that. And I know what you're doing."

"What am I doing?"

"You're trying to make me feel like shit because I'm not focusing on the charity. But there's more going on than just that. There's more at stake."

"You mean like the show going under?"

Sutton stares at me like I've stolen the breath from her lungs, and for no good reason. She looks at me like I've done it just to hurt her.

I'm worried that she's right. I wonder if I have.

"Yes," she answers softly. "The show is in trouble. These viewer votes are higher than we've had in a while. That means people are actually watching again. We could be poised to have the best season we've had in years and that means good things for the charity but it also means good things for those of us who love the show, and I won't apologize for caring about my job or the people around me who depend on theirs as well. I don't see the kids every day. I see the crew. I see the other dancers and the choreographers and directors and producers. I worry about every one of them and myself if *DNA* goes under, so I won't apologize or be made to feel like a bitch for giving a shit about the world I live in."

I nod, avoiding her eyes. Avoiding the fight that I started because I'm not even sure why I did it. "Okay. Got it. Sorry."

She doesn't reply. I wonder what she's thinking, but it doesn't matter. She'll never tell me and I'll never be able to read her. Definitely not today. I can't even read myself right now. I'm too tired. Even after a morning off, I can't get my ass in gear. I wish more than anything that I was back home on my couch, sleeping through episodes of *SVU*. When I walked in here, Sutton was in a good mood for the first time ever, and I went ahead and screwed it up. I started a fight that didn't need to happen, and I can't figure out why, other than I'm burnt out.

"You didn't bring your lunch in today," she comments softly.

"I wasn't hungry," I lie.

"But you're always hungry."

I rub my fingers over my burning eyes. "Yeah, I know."

"Are you okay?"

"I'm good."

"You don't look it."

"Thanks," I chuckle, dropping my hand. I nod to the

unit on the wall. "We should get to it, yeah? The day is getting away from us."

Sutton's brow creases as she looks down at the paper in her hands. She folds it neatly in half, pinching the crease down tight with a slow drag of her fingertips. "You know what? Maybe we need a day off instead."

"You don't take days off. We fought about taking tomorrow off. I said even God rested on the seventh day, and you said—"

"'I'm not lazy like God'," she finishes for me. She smiles wanly. "That may have been a bit much."

"I was seriously afraid you were gonna get smote."

"Is it smote or smotten?"

"When you're struck by the hand of the Almighty, does it really matter how you say it?"

"I guess not." She sighs, falling back on her heels. "But you should take a break. I've been running you ragged with rehearsals right after practice. You must be exhausted from this morning."

"I didn't go," I confess without meaning to. It just comes out, like I can't control it. "There was no practice this morning. I only told you there was so I could have some time off."

She nods, her eyes on her hands. On our scores hidden inside the little booklet she's made. "That's fair."

"I shouldn't have lied."

"You had to, right?" she asks lightly. She looks up at me with a smile. "I would never have agreed to it if you'd asked."

That smile looks so fragile on her face, it immediately reminds me of how small she is. It's surprisingly easy to forget her size when you get to know her because her personality is so big. Her temper larger than life. She's become a sort of lioness in my mind, one I tiptoe around trying not to anger, but inside she's a kitten. She's delicate in ways I can't understand, but when she looks at me like that with the sunlight in her hair and a glimmer of sorrow and sorry in her eyes, I feel it. I can feel *her*; like a dove in my hand, heart thrumming wildly against my palm. The smallest noise will make her jump. It will make her flutter her wings and fly away, but part of me is longing to hold her like this for just a little longer.

"Have you eaten lunch?"

She gives me an amused look that reminds me how little she eats. "No. I haven't eaten."

"Can I take you somewhere?"

"Where?" she asks suspiciously.

"Somewhere good. Really good."

"We have very different definitions of what's 'good'."

I smile, popping the door open expectantly. "Trust me."

Sutton hesitates. Her eyes dart between me and the digital display on the wall. She's torn between rehearsing by herself and something else. Something like me and food and a day without work; three things she is not accustomed to. It's scary for her. I can see it in the way she wrings her hands together anxiously.

For all of her bluster, Sutton Roe is afraid of a lot of things. Things a person shouldn't fear. Things like fun.

"We'll have to work twice as hard tomorrow," she warns me in a rush. "We're not taking two days off. This isn't *The View*, for God's sake."

"Whatever you say, Boss."

CHAPTER SIXTEEN

SUTTON

I'm playing hooky. I've never done that before. I feel like a criminal when I sneak out of the studio with Shane. Luckily, there's no one around to see it.

"I'll drive," I offer, pulling my keys from my bag.

Shane laughs. "There's no way in hell I can fit into your car. I'll drive."

I look at his Jeep glistening in the sun next to my Fiat. His car looks like a skyscraper in comparison, but he's right. Even with the seat all the way back, his knees would be in his face inside my car. His is missing the doors and the roof again, and I can't think of a single reason why he would keep it like that. Inside, the seats are black leather that have been roasting in the afternoon sun. They'll be murderously hot against my bare legs, a feeling I'll find divine. I can wedge my fingers between the seat and my legs and maybe, for once, they'll feel warm.

Assuming I can get up inside the damn thing.

I stand at the passenger side looking everywhere for a handle or a step or some kind of purchase to help launch me up into this beast, but there's nothing. This is a car built for a man Shane's size. Not a woman little enough to fit inside the glove compartment.

"Let me help you," he says from behind me.

Before I can argue, his hands are on my hips. His fingers wrap around me securely as he lifts me into the air and gently sets me down on the passenger seat. It's as hot as I imagined, but not nearly as hot as the searing feel of his hands on me.

Shane touches me a thousand times a day when we're dancing, but this feels different. It feels intimate as he helps me into his car. He's not my partner right now. He's not even the guy I made out with on the night of the first filming. Right now, he's a man and I'm a woman, and I'm painfully aware of how large his hands are. How capable he is in everything he does.

I compartmentalize my entire life into easy to identify boxes. Work is the biggest, fullest one. But Shane barely fits inside that box. I can't even think of how to build one large enough for him outside that context. And what would I name it? Guys I've made out with? Men I'd like to see naked?

I watch out of the corner of my eye as he steps up into the lifted vehicle like it's nothing. The Jeep jostles under his weight, tossing me toward him.

"Do you have one of those..." He opens and closes his hand rapidly, like he's trying to mime the words into existence. "A thing?"

I frown, assuming for some reason that he's asking if I have a condom. "A thing?"

"You know, a hair thing." He gestures to my hair hanging down over my shoulders. "A rubber band. It's gonna get windy once we hit the road."

"No," I laugh with relief. "I don't have a 'thing'."

"Don't worry. I got you."

Shane reaches over to pop the glove compartment at my knees. From inside, he pulls out a bright yellow baseball hat with a big, black bear on the front.

I shake my head when he offers it to me. "Shane, I'll be fine. Really. I've been in a convertible before."

"Not like this you haven't. Here," he shakes it insistently. "You'll need it."

"I doubt it." I take it anyway, if just to stop the

discussion.

Shane sees me set it in my lap, but he doesn't push any further. He brings the Jeep to growling life before putting his hand on the back of my seat to see behind us. "Eric's here," he comments as we pull out of the parking spot. "Or is that golf cart always here?"

"It's always here, but so is he," I answer stiffly.

"I bet his wife loves that."

My heart skips a beat. "How'd you know he was married?"

"He wears a wedding ring."

"Right," I mutter, feeling paranoid. "Of course."

"Have you ever met her?"

"No. Never."

"I wonder if she's anything like him."

"What do you think he's like?"

Shane shrugs, driving us slowly through the lot toward the gate. "I don't know. Phony, mostly."

"A lot of people in television are phony," I agree.

"Including you?"

I frown at him. "What is that supposed to mean?"

"It's a question, Sutton. It wasn't supposed to mean anything."

"You're asking if I think I'm fake?"

"Not anymore."

"Why not?"

"'Cause you're getting pissed off and I liked it better when you were in a good mood." He glances at my hands even though he knows exactly what's in them. "Did you bring that sheet with you? Look at the sheet. It'll perk you up."

"I don't need 'perking'," I bristle. "I need…"

He waits through my sudden silence before prodding, "What? What do you need?"

"I don't know," I answer softly.

"You know what I think?"

"Rarely."

He grins. "I think you need this day off as much as I do. Maybe more."

I don't reply because I don't know if he's wrong or right. I felt bad, that's what got me here. That's what I know for sure. I can see how burned out he is. I've seen it for the last couple of days, but I've ignored it. I've been selfish because that's what I am. I'm not phony. I'm not Hollywood. I'm a New Yorker. I'm driven and tireless. I'm selfish and angry. I'm East Coast and so lonely and homesick I can hardly stand it, and when he gave me those wounded puppy dog eyes as he apologized for calling me out on my own shit, I felt like the worst version of myself imaginable. I felt real guilt constricting my chest until it ached.

Shane takes us west – toward the ocean. I'm disappointed in a way. For a second, I thought he was going to take me to the stadium where he plays. I thought since we were taking a day off from my turf he'd take me to his, evening the imaginary score that I know we're both keeping between us. Today is definitely a point for him. He got me to ditch. He could have scored another point by taking me somewhere I've never been before to learn about a game I've never watched, but he's not pushing his advantage.

I'm struck again by the fact that Shane Lowry is a bigger person than I am, in more ways than one.

"Why'd you choose red for your Jeep?!" I shout over the wind and the world rushing around us. It's whipping my hair into my face, over my eyes, in my mouth, but I refuse to admit I was wrong. The hat sits untouched in my lap.

"It's my favorite color!"

"Mine too!"

He glances at me with a surprised smile. "Really?! We have something in common?!"

"It's a color, Shane," I tell him coolly, looking away. "Don't get excited."

He laughs, nodding slowly. "Alright, fine! Can I tell you a secret, though?"

"Sure."

"Red is one of the reasons I decided to play ball for Nebraska. Their colors are red and white."

"That's a stupid reason to choose a college," I laugh.

He's not offended. He's laughing with me. "I know."

"Was it worth it? Going to Nebraska?"

"Yeah. If I hadn't played for the Huskers I wouldn't be in the NFL."

I sputter, spitting out a lock of hair that's blown between my lips. "And you love to hit people."

"I love playing the game."

"Are you good at it?"

"No." He glances at me, grinning mildly. "I'm fucking great at it."

I blush, feeling instantly embarrassed by it. Of course, that makes me blush even harder.

It's not what he said or even the way he said it. It's the fact that somewhere in the discussion, we leaned in closer to hear each other. Both of us have an elbow on the center console. His skin is pressed up against mine. It's warm. Almost hot, like the black leather against my thighs. His face is only a foot away when he tells me how talented he is. I can see myself in the reflection of his bright orange sunglasses. I see me as he's seeing me, and it leaves me deshelled, the way his smile does.

"Hitting people can't be that hard," I say to be a

bitch, but there's no bite to it.

"It is if you're doing it right. You gotta make sure you don't murder them or yourself. But you also can't let them through the line. My job is to protect my family at all costs but keep my head enough to not mess a guy up doing it. There's a thin line and I toe it on every play." He casts me another quick glance. Another penetrating smile. "You should watch a game."

"You should watch an episode."

He laughs, smacking his hand against the steering wheel. "I knew you'd say that."

"If you know I'm going to say it, why don't you do it?"

"Because some sick part of me likes making you mad, Sutton. It's sexy."

I hold my breath and count to five. Then I do it again. I'm not containing anger. I'm holding onto something else. Something liquid and light that runs through me like cool water. His simple words do something sinuous to me. They make me want things I shouldn't want with a man I can't have. The waters around us are muddied and confusing, and I don't like confusing. I like clarity. Simplicity. I like black and white when I can get it, and Shane looks like every color of the rainbow to me.

I lean back into my seat, sliding his hat on low over my eyes to hide them. "We'll see how sexy it is when I lose my shit and stab you in the face with one of my heels!"

Shane chuckles. "Damn! That was weirdly specific!"

"Tell me you haven't fantasized about ways you'd end me!"

"Never once!"

"You're a liar! Or not very creative!"

"What if I'm just a nice guy?!"

I shake my head stubbornly, looking away. "No one is a nice guy."

Forty minutes later, Shane pulls us into the parking lot at the Santa Monica Pier. In that time, we said very little to each other. I don't like yelling and I didn't dare lean in close to him again. Eventually he gave up on conversation and just cranked the stereo. His speakers are impressive. I could hear them clearly over the wind and traffic on the 405. He listens to a lot of classic rock. It surprised me that his taste in music isn't that bad. I expected to be subjected to country or death metal. Definitely something more abrasive than Tom Petty and Lynyrd Skynyrd.

I drop down out of the Jeep like I'm freefalling from a cliff. I've never been to the pier before. It's a gorgeous day and the place is flooded with tourists on the beach, at the amusement park, and strolling along the pier that reaches out over the sparkling blue water of the Pacific Ocean. It rolls in gently, sending a breeze up the beach that tickles along my neck and my naked shoulders. I'm still wearing my workout gear – Shane promised me before we left that it would be fine – and the bare skin on my arms and legs is greedily lapping up the sunlight.

"You a fan of the beach?" he asks from across the hood of the Jeep.

"I don't know. I never come here."

"You should. It's good for you."

I cast him a wry grin. "You say that about carbs too."

"It's true."

"Maybe for you."

"Sometimes you just have to let things be good for you, Boss. Whether they are or they aren't, it doesn't kill you to imagine they could be." He steps toward the pier, motioning for me to follow him. "Come on. Lunch is this way."

I follow obediently after him. I let him take my hand as we thread our way through the crowd, something that's surprisingly easy to do with a man Shane's size. They move aside for him. People stare as he walks by, and I'm not sure if it's because they recognize him from the team or because of how large he is. Or how handsome. He looks shockingly beautiful in the sunshine with those stupid glasses on and a swagger to his walk that says he knows exactly where he's going. I'm holding his hand so we don't get separated in the crowd – that's what I tell myself. It's not because I like the warm feel of him pressed against my cold fingers or the way my shoulder brushes against the solid stone of his bicep. It has nothing to do with the possessive pull I feel in my stomach when other women turn to look at him.

"What's your stance on rollercoasters?" he asks me.

I look up at him, trying to figure out if he's serious or not. He is. "Um, I don't know. They exist?"

"Are we riding one today?"

"No," I laugh, shaking my head hard. "I'm not riding a rollercoaster."

"Why not?"

"Because I'm not ten."

"You couldn't ride one if you were ten. You'd be too small." He looks down at me with a smug smile. "You might be too small now."

"Eat shit."

"Eat meat," he fires back.

I laugh at how lame and yet accurate that insult is for me. "Well played, Lowry."

"I'm just getting started, Boss," he promises.

His mood was recovering the second we decided to

blow off rehearsal, but he's absolutely buoyant now that we're at the pier. The shift in him is amazing and I silently chastise myself for working him so hard. Yes, I want to win, but maybe I can find a way to do it without destroying him.

He takes me to a food cart that's selling hotdogs. *Hotdogs.* I almost punch him in the stomach for even suggesting it, but he's quick to point out that they have a vegetarian option and I can get it without the bun. No meat. No carbs. He's following all of my rules while still managing to make himself happy with two massive hotdogs for himself, both piled high with relish, ketchup, and more mustard than any human being should consume in one sitting.

We grab a tall bistro style table because he has trouble fitting in a picnic table. I'm starting to notice that he struggles with the world the same way I do, but in the opposite direction. While everything feels like it was built too big for me, it all feels too small for him.

We eat in silence. Shane seems content with his massive meat tubes and I'm happy with the smell of the ocean and the mist in the air as waves break against the pilons underneath us. It feels good. Peaceful. The silence between us is comfortable in a familiar way, like we're used to being like this. Like a pair of friends with nothing to prove or an old married couple who already knows each others' everything.

"Can I ask you something?" Shane asks suddenly.

I shrug. "It's a free country."

"You and Jace Ryker," he begins tentatively, "there wasn't anything there, was there? It was all for show."

I lick my lips slowly. "Why do you say that?"

"Because I can't see you hooking up with him."

"You've been picturing it?"

"Maybe. Or I've been trying to. But it doesn't make sense. He's into his girlfriend and you're just not the type."

"The homewrecker type?"

He flinches, a look of guilt clouding his eyes. "I shouldn't have asked. It's not my business. Sorry."

I chew slowly. My eyes are on the ocean but my mind is on the past. On the sins I've committed and the ones I haven't. I didn't wreck Jace's home, but that doesn't make me innocent because there's still Eric. There's always Eric.

I clear my throat roughly. "I didn't sleep with Jace," I confess because it feels good to be able to deny it. "You're right. It was all for show. I didn't want to sleep with him. He wasn't my type. Not by a long shot."

"Too pretty, right?" Shane jokes. He grins playfully. "I've always thought he's too pretty for his own good."

I snicker. "You like your men rugged, huh?"

"I like anyone that's a little rough around the edges. And you, Boss, are all edges. You're jagged as a steak knife."

"Are you saying you like me?"

"Yeah, I am," he answers without embarrassment. "Do you like me?"

"I don't *dislike* you," I hold out, feeling like a coward.

Shane laughs because he knows I'm lying. "We'll get there," he promises.

I roll my eyes like he's being annoying, but he's not. He's right. We're already there. I already like him, but to tell him that would be to give up ground and I never give up anything without a fight. I wouldn't know how if I tried.

"So if Jace isn't your type," Shane presses, "what is?"

"Trouble," I answer immediately and honestly. "My

type is definitely trouble."

"You mean badasses, like me."

I grin. "I thought you were a nice guy, Shane."

"You told me no one is a nice guy."

"I think you might be."

"Dammit," he laments dramatically. "I guess I'm out then, huh?"

"I guess so. What about you? What's your type?"

He looks at me for a long time. Long enough to draw my eyes to his. Long enough to make my stomach churn and my heart stutter painfully in my chest.

"I'm still figuring that out," he answers softly.

I take an unsteady breath. I try to hold onto it, try to count it out the way I did in the Jeep, but I can't. I can't hold onto it with him looking at me like that; like I mean something.

CHAPTER SEVENTEEN

SHANE

May 30th
KBC Studios
Los Angeles, CA

"Again!" Sutton cries.

I give her a meager head start before launching after her. She's short but she's fast. She sprints across the fake grass that's too green for reality with fierce determination that nearly leaves me lagging behind her. Nearly. I use the length of my legs and the strength coiled inside them to overtake her, passing her at the last second before we turn and run back to the starting point. We've been at this for the last hour. My lungs are screaming. My legs are on fire.

It feels so good I can hardly stand it.

Sutton is true to her word. Since we slacked off yesterday, we're working twice as hard today. I feel like I'm being punished, but I like it. I like running with her. She's a competitor, like me. She wants to be the best at everything she does and she will not rest until she's beat me back to the line at least once. I could let her win and end this whenever I want, but I'm no sucker. I don't let people win and she wouldn't be happy if I did. No, this ends when she wins for real or we both die trying.

"Again!"

I chase her across the faux field with a smile turning into a grimace. We're in the same park where we filmed the opening scene for *DNA*. It's on the KBC lot. It's been in a hundred TV shows and movies, shot from different angles and dressed up to look new every time. It's deserted now, becoming our own personal playground. And when Sutton kills me with these sprints, they can bury me here.

"I give!" I shout. I limp to a stop, my right foot hovering above the ground. "I give! Fuck! I give!"

Sutton slows, jogging back to me. "What's wrong?"

"Cramp," I growl through gritted teeth. "Hamstring."

"Get on the ground. Put your foot in the air."

I do as she says. She straddles my leg still on the ground and pushes against my foot held in the air.

I growl as it painfully stretches the muscles along the back of my leg. "Shit."

"Just breathe. Keep breathing," she pants.

Her face is flushed red from running. Her long, blond hair is pulling free from her ponytail that hangs over her shoulder, tickling my calf. She adjusts her hold on me, pushing harder. Making me bark in pain. She doesn't let up, though. She knows I need to stretch it out or it will only get worse. She uses her whole body to hold my leg straight and I'm still worried I'm going to accidentally kick her over. Her chest is pressed against my calf, her stomach flat against the back of my knee. I can feel her breathing. It's erratic and exciting.

"I think I'm good," I tell her roughly.

She shakes her head. "Shut up and breathe."

"I'm trying."

I really am. It's just hard to focus on breathing when I'm getting a boner, but I can't tell her that. If I don't get it under control soon, she's going to see for herself. Why do her breasts have to heave like that every time she breathes, glistening with sweat and—Oh shit.

"Do you watch baseball?" I ask her, staring up at the sky. Anything but the swell of her tits in that yellow sports bra. Kodiak yellow.

"No," she chuckles.

"I do. I watch the Mariners. There's a game on today."

"Wow. Great."

"It's a big one. They're playing the Dodgers."

"Shane, seriously, why are you telling me this?"

I shake my head, my eyes fixed on a cloud that looks like a teacup. It reminds me of my grandma. That helps. "I'm just making conversation."

"Okay," she mutters, unimpressed.

Her body is slick with sweat. Mine is too. It's mingling together where we're touching, turning hot. Moist.

"Damnit."

"Just a minute more," she consoles me gently.

That, her voice being tender with me, is more than I can take. It's worse than her skin against mine or her breasts bulging with every breath she takes.

I meet her eyes for a second, shaking my head. "It's fine. I'm good."

"Are you sure?"

"Yeah. I'm sure."

She lowers my leg slowly, letting me drop it to the ground. I'm relieved that my shorts aren't bulging noticeably as Sutton drops to the ground next to me. She starts stretching her own body, bending it in half with impossible ease.

Working out with her is the best and worst idea I've ever had.

"Hey," I grunt, sitting up quickly. Too quickly. My head swims a little from the blood rush. "Do the thing again. The Milan thing."

She laughs, shaking her head. "No."

"Come on!" I plead, scooting closer to her. "I'm injured. You owe me."

"I didn't injure you. Your pride did. You could have quit at any time."

"Just once."

She looks at me hard. Finally, she sits up with a sigh and I know I've won.

Sutton straightens her face like she's slipping into character before she affects a perfect British accent. "Darlings, I loved it. I *adored* it, but it didn't resonate. I didn't feel the love. Make love on the stage so I can see it, otherwise I simply won't believe it, lovelies."

"Jesus, that sounds just like her," I laugh. "That's creepy good."

"I swear, she says 'love' in some form at least five times per sentence," Sutton promises me in her normal voice. "You'll never be able to unhear it. You're going to notice it every time she talks."

"Worth it. Do Desmond now. The New York accent should be easy for you."

"It's fake!" she cries, crossing her arm over her chest to stretch it out. "He's not from New York. He's from Florida."

"No fucking way."

"Yes, fucking way. He's from Tallahassee."

"Okay, then do his fake accent."

She shakes her head stubbornly. "I will not."

"Come on!"

"No," she chuckles. "I won't offend my state like that. Pass."

"Okay, fine. Do an impersonation of McKay. Unless you're afraid of offending robots too."

"No, I can't. I love McKay. I can't make fun of him."

I fall forward dramatically. My fingers brush her leg;

soft and warm in the sunshine. "Holy shit."

"What?"

"You *love* McKay?"

She rolls her eyes. "Don't be weird about it. I don't mean I'm in love with him."

"No, I know. That would be too much to handle. This is enough. You love someone. You care about someone."

"I love Clara too. It's not a big deal."

"*Sutton has feelings*," I sing in an elementary school tone.

"Shut up, Shane," she growls, but it's weak. She's smiling. She can't stop smiling and I can't look away from her.

"Alright, fine, if you won't make fun of the people you love, make fun of someone you hate. Who do you hate on the show?"

"You?"

"Bullshit. I'm on the love list."

She laughs at me. "Just yesterday you were trying to get me to *like* you. Now you're convinced I love you."

"I'm an easy sell."

"Okay. Whatever."

She's trying to be flippant but she knows I'm right. She likes me. She liked having lunch with me yesterday. She liked walking on the beach with me afterward. She liked showing off her impersonation skills and making fun of the judges with me. She liked riding the Ferris wheel for the first time in her life with me as the sun went down over the ocean. She liked waking up knowing she would see me again today. I know all of that because I feel it too. I like Sutton Roe. More than I thought I could. More than I probably should.

"Are we doing lunch again today?" I ask her as I lean

back on my hands.

She snorts. "No. Absolutely not."

"You didn't like your veggie dog?"

"I liked it fine, but that was a one-time deal. I told you that."

"Girls say that to me all the time but they always come back for more."

Sutton laughs in my face. "Not this girl."

"You're different, huh?"

"You can't handle how different I am," she promises.

I smile at her softly. "Doesn't mean I won't give it a try."

She meets my eyes for a fleeting second before looking away. Her smile has dropped. Her face has that scared look she gets when things get too close to her, like a deer in the woods. She's on alert and I need to back off if I don't want her to run. But I'm looking at her beautiful face as she licks those pouty lips, and I'm thinking of a million things I'd like to do with her. Things she doesn't want to hear me say but they're in my head and rising in my throat, and I don't know how long I can contain them. She's hard as stone but I'd love to know what it feels like when she goes soft inside. I want to know what her eyes look like when they're half-closed with ecstasy and she whispers my name like she needs it instead of being annoyed with it.

I want to be on her list. The Love List. I want her to love me or love being with me. Some sick part of me wants her to be *in love* with me even if I'm not in love with her just because she's so damn hard, it'd be a thrill to break through all that stone to the tender part of her underneath. Has Sutton ever been in love with someone? Has she ever let anyone in that far? I doubt it, but the competitor in me wants to be the first. I don't know what I'd do with the victory once I had it, but I can't help wanting it. I can't help how deeply and irrationally I want *her*.

I want to get as close as I can to the fire in her eyes without getting burned.

"What's your family like?" I ask conversationally, switching gears for both our sake. "Are they here in California?"

She shakes her head sharply. "No. I don't know where they are."

"You don't know where your parents are?"

"I don't know and I don't care to know."

"So you guys aren't close then."

"No," she scoffs. She casts me a hard smile. "They're worse than me, if you can imagine that."

"How is even possible?"

Sutton licks her lips, her face going pale. "It's my mom, actually. I don't know much about my dad. But my mom is... she's more controlling."

"That's impossible," I tease, trying to lighten the mood I've sunk us into.

"I promise you, it's not. She's also a diva. She burned through most of my dad's money before they finally split and he stopped coming around, not that he was around much to start with."

"Where was he?"

"Working. He traveled a lot. Mom did too, but she always took me with her. She was a stage actress when she was younger. That's why she pushed me into it. Once I started working, she quit and followed me instead. She also started spending my money the way she spent my dad's. She burned through almost everything by the time I was fifteen."

"What'd she spend it on?"

"Jewelry. Clothes. Vacations." Sutton shrugs. The move looks jerky, like a shudder. "A race horse in Argentina."

"Damn. Did she leave with you anything?"

"Barely. After my first Tony, I was earning about eight thousand a week. I had over a million dollars in the bank at one point, but by the time I managed to get custody of my money, it was closer to half that. That's when I quit Broadway and moved out here. Alone."

I sit forward with a serious frown. "How old were you?"

"Seventeen."

"You divorced your parents, didn't you?"

"I became emancipated, yes," She answers stiffly. She hates talking about this. So why do I keep asking? And why are her fingers trembling? "When the judge saw what she was doing with my finances, he let me separate from her. I haven't spoken to either of my parents since the gavel fell."

"Sutton, I'm sorry. I—"

She stands suddenly. Her steps are wobbly, nearly toppling her back to the ground.

I jump up to reach for her, steadying her. "Whoa, slow down."

"I'm fine," she lies. Her face is sweating but I don't think all of it is from our workout. Her skin feels clammy against mine. "I got dizzy. That's all."

"That's not all. You look sick."

She chuckles shakily. She refuses to meet my eyes. "Thanks a lot for that."

"Let's get you back to the studio and find the doctor. You seriously don't look right."

"No. I can... I'm fine. I—"

Her eyes go unfocused. Her lower lip trembles.

She vomits on my shoes.

"Oh shit!" I jump back out of range, careful to keep my hand on her elbow to help steady to her.

Sutton gags and spits bile from her lips, her eyes closed against what looks like real pain. She's dry heaving. Everything that was in her stomach came up on that first wretch, but now there's nothing. Still, her body keeps trying. She hiccups and coughs, moaning weakly.

I come around next to her, rubbing my hand on her back consolingly. "It's okay. You're okay. Just let it out."

"So embarrassing."

"It's not. It's my fault. I made you run too hard. I shouldn't have challenged you like that."

"It wasn't the running," she whimpers pathetically.

When her body stills and the worst of it has passed, I take off my shirt and hand her a dry corner to wipe her face with.

"I'm sorry about your shoes," she mutters.

"Don't sweat it. I have others."

"This is so humiliating."

"We've all been there. But now we need to get you out of the sun. Come on." I wrap one arm around her, putting my other hand under her elbow. "You're going to the doctor."

"I don't want to go inside the studio like this."

"You're probably suffering heat stroke, Sutton. Or dehydration. You can't just go home. You can't drive."

She shakes her head stubbornly. "I can't go in the studio. Blood in the water."

"What are you talking about?"

"They're sharks," she insists forcefully. "You think they're just women, but they're sharks. They can't see me like this."

I sigh, glancing around the empty park like it will give me an answer. It gives me jack shit because it's not real. Nothing here is real. Not even the sharks she's so afraid of.

"Okay, how about this?" I suggest in my most convincing voice. "I'll take you back to my place."

"Hard pass," she laughs tremulously.

"You just vomited on my shoes. I'm not trying to hook up."

"No."

"Not even if I agree to watch an episode off the pen drive you sent me?"

She stiffens in my arms. Her eyes rise to mine; watery and intrigued. "Seriously? You'll finally watch the show?"

"I swear it. And all it took to convince me was you putting your health at risk."

"Six episodes."

I frown at her. "Three."

"Five."

"Whatever. Yes. Five."

Her hand goes over her mouth like she's ready for round two. Only problem is, there's nothing else inside her. She was all coconut water, and now that's sprayed across the ground at our feet. She's made of nothing but spite at this point. Even so, she won't let me carry her to the Jeep. We make slow progress but when we finally get there and I offer to lift her up inside, she doesn't complain.

I give her my sunglasses as well as my hat on the drive home. She doesn't like it but she doesn't fight me either. That's how weak she's feeling. She wears them both like a suit of armor against the world that roars around her. When I glance at her, I feel my heart tighten with worry. She looks like hell. Pretty hell, but still. Hell. Her face is pale, her lips almost white. I wonder if that pink hue I've always admired is lipstick. Maybe it's fake and this is the real her. White as snow. Fragile and fierce.

"Two episodes, right?" I ask her, focusing on the road.

I'm relieved when she chuckles softly. "Nice try. It's seven."

"You're a liar."

"Takes one to know one."

I smile, shifting my hands on the steering wheel. Reminding myself to watch the road and not her. "Why don't we just make it an even ten?"

"That's the entire season."

I shrug. "Might as well, right?"

"It's two o'clock. We'll be watching until midnight if we do that."

"I can hang if you can." I glance at her with a smirk on my lips. The kind she loves to hate. "What do you think, Boss? Can you handle it?"

She smiles smugly. "I can do anything you can do."

"One of these days I'm gonna get you on a football field and show you how wrong you are about that."

"Do your worst, Shane Lowry. I'm tougher than I look."

"I don't doubt that for a second, Sutton Roe."

CHAPTER EIGHTEEN
SUTTON

Shane's apartment isn't what I thought it would be. It's not as manly as I imagined. It's softer. Homier. And so is he. For the first time, I can see him with a woman. I've never bothered to imagine it before because it doesn't affect me, or I didn't want it to, but now that I'm here where he lives, I can see it so clearly. I can imagine him bringing a girl home, offering her a drink, and making her feel comfortable with his warm smile and easy attitude. She'd grin at him. She'd flirt. He'd tell her she's beautiful and she'd believe it. She'd feel it and she'd show him, following him to his bedroom. She'd giggle as he oafishly kicked off his shoes to strip away his pants. His underwear. Her inhibitions. His eyes would be like alcohol in her veins. She'd be drunk on him. She'd be naked and sprawled out on his California king, waiting for him and his huge body to be rough with her in the gentlest, sweetest way possible.

Would he whisper her name? Would he bite her neck in the tender place where her pulse runs wild with lust? Would she moan? Would she arch her back so her breasts are pressed against the never-ending plane of his chest that feels like a roof hovering over her; protecting her? Would he go slow? Would he go fast? Would he ask her how she likes it and give her what she needs? What she wants? Would he let her finish first before taking for himself? Would he kiss her slowly, savoring the taste of her ecstasy before driving in deep and bringing her to the brink for a second time?

"Sutton."

I blink rapidly up at Shane. "Yeah?"

"You okay?" He sounds worried. His face is drawn with concern.

I wonder how many times he had to say my name to get my attention. It was definitely one too many to be normal. I shift nervously on the couch, pulling the blanket he gave me up high around my neck. "Yeah. I'm fine."

"You look tired."

"Oh, that's rude."

"You look beautifully tired?"

I smile weakly. "That's better."

He grins as he hands me a glass filled with ice and bubbling liquid. "Ginger ale. It should help settle your stomach."

"Thanks."

I drink it because it tastes better than the flavor of my vomit, but it won't help. He's already made me drink two glasses of water because he's convinced I threw up from dehydration or overexertion. That's not my problem, though. It was my mother. Talking about her. Thinking about her. It brought up all the ugly I keep carefully tamped down inside me, and it had to go somewhere. It couldn't stay inside so I threw it up on his feet and the artificial field that feels like a metaphor for my life. Fake. Fake. Fake.

Shane sits down gently on the other end of the long, gray couch. His apartment is huge. It's very industrial with exposed plumbing and beams running across the ceiling. The floors are dark wood. The walls are painted a somber gray.

"I like your apartment."

He glances around like he's seeing it for the first

time. "Thanks, but it's not mine. It's Colt's. He owns the place upstairs too."

"And the garage underneath?"

"Yep. Whole building. He usually rents this apartment out to tourists but when we found out the team was being moved, I sold my place. I jumped the gun. I thought it'd take longer to sell but it went in a month and I ended up homeless. He let me move in here until we leave L.A."

I frown. "The team is moving?"

"Next year. This coming season will be our last in L.A. It'll be the last for a lot of the guys too. Not everyone wants to go to Las Vegas."

"It's not that far away."

"That's what I figure. I don't have anything holding me here. I might as well go and stay on the team I started out with."

"Do a lot of players do that?"

"It's rare. If you stay in long enough, you'll get traded at least once."

"Do you worry about that?"

"I try not to."

"Do you worry about anything?"

Shane snorts a laugh. "Sure. I worry about a lot of things."

"Like what?"

"I don't know. Nothing right now."

"Seriously?" I push aggressively. "You're not worried about anything right now?"

"Not really."

"That is goddamn amazing," I whisper.

He laughs, full and intoxicating. I smile as I listen to it. "I just don't see the point in worrying about what I can't change. And right now, there's nothing in my life

I'd change, so there's nothing to worry about."

I still don't get it. I can't imagine a world where I didn't worry. It sounds terrifyingly liberating. It makes my heart race to think about, like imagining you can fly. It's invigorating and scary and so outside sane thought that you can't really understand it. You can only dream and wonder. That's what Shane looks like to me right then. Like a wonderful, terrifying dream.

It takes some coaxing, but I finally get Shane to plug the pen drive into his DVD player. We watch the first two episodes of last season's *DNA* in quick succession, barely saying a word to one another. I doze off for a little bit about an hour in and wake up to find myself stretched out low on the couch. My head is on the armrest and my feet are in Shane's lap. His hand rests absently on my ankles, his fingers slowly rubbing them through the thick fabric of the blanket.

It's almost too much. Part of me is screaming inside, telling me to sit up. To kick off his touch. I should go home and I should be alone, but I don't want to do any of that. There's another part of me, a quieter, scarier part, that's comfortable here under the warmth of his blanket in his home with his hand on me. I feel oddly settled for the first time in a long time, and I'm not quite ready for that feeling to end.

When the second episode is over, Shane reaches for the remote with his free hand. He deftly changes the TV to a live channel. It's ESPN.

"Nope," I mumble from inside my cocoon.

His hand freezes on my ankles. "Shit, I thought you were asleep."

"Yeah, I can see that." I roll my hand at the screen. "Change it back. Next episode."

"Just let me check the score."

"To what?"

"The Mariners/Dodgers game."

"Baseball, right?"

He casts me a disappointed look. "You're being difficult on purpose."

I smile. "Maybe."

"You don't follow sports at all, do you?"

"None of them."

"Wow. Okay, yeah, it's baseball." He gestures to the screen. "The Mariners are Seattle. They're playing the L.A. Dodgers. It's a big match up for me because it's my two teams."

"Who would my team be?"

"No one because you don't care."

I kick at him gently, jostling his arm. "But what if I did? Who's the New York team?"

"There are two of them. The Mets and the Yankees."

"Okay... I pick the Yankees."

"Of course you do," he mutters, his eyes on the game.

I scowl at him. "Why did you say it like that?"

"Because the Yankees are baseball royalty."

"I don't know what that means."

"Name one baseball player," he challenges.

I roll my eyes. "I don't know any. I don't watch."

"Just name any player you can think of. Alive or dead. I'm sure you've heard names before in movies or on TV."

I look up at the ceiling, thinking. "Um... Joe DiMaggio."

"He played for the Yankees. Try again."

"Babe Ruth."

"Yankee. He played for Boston and Atlanta too, but his good years were with the Yankees." He looks at me with an amused grin. "Go again."

"I think I see where this is going."

"Come on. One more."

"Okay, fine," I sigh. "Lou Gehrig."

"Yankee."

I drop my jaw, feigning shock. "What?!"

Shane laughs. His hand rubs my leg again, and I'm not sure he even realizes he's doing it. He massages my calf gently, sending shivers down my spine. "That's what I'm saying. The Yankees are the most famous baseball team out there. They've won a lot of pennants. And you love a winner."

"I do," I admit greedily. "They're my favorite."

"Then yes, the Yankees are your team."

"Cool. Now turn the show back on."

Shane laughs but he listens. He turns us back to *DNA*, immediately going to the last episode.

"What are you doing?" I protest. "We're on episode three."

"And we'll watch episode three. But first I want to watch you win."

I smile, stretching my legs out farther into his lap as I sink down deeper into the couch. He puts down the remote to massage my calf with both hands as the opening number begins.

"Is this bugging you?" he asks quietly, his eyes on the screen.

I shake my head even though he can't see it. "No. It feels good."

"You have a knot in this one."

"I know. It's been there all week. I'll give you everything I own if you can work it out."

He snickers. "Hell of an offer after telling me you're broke."

"I might not be rolling as deep as you but I'm a far cry from broke."

"You mind if I put my hands under the blanket to get deeper into the muscle?"

"Do whatever you have to do."

He puts his palms against my skin. They're so hot it's a shock. His touch makes the hair on my arms stand on end. I'm watching the TV but I'm hyper aware of his hands. He's strong but gentle. He kneads the muscles in my legs with an expert touch, alternating between deep pressure and soothing strokes.

"Is this okay?" he asks, his voice so low I can hardly hear it.

I swallow roughly. "Yes."

On the screen, Tina and her partner dive into a Paso Doble that will earn them some of the highest marks of the night.

Under the blanket, Shane's hand drags along the back of my knee.

Inside my body, I start to burn.

He's pushing boundaries. He's doing it slowly, giving me plenty of time to complain, but I don't. I can't. His touch is everything I've wanted for weeks. I haven't been able to shake the memory of kissing him in the rehearsal room. I think about it all the time. I'm thinking about it now as he moves his other hand up my calf, around the front of my knee, and between my thighs. His fingertips brush the tender skin that's pressed together, asking permission.

I'm breathless when I give it. When I open my legs to let him in.

He doesn't dive in right away. He takes his time exploring the ticklishness that lies just at the edge of my tight workout shorts. He teases me slowly. Painfully. I'm panting with need by the time he brushes one thick fingertip under the elastic material, pushing upward until he grazes the edge of my underwear.

We aren't looking at each other. We're staring at the screen, pretending to watch the show, but in reality we're both between my legs. I'm with him as he tugs at the thin material of my underwear. We're one when he drags his finger down the center of my body, making me gasp. Making me buck.

That's his undoing and mine. We stop pretending to care about the television. Fuck the show. Fuck the whole competition. Fuck the world. Just, please, for the love of God, let him fuck me.

I toss the blanket aside as he sits up on his knees on the couch. There's a fierceness in his eyes as he leans over me, replacing the warmth and weight of the blanket with his body. It makes me tremble with desire that feels like lightning in my veins.

His kiss is tender and slow. He takes his time with me, exploring my mouth, and I moan low in the back of my throat with a devilish delight at how thorough he is. We stay like that for five minutes or an hour or a day – I lose track of time and myself. At one point I'm gasping, ready for him to take it to the next level before I lose my mind, but the next minute I'm giggling as he runs his hand up my side, tickling my skin. He smiles against my mouth and I swear to God, I can taste it. It's like icing on a cupcake I'd never eat in my wildest dreams, but I love the flavor of it. The easiness of him is something I can't understand but that doesn't mean I don't enjoy it.

I tug at his shirt, yanking it up over his head to find more of him. All of him. As I kiss him, he becomes everything I've ever denied myself rolled into one, massive package of joys. The ridges of his stomach that count out a perfect six. The thick tresses of his hair the slide smoothly through my fingers. The hard roll of muscle that builds the landscape on his back. The tattoos on his shoulders. The thick cords of strength in his neck. He's candy and cake and soda. He's birthdays and swimming pools in the summertime. He's every kiss I never got as a girl. He's the fun, flirty sex I've been too afraid to have as a woman. He's big enough to be everything I want and need him to be, and he does it so effortlessly it hurts. It almost makes me angry how good he feels.

He mumbles something about a condom. He hesitates after he says it, waiting for me to complain or pump the brakes, but I don't. I stare up at him silently, smoothing my hands over the warm skin on his chest that bristles with wiry black hair. He has a tattoo of a bear there. A Kodiak. I look into his inky eyes that stare back blankly, and I nod to Shane.

"Find one," I whisper. "Hurry."

Shane is a big guy, but he's fast on his feet. He's gone for maybe thirty seconds before he comes back with a condom in hand and a look in his eyes that asks me if I'm sure about this.

I answer by sitting up just long enough to pull off my shirt. Then my bra. I toss both at his feet but he doesn't look. He doesn't move as he watches me lay back, arching my back to slowly pull my shorts down my legs. When I'm naked and trembling from the cold, Shane undresses as well. He doesn't go slow. He's quick and efficient, bringing his body heat back to me as a kindness to us both.

I exhale slowly as he lowers himself over me. He feels bigger than he did before. He's so much it's scary, but all I have to do is look into his eyes to feel safe again. He's gentle in his eyes. He holds me steady with them as his body presses against me everywhere.

"Is this okay?" he asks again, his voice strained. He's holding back and he's hoping like hell I don't tell him no. But he's asking because that's what nice guys do. Just because I've never seen it before doesn't mean it's a myth.

I nod shakily, bracing my hands against his shoulders. They bulge against my palms; solid as stone. "Go slow," I whisper fiercely.

He smiles at my nervousness. He knows exactly what I'm worried about and the smug asshole is flattered by it.

"Whatever you say, Boss."

I'd laugh, but he's too quick. He's sliding inside me inch by agonizing inch, and I'm gasping. I'm dying. I'm flying and floating as he does something terrible and beautiful to me. I can't catch my breath but he keeps his promise; he goes slow.

"Are you okay?"

"Yes," I gasp. My eyes are wide on his. I move my hands from his shoulders to his face where I can feel stubble pricking my palms.

"Tell me to stop if you need me to," he grunts. "I don't want to hurt you."

His words make my heart hurt. They make it swell to twice it's size until I can feel it against the back of my throat, reaching for him.

Shane's face contorts with determination. He lowers his head between his arms, letting it hang as he focuses on keeping pace. He's almost all the way there. He has to be. It feels impossible for there to be much more of him. If there is, I'm not sure my body can take it.

I run my hands through his hair in a soothing

pattern. "You can go faster, Shane."

He shakes his head stubbornly. "Not yet."

"It's fine."

"It's not."

"It doesn't hurt that much. And I'm tough, remember?"

"I remember."

"Then why are—"

"I'm about to come, Sutton," he snaps.

My hands freeze in his hair. "Seriously?"

"You're too goddamn tight," he breathes. "It's killing me."

"Then just come."

"No."

I scratch my nails down the back of his neck and over his shoulders encouragingly. "I don't mind."

"I do," he chuckles tightly. "Do you have any idea how many times I've imagined this? I've been dying to get with you and now I'm going to lose my shit in the first minute."

"What have you thought about?"

He raises his head to look down at me. The rest of his body is held tensely still. "What?"

"What have you imagined?" I run my hands down his chest slowly. It's peppered with coarse, golden hair that tickles against my fingertips. I can't stop touching him. I've felt him against my hands every day for weeks but now I can feel him literally everywhere and it's like a drug. I'm drunk with it. "Were we like this?"

"No."

"Where were we?"

Shane smiles. "On the stage."

"The stage?" I laugh.

He winces. "Shit! Don't laugh. You get tighter when

you're laughing."

"Okay. Sorry. Were we alone or was everyone watching?"

"We were alone. I'd never be able to share you."

My smile softens. "Did we dance?"

"Yeah."

"And then?"

He shifts his weight on his arms, leaning forward just a little. "Then I kissed you."

"Did I kiss you back?"

"Always."

"How often do you imagine this?"

"Every damn day," he admits huskily.

I lick my lips, pinching them between my teeth. "I have to."

"Really?"

"Yes."

"Where?"

"Your Jeep."

Shane smiles. His body lowers over mine a little further. A little deeper. "Night or day?"

"Night. It's raining."

"That's so hot," he moans.

"It is. We're soaking wet and it's hard to take our clothes off so we just work around them. You're in the driver's seat and I'm in your lap and I'm grinding on you slowly."

"Is there music?"

"There's always music with me, Shane."

His eyes flutter as he starts to move again. In and out in a slow, easy rhythm that makes my heart give way. It floods my system, washing me in warmth that feels like the heat coming off his skin. Like we're the same.

"You have your hands on my hips," I whisper to him.

"You're guiding me, showing me how you like it."

"How do I like it, Sutton?"

"You like it slow. And you like to look me in the eyes when you're inside me."

He's looking down at me now with those blue eyes that always remind me of the sky, and I forget how to breathe. All I can do is feel. I feel him and the air and the heat rising in my core as my breaths and his strokes become shorter. Faster.

"I love your eyes," he pants.

"I love your hands."

He lays one on my chest; over my heart. He's supporting his body on one arm but his tempo never falters. He's a marvel of strength and tenderness that humbles me. It breaks me in two. His forehead falls against mine as he finally lets himself go and I sigh into the sweetest orgasm of my life. In that moment, I am new. I'm a meadow in the morning reborn under the rays of the sun. Baptized in drops of dew. Shane is my sky. He's the clouds and the mountains and the rain on my fields. I've never felt more beautiful than I do as he holds me to him like I'm more precious than gold.

He lowers his body slowly onto mine, careful not to crush me. Leaning on his elbow, he uses his free hand to brush my hair away from my face.

"I'll do better next time," he vows with a self-deprecating smile.

I pull his hand to my lips, kissing his palm softly. "I'd love to see you try."

CHAPTER NINETEEN

SHANE

May 31st
Eucalyptus
Los Angeles, CA

In a bar just outside the gates of the KBC lot, half the remaining cast of *Dance the Night Away* have swarmed. It's a tradition after each show. We're here for drinks and a chance to watch tonight's episode as it replays just two hours after the live broadcast. Tonight we're missing two football players and four dancers who have children and families to get to. The rest of us, even Tina and Vic who were voted off the show tonight, have come out to celebrate. They're the third couple to go, bringing our numbers down to seven teams.

The one addition to the group, and she's definitely worth noting, is Sutton. She's never come with us to watch before, but tonight she followed me out to my car and let me lift her inside without comment or question.

"I'm so sorry you guys are gone," Ana whines at Vic and Tina over her mudslide.

"I never expected to get very far anyway," Vic laughs. He casts Tina an apologetic look. "Sorry, partner."

Tina laughs at him. "I don't mind. We had fun. No reason to be sorry."

"She'll get 'em next year," Ana giggles. "And by 'them' I mean us!"

We're only halfway through the show and Ana has already had three drinks. I can see Brett looking at her with worry.

I glance at Sutton sitting demurely next to me at the bar. She's perfectly composed and dead sober. She doesn't eat and she doesn't drink. I don't know how she's alive but I'm glad she is. I have to resist the urge to reach out to touch her. I'm dying to feel the impossible softness of her skin against mine, but there are rules. Sutton made that very clear. No one, not even my friends away from the show, can know what's happening between us. Not until after the competition is over. But whatever it is, it wasn't a one-time thing. She's slept over the last two nights and I'm hoping like hell she's coming home with me again tonight.

The commercial break ends. The TV screens on the other side of the room start blaring the *DNA* theme music through the bar.

Sutton sparks to life, patting my arm excitedly. "Here we come."

On the screen, the lights are low over the studio. Sutton stands in the middle, looking beautiful in her slinky black dress. She struts across the stage through the opening of the song until I meet her in the middle. We start a push and pull until the chorus hits and the lights turn red around us. We dance together in perfect form across the stage to the cheers of the crowd.

It's weird to watch us on screen. It's like I'm merging two memories of one moment. I can smell the studio as I watch from the bar. I feel the way I felt on the dance floor. I feel the pounding in my chest that beats against hers, knocking on a door that's been nailed shut. But bit by bit, throughout the dance and the competition, it's cracking open for me.

"We look good," she whispers like she's surprised.

I laugh, throwing my arm over the bar behind her

where I can furtively run my fingertips down the naked skin on her shoulder. "We look hot."

She takes a deep breath that only I can see. It raises her shoulder, pressing her body deeper into my touch.

Watching us on screen, our size difference looks larger than it feels when I'm holding her. We fit together better than you'd think. We're more natural than should be possible, but it works because *we* work. So much more than we did the first night. You can see the confidence we have as we glide across the floor together. There's a trust between us as I lift her, spinning her around my shoulders, down my body and onto her knees where she clings to my leg with a desperation I feel in my gut.

When our number ends, the room breaks into applause.

Sutton smiles, waving her hands at the screen. "Mute it! Mute it! I can't listen to the judges again."

"Me either," Tina agrees. She lifts the remote she seduced off the bartender to silence the pompous asshats who sit in judgement over us.

I nudge Sutton gently. "Do Milan."

Sutton laughs, shaking her head.

"What does he mean by that?" Tina asks curiously.

I look down at Sutton, eyebrows raised. I'm challenging her and she knows it. And Sutton Roe never backs down from a challenge.

"One time," she tells me sternly. "That's it."

"That's all I need."

Sutton sits up straight, composing her face. She falls into character like she's putting on a coat and I wish I could have seen her perform in a theater. From what I've seen, she's an amazing actress.

"You're a doll, Shane Lowry!" she cries in Milan's

thick British accent. She even gets her hand motions right. "An absolute, drop dead, doll! I love you. Both of you. I felt the power of the dance. You were in it, darlings, and I loved every second of it!"

"What score do you give them, Milan?" Brett asks, mimicking Jerry's deep bass.

"Eight! Crazy eights! Eight! Eight! Eight!"

The room laughs at how perfect her impersonation is. Sutton covers her face like she's embarrassed but she's eating it up. She loves the attention almost as much as she loves winning.

"Do Desmond!" Ana demands.

"Don't even ask," I warn her. My phone buzzes in my pocket, pulling my attention. "She won't insult her home state with that accent."

"Boo!"

"*You* do him, Ana," Sutton laughs.

Kasian snorts. "She already did."

"*Oh!*" we all laugh as one.

Ana turns deep red. She swats at Kasian angrily. "I told you to keep it a secret!"

"How can I when you cannot."

"He's got you there," Tina laughs.

The rest of the room is chuckling as I frown at my phone and the message that's just come in. It's from Colt.

Baby is here. Get your ass to UCLA MED.

I stand abruptly. "Holy shit."

"What's wrong?" Sutton asks.

I run my hand over my head, smiling. "My buddy just had a baby. I mean, his girl just had a baby. His baby. There's a baby." I shake my head, reaching for my coat laid across the bar. "I've gotta go."

"You can't drive."

I hesitate, glancing at the bar behind me.

Two beers. One shot.

Shit.

I look at Sutton's drink next to mine. Drink. Singular. Water.

I toss her my keys. "You drive."

"What? No," she protests, her face aghast. "I can't drive that thing."

"And I can't fit in your car. We've been over this."

"Shane."

"Can you drive a stick?"

"Yes."

"Then you can drive it." I look her in the eyes. I give her the soulful stare that she hates. The one that I know makes her weak but I can't ever let on that I know because then she'll steel herself to it and my superpower will be dead. "Please."

I can feel her defenses breaking down even as she frowns at me.

"Yes, alright," she mutters, sliding down off her stool.

"Drive careful!" Tina shouts to her. "And tell the new mom congratulations, Shane!"

"I will! Thanks!"

There's a chorus of goodbyes that follows us out of the bar and onto the sidewalk. It's dusk. That in-between time of day when the temperature starts dropping with the sun.

Without a word, I drape my jacket over Sutton's small shoulders.

She looks up at me with a grateful smile.

"Thanks for doing this," I tell her.

"You didn't leave me much choice."

"You could have said no."

"And I could have looked like a raging bitch in front of everyone."

"You worry about looking like a bitch a lot."

"Maybe because people think I am a lot."

"You know how you could change that?"

"Surround myself with different people?" she asks drolly.

I smile. "You could try being nice."

"No. I'm good." She motions to my car parked right up against the curb. "What the hell is that, anyway?"

"What?"

"The big black pipe coming out of the side."

"That's the snorkel."

She snorts. "Are you serious? Why does your car need a snorkel? Is it going scuba diving on the weekends?"

"It could. That's why I have it."

I lift her up inside. I have to resist the urge to give her a kiss as I do it, but the windows on the bar are big and the street is not empty. I settle for copping a feel of her ass instead.

When I climb in on my side, she gives me a blank stare. She kicks her feet fecklessly over the open air under the dash. They don't even come close to touching the pedals.

"The seat slides forward," I tell her.

"Yeah, I know. Thanks. I'm just pointing out how ridiculous it is that I'm driving this thing."

"Got it. Can we go?"

"Hold on." She pulls her hair back into a ponytail, securing it with a black band she had wrapped around her wrist. "I have to use my *thing*."

"It's good you started carrying one. It's like you know I'm never putting the doors back on."

"What happens if it rains?"

I grin. "We get wet, Sutton. Remember? Real wet."

She rolls her eyes. "I should never have told you about that."

"Fuck that. I love that story. I want to hear it every night before I go to bed."

"If you play your cards right, you just might."

Sutton practically has to hug the steering wheel to get close enough to touch the pedals, but she finally gets there. She grinds the hell out of my gears getting it into reverse. I wince but I don't say a word. My baby can take it. She could catch on fire and keep rolling. She can definitely handle Sutton.

"Who is this we're going to see?" she asks as she pulls into traffic.

"Trey and Sloane. Trey is my quarterback."

"He's the reason you were ejected from the Super Bowl?"

"No. I'm the reason I was ejected. But the guy I hit was giving Trey shit. He spit on him. It was over the line."

"Are you friends with his wife as well?"

"Girlfriend, and yeah. Sloane is close with most of us on the team and she's Colt's agent."

Sutton snorts. "I still can't get over the fact that you know a guy named 'Colt'?"

"You know a girl named 'Ginger'." I look at her sideways. "You really wanna start this with me?"

"No. Never mind."

"And Fiona."

"I said no," she barks.

"Did you feel that? I just won an argument with you."

She glares at me out of the corner of her eye.

"Sutton?"

No answer.

"Sutton!"

"What?!"

"I won."

"I know!" she shouts heatedly.

I can make her moan my name like she's begging me for her next breath, but the sight of her angry like that is still one of the sexiest things I've ever seen. I'll never get tired of antagonizing her.

Once we're on the freeway, I'm glad I gave her my jacket because the wind is whipping cold around us. She looks so small inside it. The sleeves are bunched up around her thin wrists and she had to wrap the front over her body twice to pin it closed with her seatbelt. I open my mouth to ask her if she's warm enough but her face is so focused on the road, I don't bother her. I sit back in my seat and text Colt for an update on the baby.

It's a boy, he answers right away. *He looks like Trey, poor bastard.*

Just as long as he doesn't look like you.

The Hotness could do a lot worse than me, brother.

Has Lilly held him yet? Has she contracted baby fever?

Colt takes a minute to answer, but when he does it's a picture. Lilly is in a hospital room filled with balloons and flowers. There's a small mass of blue blankets in her arms. She's smiling from ear to ear.

You're screwed, I tell him.

No shit. Get here and take this kid from her before she steals it.

On my way.

Quit driving and texting, asshole!

I'm not, douchebag! I had a few drinks after the

show. Sutton is driving.

Oh shit. We're meeting the shrew?

I glance at Sutton. She's not paying any attention to me, but I'm worried. All the guys have heard me say about her is that she's a ball buster. I'm pretty sure that's about to bite me in the ass.

Try to be nice to her, I plead uselessly with Colt.

We're nice to everyone. Fucker.

"Great," I mutter to myself.

If she hears me, Sutton doesn't ask me what I'm mumbling about.

When we get to the hospital, she parks us in the garage in a deserted corner near the elevator. I check to make sure we're alone before I lean over, take her surprised, beautiful face in my hands, and kiss her deeply. She smiles against my mouth. I can practically taste it; sweet and bitter as dark chocolate. It makes my stomach growl hungrily for her.

"You have zero self-control," she scolds lightly when I release her.

I laugh at how wrong she is. "I've wanted to do that all night. I have more control than you're giving me credit for."

"Are you good now? Can you keep your shit together?"

"Just one more."

Sutton indulges me. She giggles against my lips as I savor her for a little too long. I take things a little too deep until we're both breathless and tugging at each other's clothes, eager for everything underneath.

"Baby," she mumbles urgently. "Baby. Baby. Baby."

"I know, baby. I know."

"No. *Baby.* Newborn baby. Pregnancy. Hospital. Remember?"

I drop my head in defeat. "That's a buzzkill."

"Diapers. Feedings. Nipple chaffing."

"Okay! Okay," I laugh. "I stopped, didn't I?"

She grins. "Butt rash."

"You're such a bitch."

With my boner appropriately deflated, we head to the hospital lobby. I go straight for the directory to search for Maternity. After scouring the endless list of departments, I find it on the third floor. I turn to Sutton to tell her that's where we're going, but she's gone. Spinning in slow circles, I look for her in the lobby. She's nowhere to be found.

"Over here," she calls from behind me.

She's coming out of the gift shop with a big bouquet of spring flowers in one hand and a tiny little teddy bear in the other. She gives them both to me.

"I wouldn't have remembered to buy any of that," I confess.

"It's a sad world when I'm the thoughtful one."

"You're a lifesaver, Sutton."

"Whatever. Where are we going?"

"Third floor."

It's not hard to find Sloane's room. First of all, it's posh. Of course it is. It's Sloane. Second, it's overflowing with people. Colt texted the entire team about the baby, but he only told about a third of us to come down tonight. The rest will filter in over the next few days. They'll bring so many gifts and flowers and balloons, Sloane will have to start sending them home with Trey. Or give them away. That seems more likely. She'll have the flowers distributed to every mother on her floor to make sure they feel the love, because even though Sloane enjoys the finer things in life, she's also a giver. She has a huge heart that's always been one of the things I love the most about her. Trey is just like her. He came from a poor family who gave away every spare thing they could to help others, and he's living his newer, wealthier life the same way. They're good people who deserve the good things coming to them.

"Lowry!" Colt shouts from inside the room.

Bodies shift to make way for me. I shake hands with my teammates as I make my way inside until I'm standing at the end of Sloane's hospital bed. Inside is exactly what I expected; Sloane's own personal gift shop. Flowers cover every surface. Balloons bounce off my head from every direction. Sloane sits propped up on a mountain of pillows dressed in a pale blue tank top and matching pajama bottoms instead of the usual hospital gown open over the ass. Trey stands on one side of her. Her best friend Hollis mirrors him on the other side. They look like guards at the attention of a queen.

I smile down at Sloane. "Congratulations, gorgeous."

"Thanks for coming, Shane."

I hand the flowers and bear off to Hollis so I can take Trey's hand and pull him into a hug. "Congrats, man."

"Thanks, brother."

"Hi," I hear Lilly behind me. "I'm Lilly. Colt's fiancé."

"Sutton. Nice to meet you."

"Shit, sorry," I mutter. I point down at Sutton with both hands, addressing the room. "Everybody, this is Sutton. My dance partner. Sutton, this is Sloane, Trey, Colt, Lilly, Sam—"

"Everybody," Sloane laughs. "Just say everybody. She can learn their names as they come up to hit on her."

"Hi," Sutton greets the room awkwardly. She moves in closer to me, as though she's intimidated. She might genuinely be. She's in a room full of strangers that are roughly half a foot taller than her and easily a hundred pounds heavier. It probably feels a little like being lost in the forest.

"We saw you guys dance while we were waiting for the baby to come," Lilly tells her excitedly. She's still holding him wrapped up in the blue blanket I saw in the picture. What I didn't catch in the photo were the wires. Little dude is hooked up to monitors that sit quietly to Lilly's right and what looks like an IV on her left. "It was so beautiful."

"Thank you."

"I had no idea Shane could move like that."

"I couldn't," I admit. "Not before Sutton got her hands on me."

She shakes her head. "He's a natural. My job has been easy this season."

"Easier than the Joey Lawrence season?" Lilly teases.

Sutton smiles. "That was rough."

"What happened with Joey Lawrence?" I ask curiously.

"We fought."

"A lot," Lilly adds.

"Oh, it was a regular season then."

"Eat shit," Sutton suggests.

I smile, nodding to the bundle in Lilly's arms. "Is this him?"

"That's the man," Sloane answers proudly. "He's sleeping, I think."

Lilly nods. "He is. He's had a big day."

"And he likes Aunt Lilly a lot. He zonked out the second she picked him up."

"Can I see him?" Sutton asks hesitantly.

"Yeah, of course," Sloane laughs. "Do you want to

hold him?"

"No, no. I just want to see his little face."

Sutton moves slowly to Lilly's side. They both look adoringly into the blanket in her arms while Sloane watches like a hawk from the bed. She's hyper aware of her baby. It's like there's a line still tethering them together. I doubt she'll let him more than a few feet away from her tonight.

"How is he?" I ask gingerly.

Trey bobs his head back and forth. "He's doing good. He's having a little trouble breathing. They had him on oxygen in the first hour but he's breathing on his own now, so that's good."

"He's a little underdeveloped even though he went full-term," Sloane admits.

"But he's got a good heartbeat. They're hoping he'll be able to come home next week. We think he'll be—"

He pauses, staring behind me. I look at Sloane, but she's doing the same.

In fact, just about everyone in the room is looking behind me. At Sutton.

I turn around to find her with little dude in her arms. Lilly has just handed him to her. She's standing next to Sutton with her hand on her shoulder and a worried look on her face. The same concerned look the rest of the room is giving her.

Sutton is openly crying.

The tears are silent but they're large. And there are so many. Her face is streaked with them. They drip down her cheeks onto the blanket surrounding the baby, but she's careful not to let any of them fall on his face. She's protecting him as she weeps over him, and I don't know near enough about women or babies to get what the hell is happening right now.

"Are you okay?" I ask her quietly.

She sniffles, shaking her head to clear the tears from her face. "I'm fine. I just... He's so perfect, isn't he?"

Hollis smiles reassuringly, handing Sutton a Kleenex. "Yeah. He is. It's like a gut punch, isn't it?"

Sutton laughs shakily. "It really is. I wasn't ready for it."

"Me either. You should have seen me when I held him. I cried too."

"You don't have to say that just to be nice."

"He's not nice," Sloane corrects dryly. "He's horrible. And he wept like a bitch. How do you think he knew where the Kleenexes were?"

Hollis glares down at her. "Excuse me for having a heart, you harpy."

"It's fine to have a heart, just have a little bit of a spine to go with it. You cry at everything lately. You're giving gay a bad name."

"I hope you get allergies from all the flowers."

"I hope you get adult acne."

Hollis stares at Sloane like he's imagining all the ways he'd murder her if there were no witnesses. "You're a bitch, but I love you so damn much."

She smiles. "So much you're going to cry about it?"

Hollis doesn't reply. He sits down on the edge of her bed and wraps his arm around her. He's crowding her but she leans into him, hugging him tightly.

"I didn't peg you as a baby person," I tell Sutton.

"I'm not. Not normally. But he's so beautiful." Her voice cracks. She glances up to frown apologetically at the group. "I'm sorry. I'm a mess. But I... I had a shit mom and he's just so precious and new and..."

"Preaching to the choir, sister," Sloane promises from the bed. "No apology or explanation needed.

Parents mess you up. It's not your fault."

"Thanks," Sutton chuckles nervously. She tries to hand the baby back to Lilly. "You should probably take him. They don't want some strange nutcase crying all over their baby."

"Why don't you hand him back to his dad," Lilly suggests. "If I hold him much more, I'll never let him go."

I give Colt a meaningful look.

He smiles in reply.

The room slowly moves back into action with people talking and laughing, but I move to the edge of it with Sutton. I park my ass on the arm of a chair and smile when she comes to lean against my side. We're almost the same height like this. I can look straight into her eyes and she can see into mine, and I feel dizzy when she does. She looks so vulnerable it hurts. I feel a pain in my chest that can't be healthy. I know she's causing it. I know what's happening to me and to her, and part of me wishes I could stop it because I don't know if I'm ready for this. I don't know if I can be everything she needs because she's a beautiful, mess of a human being. I don't think *she* is what she needs yet, but the train left the station three nights ago and there's no stopping it now. We're on a track, Sutton and me, and where it's going is not up to us. All we can do is hang on tight and hope for the best.

CHAPTER TWENTY

SUTTON

June 3rd
Carmichael Condos
Los Angeles, CA

We're dancing the Viennese Waltz this week. It's a slower, more elegant number than the other dances we've done so far. Shane will be in a full white tuxedo. I'll wear a shimmering white gown that looks like it's been dipped in gold. It's ombre, starting white at the top and turning darker and darker until it's solid gold at the very bottom.

"You look like the angel on top of my family's Christmas tree in that dress," he tells me now.

His arm is under my head. His hand plays in my hair splayed out over the mattress that's missing all of my pillows. I don't know where they went but they probably ended up on the floor along with our clothes and the blankets. It was a long, grueling day of dress rehearsal to get ready for tomorrow's show and we couldn't wait to get out of the studio. This is where I wanted to be; here in my bed in my home with the man who makes it feel like it's not nearly as empty as it actually is.

I smile at him, being careful not to roll my eyes at his sweetness. I do that a lot. He's never complained but it's a habit I don't mind breaking. "I do not look like an angel."

"Not right now you don't. Right now you look like—"

"Choose your words very carefully because there is nothing between my knee and your balls but air and the next thing you say."

His eyes go wide. "Damn. What do you think I was going to say?"

"Whore crossed my mind."

He frowns at me impatiently. "For real, Sutton. Who hurt you?"

He's joking because he doesn't know that his question has an answer.

I make sure to keep my face perfectly blank so he never has to know.

"For real, Shane," I tell him lightly. "No one can hurt me. I'm invincible."

"Devil."

"Excuse me?" I laugh.

He smiles. "That's what I was going to say. You don't look like an angel. Right now, you look like a devil." He puts his palm on my naked thigh. It rises slowly, caressing my ass. My hip. My side that tickles so badly I squirm under his touch, but I lean into it too. I want it more than I want anything else in the world. "You look like a gorgeous," he kisses me softly, "insatiable," another kiss, "naughty as hell little demon. And I am into it like you wouldn't believe, baby."

I kiss him hungrily as his hand rises to my breast. He cups it as much as he can but his palm is big and my breasts are not. Still, he makes it work. Lord Jesus Mary and Joseph, this man makes my body work.

I swing my leg over his hips to straddle him. We're animals here, alone. We're easy. There are no questions asked. There are no assumptions made. There's no doubt. Not for either of us. Here we are safe and together and no one can screw that up for us. Not even me.

I'm not the woman I thought I was when I'm with

Shane. I'm better than I ever thought I could be. I'm happier. Kinder. I feel my age when I'm with him. I'm younger than I've ever been before. Freer than I believed a person could be. He lets me be whatever I need to be – whether I'm a bitch, an angel, or a devil – he takes me as I am in every moment, and I want to give him every ounce of goodness I have inside me. I'll run dry eventually. It's unsustainable because that's the way all good things are – fleeting. But for now, my soul is an ocean.

I shudder against him as he pulls my body down hard over his. It hurts but it's good. So fucking good. I bite down on a scream that rises in my throat as he grunts. He shakes and grips at me with a controlled strength that should terrify me but it makes me feel whole. I feel safe in the steel cage of his arms, held tight to the rock solid span of his chest. He's warm stone under the heat of a desert sun and I'm a cold blooded creature curled up against him, desperate for his heat.

We fall back against the bed together, tangled in a mess of limbs, hair, and hands. He loves to play with my hair. He tells me it's like sunlight. I tell him the nickname that Kasian gave me. He laughs, saying he likes it, but he likes his nickname better. Deep down, I do too. We stay in bed for way too long like that; just talking. Laughing. I'm never this lazy but I could get used to it with Shane. We lose hours that way, but we'll never miss them. We pass them teasing each other with our words and our bodies. We have sex again, this time in the bathroom where he pins me against the shower wall with my legs around his waist and hot water pouring over the rippling muscles along his back. I can't stop touching him. He can't stop tasting me. He says he could eat me for breakfast, lunch, and dinner, and I smile at the insatiable need of this carnivore.

Finally, around midnight, we realize we need actual food. We get dressed for the first time since we left rehearsals and order Chinese takeout from my favorite place down the street. They're fast, cheap, and have amazing soup. It's my one indulgence that I allow myself only a few times a year, but tonight I don't worry about my diet. I order egg rolls and I promise Shane I'll try a bite of the orange chicken he ordered.

"You'll love it," he promises.

"I doubt it," I laugh. "But I'll try it."

"You're getting brave, Boss."

"I've always been brave. I think you're getting pushier."

"Now that I know your bark is worse than your bite, you're not nearly as scary as you used to be."

"No," I lament dramatically. "There goes all my power."

Shane reaches across the kitchen island to take my hand with a smile. "Nah, you've still got it. You're the strongest woman I've ever met."

I don't believe that at all, but I smile anyway because I want to believe it. I want to think I'm strong. I used to. I did when I left New York and my old life behind, but for the last couple of years I've started to doubt myself. I think it's easy to confuse strength with anger. And anger is almost always rooted in fear.

Ten minutes later, right on time, there's a knock at the door.

Knock. Knock. Knock.

Only it's the wrong knock.

My hand tightens on the plates I was pulling from the cupboard. I worry for a split second that I'll drop them. That they'll shatter on the floor into shards of ceramic that I'll never be able to put together again.

"I got it," Shane tells me amiably.

"No!"

He freezes halfway off his stool. "What's with you?" he chuckles.

His smile fades when he sees my face. I can't cover the dread I feel. It's written in my eyes and I let Shane read it. Every word.

"Who's at the door?" he asks quietly. His voice is low. Deep. I've never heard him speak like that so I have no idea what it means, but it makes goosebumps burst out over my skin.

"Sutton, who is it?"

"It's Eric," I confess without feeling.

Shane's face darkens dangerously. It's amazing how fast the light leaves him. He's at once jealous and territorial. "What is he doing here?"

"That's a really good question."

"I'm looking for an answer, Sutton."

"Me too. Just sit. Stay right there. I'll deal with it."

"What are you dealing with? Why would he come here in the middle of the night like this?"

I look at him hard. "You know why."

Shane sits down heavily on the stool. His face is a swarm of shadow, his normally brilliant eyes as dark as midnight. "Got it," he replies numbly.

I want to reach out to him. I want to hold him and kiss him and tell him that it's nothing. That it was never anything but ugly.

Knock. Knock. Knock.

But first I have to make the asshole go away.

"Give me a minute," I tell Shane.

"Just tell me one thing first," he says quietly. "Who's intruding here tonight? Me or him?"

I feel like he's knocked the air out of me. It hurts to hear him ask that.

"Him," I answer firmly. "He's always been unwelcome. Always."

Shane nods stiffly. He's not looking at me but he's done asking questions.

I storm out of the kitchen to the front door with murder on my mind. I don't open the door. I don't want to see him, I don't want him to see me, and I sure as shit don't want him to see Shane. The look on Shane's face has me on edge. I'm not sure what he'll do if he's face-to-face with Eric right now. The absolute worst thing I can imagine is that he'd leave.

Knock. Knock.—

"What?" I demand through the door.

Eric hesitates. "Sutton?"

"Who else would it be?"

"I don't—"

"What do you want?"

"I want to see you."

"No."

He waits for me to say more, but I won't. He wants an explanation but he can get fucked. I don't owe him anything.

"Are you going to open the door?" he asks quietly.

"No."

"Why not?"

"Because I don't want you here. Go home."

"You're my home, Roe."

"Fuck you," I scoff. "I'm sure you say that to your wife too. It's a tired line."

"You want me to leave her?" he asks, his voice gaining strength. "Is that what's wrong with you lately?"

"There's nothing wrong with me."

"Baby," he coos sadly, "we both know that's not true."

His words, his knowledge of me, they cut me down in an instant. The hot air of my anger is deflated from my body, leaving me limp and spineless.

I let my head fall hard against the door. My eyes close as I bang it gently against the cold surface. "Just go away, Eric."

"I don't want to lose you, Roe."

"You never had me."

"That's not true either."

"It's over. I told you I never wanted it in the first place."

"Sutton, open the door."

"I don't want to."

"You don't know what you want." He goes silent for a second and I think maybe he's leaving. Maybe he's giving up. But then he says, "You're thinking about Garret again, aren't you?", and I think I'll throw up on the door.

I feel tears sting my eyes. They're like needles filled with poison. I think I'll go blind from the rage of them. "Don't talk about him. Please."

"He's important, baby. He made you the way you are. He broke you, but you know I can put you back together. Just open the door."

"No."

"Yes," he insists. "You're confused. Let me see you. Let me talk to you about this. I just want to talk."

He's lying. Men always lie. Or they tell the truth and it's so ugly, you wonder why they didn't do you the courtesy of lying to you.

I'm shaking scared. I'm sick to my stomach, hiccupping on fear and hate. My stomach clenches painfully as I gag on a sob of so much ugly I can't bear it. I can't stand me and my body that he's touched. Kissed. Licked. Fucked. Used. That's what I am. I'm used up. I'm twenty-one and I'm nothing but a cold condom forgotten on the floor.

A warm hand touches my shoulder gently. Shane turns me away from the door. He looks down at me with that darkness in his eyes and his hand on the knob, and I think this is it. He's done with me. He's leaving.

He holds my eyes for one inscrutable moment before yanking the door open hard. I'm hidden safely behind it. I can't see Eric's expression but I recognize the shock in his voice when he comes face-to-face with Shane.

"You," he says simply.

"Yeah," Shane growls. "Me."

"I didn't know—"

"She's made it clear, man. She doesn't want you here. Go home."

"I came to talk about the show. We have—"

"You're not here about the show. You're here to fuck her."

Eric pauses, adjusting his tactic to Shane's attitude. "I guess I missed my time slot. It's a busy apartment."

"Watch yourself."

"Or what? You'll hit me?"

"You come around here harassing her again and I'll do a lot more than hit you."

Eric takes his time responding. I hold my breath in the silence, watching the white-knuckled grip Shane has on the door.

"Well, I wouldn't want that, would I?" Eric asks quietly, his voice dripping with sarcasm.

Shane doesn't answer. He stands stone still waiting

for Eric to decide how this night ends. I can see it in the hard set of his jaw that Shane is up for anything. It can end well or it can go very badly. It's all the same to him. He's game.

Eric is not. Shane's eyes track him as he moves away. He waits for a good ten seconds, probably until Eric is in the elevator, before he closes the door. He throws every lock on it before his shoulders relax.

"I'm sorry," I breathe.

Shane looks at me with a surprised frown. "Why are you sorry?"

"I didn't tell you."

"Have you been with him since we—"

"No."

"Then it was none of my business."

"It started last year but it'd been building for a couple of years before that."

"Sutton, you don't have to explain it to me."

I ignore his protests because I'm not doing it for him. I'm saying it for me. I want to purge this pill that I swallowed because it's been killing me slowly. I'll feel better to have it out. I'll be humiliated. I'll be ashamed. I'll hate every second of talking about it, but when it's over, when it's all out, I'll be stronger. I have to be. I *need* to be because I can't keep going the way I am. I'll never survive myself.

"I didn't get emancipated from my parents because of the money," I admit anxiously. I'm having trouble meeting his eyes. My heart is in my throat, beating slow. "I did it because when I was sixteen my mom convinced me to have sex with a thirty-seven year old director."

Shane stares at me blankly. "The hell," he mutters.

"He was planning a production of *Les Mis*," I

continue without thinking. It's the only way to get through it. Thinking means remembering and remembering is feeling and feeling is agony. "It was my dream. My entire life I'd wanted to be in *Les Misérables*. I was desperate to do it. I auditioned three times and Garret said it was down to me and another girl but he couldn't decide. He said he was torn. He needed help making a decision."

Shane runs his hand over his mouth, shaking his head. "I don't think you should tell me the—"

"My mom told me what he wanted. She knew. She'd been through it. She grew up in the theater. She said I was lucky he was attractive. A lot of the men she'd slept with were older and uglier. She said I should be grateful I had it so easy. I didn't feel lucky. I wanted the part so bad I could taste it, but I wasn't sure I could do what I had to do to get it. I wasn't a virgin but I wasn't very experienced either. The idea of sleeping with a strange man scared the shit out of me.

"Mom told me that if I didn't do it, the other girl would and I'd be out of luck. She said landing that part would launch my adult career. I could stop doing kid's shows and start the next part of my life. She said I needed something and he needed something, and if we could help each other out, we'd both be happy in the end." I shrug but it turns in to a shake I feel down to my core, chilling me like I've been dropped in an ice bath. "It was only one time. It was in a nice hotel room. My mom bought me a beautiful yellow dress and took me to the salon beforehand. I felt... I felt grown up. I told myself I was taking care of my business, the way all women do."

"Did she make you work with him afterward?" Shane asks tightly.

"No. I never made it to the production, but I went to the hotel. We had sex."

"Fuuuck," Shane groans, rocking back on his heels. He takes a step away from me, his hands on his hips. His head down.

"When I left, he said I got it. We were going to start working a month later, but I couldn't sleep that night. I felt sick. No matter what my mom was telling me, I knew what had just happened." I lick my lips, tasting salt tears I didn't know I was crying. "I knew I was raped."

"And that son of a bitch," he points angrily at the door, "he knows about this?"

"I told Eric about it two years after I got to L.A. When I got on the show, we hit it off right away. He treated me like an adult. He asked my opinion on things and he respected it. It felt good to be seen as an equal, for once. We started flirting. It was innocent at first but it got serious fast. It was like something had to happen or we'd both go insane, and then it did and I felt sick with myself. I felt like I was making the same mistake all over again. He's older, he's my boss, he's married. It always felt so good when it was happening, like scratching an itch, but I felt like shit afterward. I cried every time. I hated myself. I hated him. I told him I never wanted to do it again but Eric said it would always happen because we're meant for each other. He's told me a thousand times that he loves me."

"Do you believe him?"

"No," I laugh shakily. "I'm a masochist but I'm not an idiot."

Shane stands still, his eyes on the floor. He's thinking. It's a lot to process and I'm relieved I got through it all without him running out the door away from me. He still might. I wouldn't blame him. But he's made it this far and that's more than I would expect from anyone.

"I don't know what to do with any of this," he admits, his voice rich with emotion. He looks at me with an open expression that shows me the frustration, rage, and sorrow that's brewing inside him. I hate that I put it there. That I fed him the poison I'm so desperate to purge. "All I want to do is hug the absolute shit out of you but I'm worried that's the exact opposite of what I'm supposed to do."

I smile faintly. "I don't know what you're supposed to do either, but I would never say no to your arms."

"Get over here," he demands gently.

I step into his embrace with a sigh of relief that I feel down into my toes. His warmth caresses me inside and out. It dries my eyes. It evaporates the tears from my cheeks. It washes away the dirt and grime that hides in my heart until I feel fresh. Not clean. I'll probably never feel clean again, but I don't feel half as sullied when he holds me.

"Don't ever tell me Garret's full name," Shane pleads quietly, his mouth pressed against the top of my head. "I'll fucking murder him if I know and I'll end up in jail and you'll have to come visit me every Friday to tell me how my Kodiaks are doing."

"Oh, Shane," I sigh sadly. "There's no way I'm watching football. Not even for you."

He chuckles, leaning back to look down into my eyes. "You are the most stone cold bitch I've ever met in my life, Sutton, and I want you to take that as a compliment because that's how I mean it. You are a badass bitch."

"I thought I was a devil."

He kisses my forehead before pulling me against him

again. "You're everything, baby."

CHAPTER TWENTY-ONE

SHANE

June 6th
KBC Studios
Los Angeles, CA

Tomorrow is the fifth show of the season. The halfway point. Sutton and I are still hanging steady at the top of the pack, though last week after our Tango to *Sorry Not Sorry*, we slipped down a notch. We're number two under Brett and Ana. They brought the house down with an emotional Waltz that legit made Milan cry. She's a softy. She goes nuts for anything that's 'lovely'. Sutton says I need to be patient. Our Waltz will come and when it does, Milan will ugly cry again. But this week we're focused on impressing Desmond with our Jazz routine.

I lay back on the floor of the studio, throwing my arms high over my head to stretch my body out. "What a *glorious* morning."

Sutton glares down at me from the ballet barre. "I thought we agreed yesterday that you were done doing that."

"Doing what?"

"You know exactly what."

"I can't help it, Sutton. I feel so *glorious*. Don't you?"

"I will change the song. I swear to God."

"Don't," I laugh. "I'll stop. I like the song. And besides, I told my mom it's the one we're dancing to. She already downloaded it so she can be ready."

"Do you immediately call your mom about everything we're doing on the show?"

She's giving me shit again because I call my mom after each episode. We dissect the other dances and talk trash about the judges. Mom hates Desmond. She thinks he's a 'poser'. Her words, not mine, but when I told Sutton her summation of the guy, she laughed at how right my mom got it. It endeared Mom to Sutton immediately, and that made me happier than I can admit out loud.

"Oh, yeah. For sure," I answer Sutton now. "She'd kill me if I didn't. She's obsessed."

"Why hasn't she come out for a filming until now?"

"Because she wanted to come to the Super Bowl ring ceremony too."

"Right," she mumbles, switching legs. "I forgot about that."

I sit up straight to look her in the eyes. "Are you bailing?"

"No. I just forgot is all. It's a busy week."

"Well, write it down. It's a big deal."

"I understand that."

"And you're excited about it," I say sarcastically.

Sutton looks down at me impatiently. "You know why I'm nervous about going."

"I know you're nervous for no reason."

"People are going to assume we're hooking up if we go to a party together. *With your mother.*"

"We *are* hooking up."

"And I don't want anyone to know that."

"And I try to pretend that that's not a really hurtful thing to say."

She rolls her eyes. "You know what I mean. We're still in the competition and I don't want anything to mess with that."

"People thought that you and Jace were boning and

you said the rumors helped you win."

"Yeah, and because of that I don't want anyone thinking I'm sleeping with you too. They'll think I'm a slut who falls into bed with every partner she has."

"Are you sure that's all it is?" I ask heavily. "You're worried about what it will look like if you're sleeping with your partner? Or do you regret—"

"No," she answers immediately. She meets my eyes in the mirror, holding them steady with the seriousness of her expression. "I don't regret it. And before you ask, I don't want to stop."

"Good," I grin. "because I don't think I can stop."

She smiles softly, affection brewing in her stormy, gray eyes. "Neither can I."

I lick my lips, feeling my pulse quicken. "I wish I could kiss you right now."

"I do too, but someone could come in at any time. And they'll probably have cameras."

"Perverts."

She laughs, turning away from me to focus on her stretching.

I stay where I'm sitting, focusing on her ass.

It's magic hearing her laugh like that. It's so free and unafraid. She's still a bitch most of the time, I doubt she'll ever stop, but I'm good with it. I understand it better now than I did before.

I always liked Sutton, even when I thought she was utterly unlikeable, but now that I know where her aggression is coming from, I'm proud of her for it. What her mom put her through was unimaginable. I try not to think about it because I just get angry every time. I tried to stop her from telling me everything the other night. Not because I was disgusted or thought any less of her for it, but because I wasn't sure I could handle it. The anger that I felt toward her mom, that piece of shit director, and Eric was blinding. I had to stop myself from running out of the apartment to chase Eric down and kick his ass into the hospital.

Sutton told him everything she told me. She told him she didn't want to get involved with him from the start, and that asshole still pursued her because he saw the weakness there. He's been exploiting her for a year. She was legit shaking when she told him to go. She couldn't even open the door to face him because she's so shaken by the idea of him, so I know she understands what he's been doing to her. She definitely wants it to stop and I'm glad I was there to help her make that clear to him. It hurt to see my lioness brought low like that, but it's comforting to see how much strength she still has in her. It's not a solid thing. It's not a stone that can be cracked when it's battered for too long. Her power is pliable. It bends and gives without snapping, like a tree in the wind. The world will not break her. She'll change with the seasons, adapting to every storm, but when it's passed she'll still be standing. I think women are just like that.

Resilient as fuck.

"What's been your mom's favorite dance so far?" Sutton asks curiously.

"I think it was the Jive. She said we looked really in sync on that one."

"I agree with her. She has a good eye."

"She hated the song, though."

Sutton laughs, glancing over her shoulder at me. "Seriously? Why?"

"She said it's depressing."

"No."

"It's called *Breakup Every Night*. The girl comes over

for a quicky every night and then bails. It's a bummer."

"Why? Because a woman is acting like a man? Does that depress you, Shane?"

I smile. "Easy, Boss. I'm saying it'd be a depressing song no matter who did the bailing. A guy or a girl."

"Are you saying you've never had a one-night-stand?"

"No, but that's different."

"How?"

"A one-night-stand is two people having a hookup. That song is about a girl who comes over saying she wants to be with him, she wants to be in love, but then in the morning she's gone. Every single time. She's addicted to the drama. That's messed up."

"Hmm," she hums with a frown.

I chuckle knowingly. "I know that 'hmm'."

"You do, do you?"

"I do. It means, 'You're wrong, Shane, but I'm not going to fight about it because it's not worth it. I'll wait to fight about something fun, like how big your hands are and what your feet smell like'."

Her body sags impatiently. "Okay, first of all—"

"Here we go," I laugh.

"—your hands *are* huge. That's not my fault. And second, your feet smell like rotten asparagus."

"I started spraying all of my shoes with deodorizer!"

"And the world thanks you for it!"

"I'd be happy if just you thanked me for it. Just once."

Sutton sighs heavily as she leans forward to touch her toes. "Thank you, Shane."

"I'm sorry. I couldn't hear that."

She turns her head to shout at me with a smile, "Thank you, Shane!"

"You're welcome, Sutton!"

I stretch forward over my legs, touching my toes the way she is. I've gotten more limber in the last five weeks. I was always in shape but now I can stretch in ways I never knew I should. I feel it when I'm on the field, too. I'm more elastic in my muscles and joints. I like the feeling. I plan on keeping some of the moves Sutton has taught me in my workout routine to maintain it.

"Is your mom excited to come to this week's show?"

"God yes," I laugh. "Are you still going to the airport with me to get her?"

"Why wouldn't I?"

"Because you don't want to be seen with me."

"Don't be a dick."

I smile, burying my face in my knees. I let the weight of my upper body fold me in half over my legs. It hurts but it feels good too, like a lot of things in life.

"I can't wait to meet her," Sutton continues. "I can't imagine a woman large enough to give birth to your big head."

"Shmf mrden ighta nfoo," I answer into my lap

"Nope. I didn't get any of that."

I sit up straight. "I said, she's excited to meet you. She can't imagine a woman patient enough to put up with my shit."

"That's not what you said. That's not what she thinks. And I'm *not* patient enough for your shit. You drive me nuts."

"You act like it, but it's not true." I bend my legs, bringing my heels together in front of me. "You like me. You might even love me. I've made it onto The List. Everyone can see it."

"Oh, they can, can they?"

"Stalling."

"What?"

"You're stalling," I repeat clearly. "You always ask questions like that when you're stalling or uncomfortable with what we're talking about. 'They can, can they? You do, do you? I have, have I?' It's your tell."

She's not convinced. "Really? And what does it tell you?"

"Not much. I just noticed it is all."

"Yeah, well, stop noticing me."

I laugh. "Fine. I'll stop."

The door to our rehearsal room opens without a knock. Sutton turns to glare at whoever is barging into her sanctuary. Her scowl deepens when she sees the camera crew.

"Do you have time for us?" Deb asks, but she's only being polite. We don't have a choice in this. If we don't let them film us right now, they'll be back in an hour. They'll keep popping in until we give them what they need, and Sutton will go absolutely insane with the interruptions.

Sutton nods reluctantly. "Sure. Why not?"

"McKay wants us to get some footage of you practicing the lift in your number."

"He does, does he?"

I snicker at her feet.

"Oh, shut up," she snaps at me. "It doesn't always mean I'm uncomfortable. Sometimes I do it because I'm pissed."

"You do, do you?"

"Fuck off."

Deb's eyes bounce between me and Sutton. "Are you sure this isn't a bad time?"

"Interrupting rehearsals is always bad timing," Sutton answers coolly. "But we have to do it, right?"

"Right."

"Great. Then we're ready for you." She puts her hands on her hips, watching Scott set up the camera. "Anything you want from us besides the lift?"

Deb checks her clipboard. "McKay was hoping you could talk about the Jazz genre a little. Can you explain to Shane and the viewers what makes a dance Jazz?"

"Sure."

"You want me to ask about it so it looks natural?" I ask Deb.

"That'd be ideal, yeah. Thanks, Shane."

"Anything you need."

"Quit sucking up," Sutton scolds. "Let's get it over with so we can get to work."

I rise slowly, smiling at Deb. "Do you guys ever think about airing footage of her talking like that? Just for the fun of it?"

"All the time," Deb answers drolly.

"You can," Sutton tells her plainly. "I don't care. I'll be real for the camera."

"Nope. Sorry. Real is not what the doctor orders."

"McKay is one of the only people in the world you're nice to. He thinks you're sweet," I remind Sutton. "He probably wants everyone else to think the same."

Deb shakes her head. "Nope. It's not McKay. He knows what she's really like. He wants to shoot the real her but Eric won't let us. He's hell bent on making Sutton America's sweetheart."

I make a point of not looking at Sutton when Eric's name is mentioned. I don't want anyone catching it. If we start sharing furtive glances every time he comes up, people will talk. Questions will be asked and rumors will start going around. I wonder if they already have. When Sutton and Eric were flirting years ago, did anyone notice? I caught on to the weird vibe between them when I first started the show, but I didn't realize what was really going on. Sutton has been alone with it for over a year, and my heart beats hard with frustration that there was no one to help her.

Her fuckin' mom. If I was the kind of guy who was willing to hit a woman…

"Can we start?" Sutton asks briskly.

I smile at her clipped tone. At her absolutely unbreakable will. "Ready when you are, Boss."

Deb nods silently when the camera is rolling. Before the lift, we run through the opening of the dance where it kicks into gear. I can see it all in my mind. The stage will be dark, the lights pure white. A stained-glass window will be up behind us, implying we're in a church, and we'll both be dressed in bright, happy colors that imply springtime and rebirth. This number is pure joy and I can feel it when I start to move. I feel the lightness in my limbs.

Sutton smiles at me proudly when we finish the first combination. We run through the start of the number again, giving the cameras a second chance at different angles. They'll chop it all together later in the comfort of the booth upstairs. Eric will probably be there, watching. I take some serious joy in the fact that he'll see Sutton smiling at me. When she hugs me after the second run through, I hold her a little longer than I normally would. Just for good measure.

I'm getting territorial about her. When I look at Sutton, I feel pride, desire, and something else. It's new for me. It's a need I can feel in my heart and my head, but I don't know how to satisfy it. Fucking doesn't quench it. Kissing doesn't curb it. The only time I feel the least bit of relief from it is when she looks up at me with her eyes full of a softness that I never see her give to anyone else. When she melts into my arms against my body and she feels like forever, like she's doing right now. I feel sated when I hold her like this.

I'm not an idiot. I've never felt it before but I know what it is.

I'm falling in love with her.

CHAPTER TWENTY-TWO

SUTTON

Shane's mom is like a kid at Christmas. The second we brought her onto the KBC lot, she was wiggling in her seat excitedly. She can't believe she's about to see the stage where her favorite show goes down. She's been protesting for the last hour that she doesn't have to see it, she'll see everything tomorrow when the show airs, but it's half-hearted politeness. She's dying to get her feet on that stage.

Shane was worried about bringing her here after dinner. I think he's afraid we'll get in trouble with Eric, but I say fuck him. What can he do? Fire me?

"It looks deserted," Lynn comments as we pull through the gates onto the lot.

Shane has finally put the roof and doors on his Jeep. He did it for his mom. When I saw the way they greeted each other at the airport, I felt a tug in my stomach that felt a lot like homesickness. I miss my mom and that feels messed up. It still hurts, though. Even after everything she put me through and the hundreds of ways she screwed me up, she was still my mom. My dad was never around. I barely knew the guy growing up, but my mom was there for all of my firsts. She gave me flowers after my first performance on Broadway. She was there in the audience when I won my first Tony. She was my date to my first gala event, giving me my first sip of alcohol that would turn out to be my last. She taught me how to sing. She taught me how to dance.

For better or worse, she molded me into the woman

I am today, and when Shane's mom immediately pulled me into a bracing hug at the airport, I felt an emptiness in a dark corner of myself that I know no one will ever be able to fill. It will be my mother's greatest legacy.

"It's pretty empty right now, but there are people filming," I assure her. "TV shows and movies that are getting night shots will be on the outdoor sets. Some of them might be inside burning the midnight oil."

"Will anyone else be inside the *Dance the Night Away* studio?"

Shane chuckles. "What's the matter, Mom? Me and Sutton aren't celebrity enough for you?'

"No! Of course you are. But I wouldn't say no to meeting Jerry Feagan." She turns in her seat to look back at me where I'm sitting behind her. "I was a huge Paper Turbine fan in the nineties. I had every album."

"I've never listened to any of their music," I confess.

"That's fine. They were terrible. But Jerry was so sexy, I'd listen to him read me the phonebook if he wanted to."

"Gross," Shane mutters.

"I can see Jerry being sexy," I admit. "He's sort of a silver fox now."

"He was a ginger back then," Lynn tells me excitedly.

"Also gross," Shane mumbles.

"Don't be mean, Shane. Sutton is probably friends with Jerry and she doesn't want to listen to you insulting him."

"Sutton doesn't have friends, Mom."

"Shane!"

"No, it's true," I agree with him amicably. "I don't usually like people."

"But you and Shane seem to get along well."

"Shane isn't like most people."

I feel Shane glance at me in the rearview mirror, but I don't meet his eyes. I'm worried that if I do, his mom will see what's between us. I don't want any questions about what we are or where we're going. I can't answer them tonight and I definitely don't want to lie to Lynn. She's as sweet as her son. They're both the kind of inherently good people that make my stomach squirm with nervousness, worried they'll see what a mess I am inside.

"We're here," Mom whispers to herself happily.

Shane chuckles as he pulls into his usual parking spot. "You don't have to whisper, Mom. It's not a church."

"Maybe not to you," I remind him.

"Right. Sorry, ladies. I'll mind my manners."

We tumble out of the Jeep together. Lynn is barely taller than I am and I'm a little relieved to see her struggle with the monster as much as I do.

"You should really get running rails on this thing," she complains to Shane.

"I can't. It'd ruin the lift height."

"What's a running rail?" I ask.

Lynn gestures to the doors we just fell out of. "It's a bar that sits a little below the door to give you something to step on to climb up inside. Most lifted trucks have them."

"Most lifted trucks are lifted for show, not to clear a log in the middle of the woods," Shane complains. "I'm not getting them."

Sutton stares at me in amazement. "We've been mountain climbing our way up into that thing all night and you could have step stools installed?"

"Hey! I help you get in."

"Maybe we want to get in without help!"

"Are you going to stay out here yelling at me all night or should we go inside?"

"It's nice to see that you have a woman who's yelling at you," Lynn tells him fondly. "You're the kind of man that needs yelling at."

"Wow. Thanks, Mom."

"You are who you are, Shane."

When we get to the door, it's locked. The place is as deserted as the rest of the lot. Lynn's disappointment is palpable, though she tries to hide it. She suggests that we call it a night. It's been a long day of traveling for her, and me and Shane have to be back here early tomorrow for the dress rehearsal. All good points, but I'm no quitter.

Plus, I have a key.

"Do all the regulars have a key?" Shane asks quietly when we get inside. He watches as I punch a series of numbers into a lit pad before flicking on a light to scare away the darkness. "And an alarm code?"

I give him a stern look that tells him to stop asking questions.

He promptly shuts the hell up.

The truth is, no one else has a key. Or codes. I shouldn't have them either, but I got them from Eric over a year ago. He saw the obsession in me. I refused to leave when everyone else was supposed to so he caved and gave me my own means of locking up. He had other reasons for the generosity, though. One late night when he 'just happened' to come back to the studio was when we first had sex. A lot of what went on between us happened in this building. It's haunted in that way. I can feel his hands pulling at my hair as I pass through the shadows of the coffin room. I can taste his beloved lemon drops on his tongue when we make it to the stage. But once I flick on the main lights and Shane's mom giggles with delight, the ghosts are gone. They're run off by new feelings, new smells, new sounds that make me sigh with relief down to my marrow.

"It's smaller than I imagined it," Lynn confesses in a hushed voice.

"The angles they shoot from make it look larger," I explain. "And the edges of the audience are always dark so you have no idea how far back the seating goes. It's not as much as you'd think."

"Where will I be sitting tomorrow?"

Shane points to the front row along the right side of the stage. "Right there. Across from the judges."

"Up close and personal with Jerry," I tease.

Lynn smiles ruefully. "I'll be sure to bring my camera."

I frown apologetically. "You can't. They don't allow phones or personal cameras in the studio while we're filming."

"But you'll be able to have it after the show when we take you backstage to meet everyone," Shane promises.

Lynn smiles gratefully. She rocks on her feet, her hands held loosely together in front of her.

"You can go on up if you want to."

The words are not even fully out of my mouth before she rushes for the stage.

I laugh at her excitement. She's so enthralled by the entire thing, it brings me back to the first time I stepped into the studio. I felt the same way she does now – like I couldn't wait. Like I wanted to take the world in one bite and swallow it whole.

"Thank you for this," Shane tells me quietly.

I glance up at him. His handsome face is happy and

smiling. Relaxed like I've never seen him. "It's not a big deal."

"It is to me." He looks at his mom exploring every corner of the stage with a massive grin on her face. They have the same smile. They have the same kind of easiness inside of them. It makes me very aware of how complicated I am. "She follows football for me, but she doesn't love it. She never has. This show, though," he chuckles to himself, turning his eyes to mine. "She loves this show. She loves you and she loves us together on it. Calling her after every episode to break it down with her is the closest we've ever been and it's awesome. It means a lot to me. So, thank you, Sutton, because I wouldn't have made it this far without you and that means I wouldn't have that connection with her." He nudges me gently with his elbow. "I owe you."

"I'll remember you said that," I promise, feeling warm inside. Toasted as a marshmallow over a campfire.

I bet Shane and his family go camping. They're wholesome like that. I've never been and I suddenly really wish I had. I never cared before because I thought you just go lay in the dirt and get cold, but there's got to be more to it than that.

I wish I had a different kind of life. A warmer one with a sibling to hate the way Shane hates his brother. With a dad who's there at dinner every night and a mom who's there to lovingly make it. I wish I'd had a bike and a pair of roller skates. I wish I believed in Santa, just for a second somewhere in my life. I wish I'd gotten candy from the Tooth Fairy when my teeth came out instead of a pair of veneers to cover it up. I wish my first kiss had been in the rain instead of on a stage with a stranger while thirty people watched and critiqued. I wish I'd waited to have sex for the first time instead of rushing it with a boy in the chorus who couldn't find the clitoris if it slapped him in the face.

I wish I'd met Shane when I was sixteen; before everything went bad. Could he have saved me? Would I have felt for him then the way I do now? Would I be a different girl? A better girl? A fuller, more beautiful woman, inside and out? Would I dream of having children instead of dreading them? Would I eat meat? Would I own a sleeping bag? Would I understand myself better? Would I be able to say the things that are in my heart instead of locking them up in a cage in the dark, treating their beauty as danger?

Would I be able to admit to him and to myself how very much I love him?

I'll never know because I'll never be that girl. All the wishing in the world can't change that. It's like Lynn said;

You are who you are.

CHAPTER TWENTY-THREE

SHANE

June 8th
Charles Windt Stadium
Los Angeles, CA

"I cannot believe you talked me into this," Sutton mutters under her breath.

I look down at her with a proud smile. "I can't either. You're such a sucker."

She glances around to make sure we're out of earshot. No one is close by. Mom has disappeared to the bathroom and everyone else attending the ring ceremony is either at the bar, on the dancefloor, or around one of the fifty tables set up in the hall. It looks a lot like the Draft parties we have every April. Same decorations. Same caterers. Same lame DJ. The only difference is the atmosphere. The energy is higher. We've never had a Super Bowl win before. Every Kodiak in the room is proud to be a part of making history for the franchise. We'll be remembered forever for this. Someday we'll be old men sitting in nursing homes with bad knees, head trauma, and milky eyes, but we'll remember this moment like we're living it again. Like we're immortal.

"You asked me to come to this party with you when I was still hoarse from a screaming orgasm," Sutton whispers to me ferociously. "That's entrapment in any country."

"Tell it to the cops," I reply flippantly.

"Don't think I won't call them."

"Do it. I'll tell them I want you arrested for the hate

crime you committed on my shoes."

"Yes," she agrees dryly. "Because I meant to vomit on your shoes. That was the whole reason I did it. To mess up your kicks."

I snort. "Don't say 'kicks'. You're way too Upper East Side to get away with it."

"Fuck ya mutha," she tells me in a thick New York accent that is anything but Upper East.

I smile down at her. "You sounded like Joe Pesci. How was that hot?"

"Because you're weird."

"I think everything you do is hot. Even puking on my shoes."

"Oh my God," she groans. "Send me the bill. Let it go."

"Which bill? For the shoes or the emotional scarring?"

"All of it. It doesn't matter. I won't pay any of it."

"Pay for what?" Mom asks, appearing out of nowhere like a fifty-year-old ninja. My skills are slipping. I forgot how light her tread is. She used to sneak up on Clint and me doing all kinds of bad shit when we were kids. It wasn't fair. It was like living with the CIA. She saw everything...

"My shoes," I answer dryly. "Sutton puked on them."

Mom waves me away dismissively. "Shane, you spend more money on tennis shoes than you do on food. You can do without one pair."

I nod slowly. "So this is how it's gonna be, huh? You're just gonna gang up on me?"

"Yes."

"Cool. This'll be a fun night. I'm going to the bar. I need a beer." I swing my hand between the two of them. "Do either of you need anything?"

"Ice water, please," Sutton replies cordially, like she's a perfect little angel.

"Lemon?"

"Perfect."

"Mom?"

She eyes the bar like there's a menu to read from. There's not. "Do you think they have whiskey?"

"I think they mostly have whiskey."

"The good stuff, too," Sloane says from behind me. I turn to find her smiling in a little black dress with a gray baby sling strapped across her chest. She holds up a glass with about two fingers of amber liquid at the bottom. "Eighteen year old Macallan."

"Oh!" Mom cries excitedly. She opens her arms to give Sloane a quick hug before looking down into the bundle pressed to her body. "This must be Ben. He's so beautiful, sweetheart."

"Thank you, Lynn."

Mom has met Sloane before. They bonded over a love of alcohol at Colt and Lilly's engagement party and have been Facebook BFFs ever since. Sloane has a soft side that not everyone gets to see, but my mom brings it out in her. They share adorable pictures of animals back and forth, and Mom has been working on teaching Sloane how to cook. She sends her crockpot recipes and Tasty videos that she feels are in Sloane's depth. I think Mom sees Sloane as the daughter she always secretly wanted.

"How's he doing?"

Sloane smiles proudly. "He's getting chunky. He's doing great."

"Good job, baby boy," Mom sings to him. "You gave us all a scare there, didn't you? Yes, you did. But you're strong like your mommy and you're going to be big like

Daddy, aren't you? Yes. Yes, you are."

I look Sloane dead in the eye. "She's gonna steal your baby. Keep him close tonight."

"Shut up, Shane," Mom sings to me, still looking down at Ben. "I'll take what Sloane's having. Macallan, neat."

"You got it."

"I'll have the same," Sutton calls after me.

I turn slowly to look at her. "Are you sure? Neat means there's nothing diluting it. You're ordering straight whiskey."

"It won't kill me to try it. And besides, how bad can it be?"

"It's good," Sloane assures her happily. "It's so good I pumped all day to make sure I had enough milk to drink my ass off. Ben and I are both on the bottle tonight."

Sutton shrugs. "I'll give it a shot."

"Your funeral. Two Macallans coming right up."

"Thank you!" Mom and Sutton shout after me.

On the way to the bar, I stop by one of the TVs set up around the room. They're playing the Super Bowl game. Some are hitting the highlights but this one is playing every single second of it as though it's airing live right now. It's the fourth quarter. We're up, but the fight isn't over yet. The defense just forced a turnover. The ball is ours again.

I feel a knot rise in my throat when I realize what's about to happen.

The ball is snapped. You can see it better on the tape than I could there on the field in the fray, but the reality is the same – they're blitzing our quarterback. Domata falls back. He sees the pocket shrinking but he doesn't panic because that's just not what Trey 'Ice Man' Domata does. He keeps his cool, his eyes downfield, and just as one of the Pat's linemen is making a charge at him, he launches the ball in a tight spiral that nails Kurtis Matthews in the chest like a bullet. And then that guy is gone. Good night and good luck, you're never gonna catch that man. He runs through coverage, assisted by blocks coming from Lefao and Hibbert. He's at the twenty. The ten. Touchdown. The crowd goes wild.

But that's not what I'm watching. That's not the highlight of the play, not for me. My moment is about to come in three... two... one.

Boom!

Domata takes a late hit from some lard ass in blue. The ball has been out of Trey's hands for at least three seconds, and Fattie still lays him out like a rug. Angry cries rise from around the stadium. A whistle is blown, flags are on the field, but I don't give a shit. Not then and not now. I feel an echo of the anger I see in the video as I watch myself rip off my helmet, rush toward Domata, and grab the collar of the Pat getting up off him. He's talking shit, which already pisses me off, but when he spits on Domata's jersey, I see red.

I yank back hard, throwing him off balance. He's three hundred-plus pounds of defensive linemen, but I throw him to the ground like he's made of feathers. His helmet pops off, and right there I'm in trouble. I know it. He'll get a penalty for the late hit but I'll probably get benched for manhandling him. But Domata is down and it's my job to protect him, so when I see the Pat's sweaty face glaring up at me, I don't hesitate to punch Fattie hard in the nose.

More whistles. More flags. Blood on the field and arms around my waist to pull me back. I didn't know it was Hibbert at the time but it's good that it was. He's one of the few guys on the team bigger than I am.

Coach Allen stands on the sidelines without moving. He's a statue as he watches me shout shit I can't remember at the guy on the ground. His teammates rush in to help him up. My teammates work together to hold me back. A ref gets in my face (this part I actually remember) and tells me I'm out of the game. I'm being ejected from the Super Bowl and I'm not the least bit sorry.

I leave the field with my head held high.

The TV blinks off. The lights flicker, bringing everything in the room to a halt. All eyes turn to the stage as Trey goes to stand behind the microphone. The room erupts in cheers as he walks across the platform with a smile on his face. He's dressed in a sharp blue suit. He holds a beer in one hand, his long fingers wrapped loosely around the neck so it dangles at his side. His other hand is stuffed in his pocket casually. He looks totally at ease standing in front of a crowd of over a hundred people, a hundred sets of eyes watching and waiting, and it's clear why he's one of the best QBs in the nation. Trey Domata has pure ice water in his veins. Nothing shakes him.

"How's everyone doing?" he asks the room.

We cheer loudly. Women 'woo!' Men whistle.

Trey smiles at the enthusiasm. "It's a good night, am I right?"

"Fuck yeah!" Hibbert cries above everyone else.

Trey chuckles. "I hope no one has their kids in the room because I have a feeling that's going to keep happening."

"Just yours!" Sloane shouts laughingly.

"Get him a beer. He'll be alright."

The room laughs quietly. Eyes linger on Sloane and

Ben, but I'm looking at Sutton smiling next to her. I've always thought Sloane was hands down one of the most beautiful women I've ever seen, but standing next to Sutton, she pales in comparison. My girl could outshine the sun.

"This is a big night for the Kodiaks," Trey continues. "We are the first ever Super Bowl champions for this franchise."

"Yeah!" we roar.

Trey waits patiently for us to quiet down. "It's been a long road full of injuries and close calls, but we came out on top. We finally brought it home. And this coming year, I know we can do it again. You feel me?!"

"Yeah!" the Kodiaks shout in unison.

Trey starts our cheer with, "Raise the banner!"

"*Fly it high!*" we call back.

"Bang the drum!"

"*We hear it cry!*"

"Bring it home!"

"*It's do or die!*"

"Who dat?! Huh?!" he chants, riling us up higher the way he does on the field before the game. "Who dat?!"

"*The Kodiaks!*" we roar. "*What*?!"

"Who dat, huh?! Who dat?!"

"*The Kodiaks!*"

"The Kodiaks!"

"*The Kodiaks! Hoo!*" Trey sings with us.

He claps, leading us all to clap with him. We're applauding ourselves and our brothers. Our team. Our victory. It feels so good, I have tears in my eyes as I shout to the roof.

"Go Kodiaks!"

"Our rings are here!" Trey cries over the din.

"*Yeah!*"

"Are you ready for them?!"

"*Yeah!*"

"I can't hear you!"

"*Yeah!*"

Trey smiles, bringing his hands down slowly. It immediately lowers our applause with it, quieting the room. In the corner, I can hear Ben crying angrily at the raucous we've caused. "Sit tight. Those are coming at the end of the ceremony. First, we have awards to give out and a couple surprises up our sleeves. Colt! Tyus! Come on up guys. Floor is yours."

We applaud as Trey hands things over to Colt and Tyus. They wheel out a table covered in small gold trophies that look a lot like the kind you give a kid who just played soccer for the first time. This part of the ceremony isn't serious in any way. Some of the awards going out will be for real achievements like the MVP and Best Rookie. But the others are for fun. Shit like Most Tacos Eaten in Texas with a follow up award for Laid the Biggest Dump in Texas.

I get my beer and the whiskeys for Mom and Sutton before heading back to our corner. Trey gets there about the same time. The girls have scored a table all to themselves, and he leans down to kiss Sloane on the cheek. Ben gets one on the top of his bald little head. He's quieted as Sloane rocks him back and forth in her arms, but she doesn't let up. Once she does, he'll probably go off again.

I hand my girls their drinks just as the first award is being announced.

"The MVP isn't going to be a surprise to anyone," Colt announces. He holds a legit trophy in his hand. It's curving glass on a smooth black base that looks like a flame from a candle. "He's the reason we've gotten anywhere these last couple years. He's smooth. He's sharp. He's devilishly handsome. He probably should have stayed up here because now we're calling him back – Trey Domata!"

"Shit," Trey chuckles, running up to accept his award.

"The MVP is the Most Valuable Player, right?" Sutton asks quietly.

"Yeah. He won it last year too. And Best Rookie."

"The quarterback almost always wins MVP," Sloane explains. "They're in the spotlight a lot. It's easy to get noticed."

"He's the face of the team. When people think Kodiaks they think Trey Domata."

"What position do you play?" Sutton asks me curiously.

I meet Sloane's eyes over her head. She winces at me sympathetically.

"Left guard," I tell Sutton patiently.

"Do you ever win these awards?"

"He did last year," Mom tells her proudly. "He got the Pumpkin King award."

"What's that?"

"A made up thing," I mutter like it's nothing.

Sloane isn't having that. She happily explains to Sutton, "We had a family day at the pumpkin patch and Shane was playing with a bunch of the kids. They dared him to eat a whole, raw pumpkin. Seeds and all."

Sutton looks up at me aghast. "And you did?"

"Hell yeah, I did," I laugh. "No regrets."

"He even ate the stem," Mom adds.

"I pooped orange for like three days after."

Sutton's lips curl away from her teeth. "That's disgusting."

"You're not proud of me for eating my vegetables?"

"No."

"Hater," I mutter.

The night moves on slowly. Tyus and Colt hand out a shit ton of awards for some seriously stupid stuff, but it's fun. Matthews gets the Media Hostility award for never speaking to the press. Swanson gets the Benjamin Button award for shaving his beard and shocking us all with the baby face he was hiding underneath. An hour later and the table is looking sparse. The food has been eaten. Guys are getting anxious to get their Super Bowl ring already, including me.

"How much longer do these awards go on?" Sutton whispers to me.

I check my watch, grimacing. "Probably another hour."

"Oh. Okay."

She says it like it's no big deal, but I can see the anxiety in her eyes. She's miserable. When I look around the room, I know that she's not alone. These awards are fun for the guys on the team because most of them are inside jokes that have built up throughout the year. For anyone on the outside, though, it's lame. It doesn't make much sense and it's dragging on for way too long. It's like if Sutton made me go to opera or something. I wouldn't know anyone or what was going on, and I'd be checking my watch every twenty minutes to see if the torture was over yet.

I bump her leg with mine under the table. "Hey. You wanna sneak out for a minute?"

She eyes me suspiciously. "Sneak out to where and to do what?"

"What are you up for?"

"Not *that*," she warns sharply.

I grin, shrugging my shoulders. "I had to ask. That's not what I meant."

"What'd you mean?"

"Do you want to see the field?"

Sutton glances around the room before deciding anything has to be better than this. "Yes," she answer firmly.

I whisper to my mom that we're taking a walk because Sutton is bored. She nods in understanding without looking at me. She's too busy playing *Candy Crush* on her phone.

Sutton and I slip out of the room without much notice. Sloane and Trey see us, but they don't care. They look worn out and uninterested in anything but alcohol and their baby, like every other parent of a newborn.

It takes a while to make our way through the building to the field. We're in the big hall on the second floor by the offices for administration and coaching staff. To get to the field, we have to cross to another building, go down a massive freight elevator, and walk through the long tunnels under the seating surrounding the stadium. Sutton perks up once we're 'backstage'. It probably feels somewhat familiar to her to be behind the scenes where things aren't nearly as pretty as they are up front. This is where the real work goes on and it's gritty and massive, but she takes it in with a genuine look of interest in her eyes.

I didn't realize until now how much I want her to like the stadium. I'm anxious about how she'll react to being on the field.

"Locker rooms," I tell her as we pass them. "Utility room. Storage. Clinic. Saunas."

"Is this how you come out to the field?" she asks

curiously.

"This is the tunnel. On the other side are the locker rooms for visiting teams. They come out that tunnel. The shitty one."

"What makes it shitty?"

"It's for teams other than ours."

She snickers, the soft sound echoing off the walls around us, mingling with our footsteps. Hers are faster than mine. Even though I'm trying to keep a slow pace for her, the difference in the length of our legs forces her to work harder to keep up with me. She doesn't complain, though. That's something I've noticed about Sutton. Despite her anger and irritation, it's rare that she actually complains about anything. Scolds, yes. But she doesn't complain.

The field is dark when we get outside. It's underwhelming. There's a lot more impact when you come out with all of the lights blazing and fans in every corner screaming your name. Calling for blood. Tonight it's silent and still. It's just a field surrounded by cement, and I nearly apologize for bringing her out here.

"How many people can fit in here?" she asks curiously, her voice quiet. Almost hushed.

"Over ninety-thousand."

"Wow," she whispers. "That is... wow."

"It's the largest football stadium in the world."

She smiles sideways at me. "Do you know what the largest theater on Broadway is?"

"No clue."

"Gershwin. It has one thousand nine hundred and thirty-three seats."

"Broadway needs to up its game."

She chuckles quietly, her eyes still scanning the stands.

"Have you performed there?" I ask seriously.

"Yes. We sold it out with *Peter Pan*. I thought I was pulling in a big crowd, but this…" Sutton laughs in amazement. "Your audience is nearly fifty-times that size."

"It's not *my* audience," I remind her.

"You know what I mean."

"I do, but it's different. If you were in a production of *Cats* that was going head to head with a production of *Rent*, you'd pull in more than two thousand people."

"Going head to head doing what?"

"I don't know. Mud wrestling?"

She frowns. "What?"

"Whatever," I laugh. "The point is, ninety thousand people don't come here just to watch the Kodiaks. It's two different fan bases. There's nothing to compare here."

She shakes her head, looking around at the stands again. "I don't know. I think you won this one. Hands down."

"Maybe, but I'd buy every seat in the Gershwin to see you perform."

"Tough luck. I don't do that anymore."

"You could."

"No," she laughs dismissively. "I really can't."

"Could you try? Right now? For me?"

She looks at me in surprise. "What are you asking me to do? Dance for you?"

I shake my head, backing away toward the stands. "Nope. I've seen you dance. You're decent."

"Gee, thanks," she replies dryly.

"I want a show I've never seen before." I can't get up into the stands. The gates leading to them are locked and I'm not about to climb the wall in my suit. But I'm able to take a seat on a bench on the Kodiak's sideline. "I want to hear you sing," I call to her.

Sutton laughs. Her voice echoes over the field, bouncing off the cement surrounding us. "You do, do you?"

"Stalling!"

She scowls at me viciously. "Don't be an idiot. Come back over here."

"Not until you sing for me."

"I don't sing for free."

"I'll give you all the money in my wallet."

"How much is that?"

"I don't know. Four hundred, I think."

She gapes at me. "You're running around with four hundred dollars in your wallet?"

"Stalling!" I laugh.

"Ugh," she groans miserably. She's legit torn. Part of her wants to do it, maybe just to see how it would feel to perform on the largest stage she's ever seen. But another part of her doesn't want to dredge up her past. I wonder if it's wrong of me to push her. Am I treating her like her mom did? Am I forcing her to do things she genuinely does not want to do? Or am I helping her reclaim that part of her that was stripped away too soon?

I honestly don't know and I'm about to stand up and tell her to forget I said anything when suddenly she lifts her head. She points her face to the stands behind me. She inhales deeply and she starts to sing.

I've never heard the song before but I don't go to the theater. Ever. It's probably famous as hell. It's probably been sung by a thousand actors and actresses before her, earning awards for some. Standing ovations for others. More than likely, it's been done to death, but for me it's brand new. It's fresh as the night air it dances along, her perfectly pure voice rising and falling on the waves of the wind. It's a beautiful sound. Better than this stadium deserves. Bigger than Broadway could contain. It's a shining silver piece of her that's been kept locked in for years, sheltered from the world and the tarnish it brings.

It's the achingly beautiful sound of Sutton finally freed.

CHAPTER TWENTY-FOUR

SUTTON

June 10th
KBC Studios
Los Angeles, CA

"It's an eight count, Ginger! Not a four! Back to the start, everyone!"

I hear groans all around me, but I don't join in. I spring into action to move to the back of the stage where the group number starts. Clara is at the bottom, watching from the floor like a hawk stalking its prey. She's picking us apart today. We're four days from the next show and she's not letting us get away with anything. Shane got yelled at just ten minutes ago for 'making a stupid face'. It sounded harsh but it may have been true. Sometimes when he's concentrating really hard, he runs his tongue along the front of his teeth, bulging his upper lip out. I wouldn't say he looks stupid, I'd still hit that any day of the week, but he doesn't look show ready. That's what Clara is looking for at this stage – perfection. And we're a far cry from it.

I'm doing better about giving Shane breaks from rehearsals when he absolutely needs them, but with his practices for the Kodiaks ratcheting up, he's getting exhausted faster. I've cut our rehearsal time down from six hours a day to four to try and ease his load, but not all of the dancers are doing the same. I heard Melisandre kept Aaron Fitzpatrick here until midnight before he had to fly out to attend his own practice with the Broncos the next morning. These guys are racking up a lot of frequent flyer miles making the trip out here to film these episodes, and the wear is starting to show. I'm the lucky one with a local athlete. I guess I should be thanking Eric for pushing for that, but we haven't spoken in almost two weeks. Not since he showed up at my door and Shane sent his ass packing.

His absence has been bliss. I feel lighter than I have in a year. I'm having more fun. I'm enjoying my job in a way I never thought a person should. And even though I know a lot of it is being free from Eric, some serious credit has to go to Shane. He has me laughing more than I have before. He has me smiling more than I have a right to be. And he doesn't want anything in return. Just my joy, something he inspires in me with every word he speaks.

"Pee break!" he shouts to Clara. His hand is raised in the air like a kid in school.

Clara shakes her head stubbornly. "You can pee when you can get your timing right, Lowry!"

"On the stage? Because that's where it's going to happen. Soon."

"Oh my Christ," Clara mutters.

Shane's hand wavers in the air. "Is that a yes or..."

"Go!"

"Me too?" Aaron asks.

"Yes! All of you! Please, children, use the restroom! Then get your asses back here for the rest of the number!"

Melisandre, Ana, and Derrick disappear as well. Everyone else mills around patiently waiting for the rehearsal to kick off again.

I sit at the end of the stage with Clara, out of earshot from the others.

"What's up with you today?" I ask quietly.

She casts me an irritated stare. "Everything. I never

want to do another one of these athletes-only productions again."

"It's tough with them leaving all the time."

"Thank God you have Shane. At least he's local."

"Didn't they have more free time earlier in the year? Why didn't we do it then?"

"Because our producers are short-sighted asshats."

I smile fondly. "That's true."

She glances over my shoulder to check that we're alone. When she's satisfied, she hops up on the stage next to me. "I shouldn't complain about them."

"They shouldn't give us impossible tasks."

"No shit." Clara sighs, settling in. Settling down. "It's been a long six weeks."

"And there are still four more to go," I remind her brightly.

"What an awful thing to say to me."

I smile apologetically. "Sorry."

"You should be. You're half my problem."

"How am I a problem? I'm the best dancer you've got."

"Come on now. You're not the only award winner here."

"Are any of their awards Tonys?"

"Nope."

"Then they don't count."

Clara laughs, shaking her head. "You're such a snob."

"So are you. It's why we're friends."

She looks over her shoulder, scanning the stage.

I frown at her. "Who are you looking for?"

Her face snaps around to mine. "What? I'm not."

"And now you're lying. Seriously, what's up with you today? How am I half your problem?"

"It's Eric," she whispers, giving me a jolt.

His name is the last thing I expected her to say.

"What's he done?" I ask cautiously.

"Nothing that I know of. Not yet. But he's on the warpath lately." She looks at me curiously. "You haven't noticed?"

I shrug. "I haven't seen him."

"You're lucky."

"How is it my fault?" I demand.

Clara looks at me long and hard. She doesn't say anything but her silence speaks volumes. Inside it, she tells me she knows everything. Maybe first hand from him or by deducing it from our actions, I don't know. Maybe she saw us one of the times we had sex here in the studio. It was always late and we thought we were alone, but this is a busy space. Anyone could have walked in at any time.

It's only now that I'm outside the situation that I see how truly careless we were. There wasn't always a condom. There definitely wasn't assured privacy. Even the way we treated each other after-the-fact was not discreet. It's as though we wanted to get caught. Or, at the very least, like neither of us cared if we did.

I look away from Clara, feeling too ashamed to hold her eyes. "It was stupid," I mumble. "It never should have happened. I wish to God it hadn't."

"But it's over now?"

"So over. Dead and buried over."

"He's not taking it well."

I laugh without meaning to. "Tough shit for him."

"And the rest of us. He's making us suffer for it."

"What do you want me to do?" I ask sharply. "Sleep with him again?"

Clara's eyes dart behind us before landing on mine again. "Keep your voice down. And, no, that's not what I want. I wish you'd never done it. It was never going to end well."

"I knew that before it even started."

"Were you hoping he'd leave his wife for you?"

"I was hoping he'd leave me alone. I didn't want to…" I catch myself and my breath, holding it all tight inside me. It gives me that familiar feeling like I'm drinking poison again. I can taste it on my tongue; bitter like lemons. "I wasn't thinking. I didn't plan it and I didn't think it'd go on for as long as it did, but it's over now and I never want it to happen again."

"Because you're in love with Shane?"

Her words should be a shocking revelation to me. I should be stunned or offended or wild with fear, but I'm not. Instead, I'm nodding. I'm sniffing softly as warm tears fill my eyes.

"It's turning me into a basket case. Why am I crying?!" I whisper fiercely.

"Have you told him?"

I laugh shakily. "God no. I can't even tell you that I love you. How am I supposed to tell him?"

She takes my hand, warming it between hers in that motherly way that she does. "The same way you just told me. You say the words, however you need to."

"I'm back!" Shane shouts triumphantly behind us. "And my bladder is empty."

"Good job, Lowry," Clara calls to him without turning. She leans in closer to me, whispering, "Are you going to be okay?"

I sniff sharply, nodding my head. Willing my eyes to dry. I give her a winning smile that I almost feel. "I'm great."

Clara squeezes my hand before letting it go. She leaps down off the stage to do a headcount on her performers. The fact that she comes up three short sends her into a rage-fueled hunt backstage to find them.

"Everything okay?" Shane asks gently.

I look up to find him standing over me. He looks a hundred feet tall from here. I feel deliciously small at his feet with his body wide as the sky above me. Nothing bad could ever touch me with him around. And the good I have in my heart has yet to run out. In fact, I think he refills it every time he smiles. He sustains me with his beauty and brilliance, and I wish I could bottle the way he looks at me so I could keep it with me always because I'm better when I'm with him.

"Sutton?" he asks again.

"I love you," I whisper breathlessly.

If he has a reaction to my confession, it's lost in the sea of tears swelling from my eyes. The world is underwater. The lights behind his head blur and distort his face until I can't see him anymore.

I feel a little lost all of a sudden. I feel like I let some part of me go with those three words and I've no idea where it's gone. I don't know if I'll ever get it back. That's the scariest part about loving someone. At the start, you can never be a hundred percent sure that they love you too. Not until they tell you, putting you out of your misery. One way or the other.

"Sutton, I—"

"Sutton!" Eric shouts.

I close my eyes. Tears pour down my cheeks from my eyelashes. I brush them away as quickly as I can so I can stand and face what's coming. Whatever it is, it can't be good. It's nothing I want to deal with right now with my heart on a platter at Shane's feet and no answer yet as to whether he wants the damned thing.

This is the exactly wrong time for Eric to be messing with me.

"What?" I ask roughly.

I open my eyes when I hear him treading heavily toward me. I stare straight ahead as I wait, but I can feel Shane take a step closer to me.

When Eric stops just a few feet away, he glances up at Shane over my shoulder.

"Oh good," he says evenly. "You're here. Perfect. I need to talk to both of you about your number this week."

"What about it?" I demand.

"It's not going to work."

"What part?"

"The music. We can't get the rights for your song."

I frown. "What are you talking about? It was on the list of licensed music we were given at the start of the season."

"Legal made a mistake. It wasn't supposed to be on there. We wanted it but we never secured the rights to it. We can't air it. You can't dance to it."

"I've already choreographed it," I snarl. "We've been practicing it all week."

He opens his hands to show he's defenseless. "I can't change the law, Sutton."

"Then get me the song, Eric."

"Not gonna happen. You need to do something else."

I leap off the stage to stand in front of him.

Shane jumps down with me, keeping close to my back. He's letting me run the show but he's making sure I know he's there. That he has my back.

"This is bullshit!" I cry.

We're being watched. Over Eric's shoulder, I see

members of the crew stop to check what's going on. It doesn't encourage me to lower my voice. If anything, I want to shout at Eric louder to let everyone know what a son of a bitch he is, because make no mistake, this is a lie. We have the rights to that song. Bill/Bob doesn't make mistakes.

"I know you're disappointed—" he begins coldly.

"I want to talk to Taj about it. Where's Taj? Where's Clara?"

"You're talking to me about it. I'm the producer and—"

"Clara!"

Eric scowls. "You're making a scene."

"No. *You're* making a scene. You did this, you unbelievable asshole. You're trying to tank us. There's no way in hell we can choreograph, rehearse, and perfect a new number in four days."

"Last week you retook the number one slot on the board. The fans adore you. Why would I want to tank you?"

I bite my tongue even though I'm dying to say it. I'm dying to tell the room the truth, but I know better. I know how this business works. He's being completely calm and rational while I'm shouting my head off. I'm emotional. If I go shouting to the rooftops that Eric is trying to sabotage me because I refuse to keep sleeping with him, they'll all think I'm saying it out of spite. I'll sound crazy and he'll have won. He'll get away with it. I cannot let that happen. No matter how much I want to rip his face off and burn it in the parking lot.

I take two steps closer to him until we're nearly nose to nose. I look up at him with hate in my eyes and venom in my veins as I whisper, "You are a sad, pathetic man, do you realize that?"

He smirks at me. "I'm pretty happy at the moment, actually."

"What is your end game? You want me off the show? Fine. I'll quit after this season. But don't do this to us now. Not after we've come so far."

"No, Sutton, I don't want you off the show." He nods over my shoulder to Shane. "I want *him* gone."

"It won't change anything between us."

"Don't kid yourself," he says severely. "He changed everything between us."

"I'm not worth it."

"No, you're right, you're not. And I don't want your worn out ass anyway. But he threatened me. And I don't like being threatened."

"So this is a pissing contest?"

He shrugs, taking a step back. "Call it what you want, but I wouldn't waste any more time talking. I'd get to work looking for a new song because the one you had is gone. You're starting from scratch, guys. Good luck."

It looks like Eric is leaving, but he stops suddenly, snapping his fingers together with a smug smile.

"Oh, and Shane," he says quietly, his words just for us. "Enjoy my salty leavings, man. She's busted in the head but she's one hell of a ride, am I right?"

Shane shoves me gently out of the way, but when he gets to Eric, all tenderness is lost from him. I see it in Eric's face when he realizes he fucked up. He thought Shane wouldn't do shit in front of an audience, but it's a bad assumption. Shane knocked another player out in the Super Bowl in front of the entire world. The man doesn't give a shit.

He punches Eric in the face. Hard. It's just once, but it's enough. It lays Eric out on his back on the floor. His head rolls to the side. His eyes are glazed, but open and blinking. He's still conscious. His face is turning red around his left eye and I have no doubt it'll be purple within an hour.

Security is everywhere in this building. All it takes is one shout from the crew by the coffin room, and two guards come running through the door. It's easy to see what happened. Eric is flat on the ground and Shane is standing over him with his fist balled tightly at his side, his chest heaving angrily. I've never seen the look that Shane is wearing before. It's the animal inside him. The one that plays at hitting men on the field and makes mountains of cash by being the biggest, strongest, angriest son of a bitch in the room. That's who he is right now. That's who I'm seeing. A month ago, it would have sent me running. I would have turned my head in disgust at the violence I've seen because it's an intimidating, terrifying sight.

But I don't run because I'm not afraid of him.

Right now, more than anything, I'm afraid *for* him.

"Back up!" a guard barks at him, his hand on the Taser at his side. "Back off! Now!"

Shane puts his hands up, taking a slow step backward. His face is resigned. He knows what he did and he knows the drill that comes after. He doesn't fight it so I don't either. I move to step in close to him, but he shakes his head at me sternly. His eyes dart from me to the Taser on the guard's belt, then back again.

I hold my ground, holding my heart in my throat as the guards work together to get Shane on his knees. He goes willingly. He listens when they tell him to put his hands behind his back.

"Someone call the cops!" a woman shouts from the wings.

"Get the doctor for Eric!"

"We need to call his wife!"

"Where's Taj? Find Taj and tell him what's happened!"

The studio leaps into action around me, but I stay separated from all of it. I keep my eyes on Shane where he kneels between the security officers with his head down, his shoulders set stubbornly.

"Where will they take him?" I ask numbly. "How can I follow him?"

One of the guards looks Eric over before answering me. "I don't think he needs to go to the hospital, but if he does, Valley Pres in Van Nuys is the closest."

"No. Not Eric. Shane. Where will the police take Shane? Is he going to be arrested?"

"I don't know, ma'am. That's for the police to decide."

I nod in understanding but I don't say another word. I sit down on the floor right where I'm at, as close to Shane as he feels safe letting me get, and I wait.

"I'm sorry," I whisper to Shane. I can't look at him, but I can apologize. It's the least that he deserves but it's all I can manage.

I hear him sigh. I see his hands shift behind his back, testing the strength of the cuffs they've put on him. "It's not your fault," he answers roughly through a tangle of emotions.

"Don't lie to me."

"I'm not lying."

"You never would have hit him if it weren't for me."

"Like hell I wouldn't," he laughs darkly. I can feel him look at me, but I can't meet his eyes. "If I heard him say that shit about any woman, even one I didn't know, I'd have done the same thing. I don't regret it."

"Not yet."

"Sutton, stop. You—"

"Quiet," a guard barks at us. He shifts on his feet, his black boots squeaking sharply on the floor. "Keep quiet until the authorities get here."

I can feel the annoyance rolling off Shane in hot waves. They hit me like fire, burning my flesh until I feel like I'll scream from the pain. I know it's not directed at me, but I absorb it silently like a punishment that I wholeheartedly believe I deserve. It doesn't matter if he agrees. He's too good to agree, and that only makes it worse.

The police show up within six minutes. It's an impressive time considering they had to come through the security gates. Then again, the studio guards were probably waiting for them. The entire lot is probably buzzing with what's going down at the *DNA* building. During those six minutes, Eric is taken away to his office. He needs help getting up. His head wobbles on his shoulders like a doll without enough stuffing. Brett puts his arm under Eric's and shuffles him away from Shane, followed closely by Taj and the show's doctor. I don't know if he's going to the hospital or not. The only reason I care is because it matters to Shane.

The cops come in asking a lot of questions that only me and Shane have the answers to. I tell the basics of what happened without the details of my relationship with Eric. When they start to dig too close to that truth, Shane asks them if we can finish this at the station, away from the crowd that's listening so closely. He's not being arrested, the cuffs are taken off of him, but he goes willingly with the officers into the back of a police car. They ask me to come down to the station too to finish giving my statement.

I'm gutted as I watch the car pull away with Shane

wedged in the back.
	This is my fault. This is all because of me.
	This is the ugly that is knowing me.

CHAPTER TWENTY-FIVE

SHANE

June 14th
Eucalyptus
Los Angeles, CA

Eric decided to press charges because he's a cunt. I won't apologize. He earned the hit he got, and if he had any honor, he'd take it like a man. But, no, he's being an asshole about it. He went to the hospital even though the *DNA* doctor said there was no reason to. He didn't have a concussion. Just a hell of a black eye and some wounded pride. I didn't hit him nearly as hard as I hit the Pat's player. He couldn't have handled how hard I hit that guy. In the end, the hospital agreed with the *DNA* medic. I heard they prescribed him a Tylenol 3 and sent him home to ice his face.

Three hours after I hit him, I was told he was pressing charges. I was already at the police station giving my statement, so it was easy for them to book me. Sutton was there too. I didn't see her but they told me she stayed even after they were done hearing what she had to say. They couldn't get her to leave. She insisted she was staying until she knew what was going to happen to me. Two hours later when my lawyer came down to pay my bail, she was still there. Her eyes were tired but they were dry. She was quiet but stoic as she drove me to my car in her tiny little Fiat. I still don't know how I origamied myself into that thing but my neck was jacked for two days afterward.

It's been four days but Sutton has been with me every single one of them. She's basically living at my place with me like she's afraid to leave my side. The fact that I'm being charged with Assault has her more stressed than it should. She doesn't listen when I tell her that we'll probably settle out of court, just like last time. Or when I explain that I was charged with Assault as a misdemeanor, not a felony. I could see a max of six months in jail or be made to pay a thousand dollar fine.

What I don't tell her is what my lawyer told me – it's my second offense and I'm a wealthy athlete in a sport that encourages violence. Those two things combined could make a judge very unsympathetic. He might be inclined to give me the maximum penalty, and, given my wealth, send me to jail for the full six months. No fine. Just time. Assuming I went in sometime in the next month, I'd be gone until January. I'd miss this entire coming season. I could lose my slot for next year and the year after that. I could become useless to the Kodiaks, meaning they could back out of my contract.

There's a lot at stake for me right now, but I don't tell Sutton any of that. It'll just worry her and she already feels guilty enough for what went down.

"There it is," she mutters softly. "It's starting."

On the TV across the bar from our table, *Dance the Night Away* is starting to air. Right on time. On the KBC lot just a mile and half away from here, the show goes on without us. I wonder what they'll say about why we're missing. I don't really care. It'll be a lie and people will know it's a lie. The day after the fight at the studio, newspapers published pictures of me in the police car being driven off the lot. They know I was booked for Assault, but not against who. So far, KBC has no comment. Neither do me or Sutton. People are speculating but no one's gotten it right yet.

"It's official then, isn't it?" I ask Sutton grudgingly.

"We're really off the show. We lost."

Sutton nods slowly, her eyes distant. "We lost. Yep."

"I'm sorry."

She looks at me with sad, swimming eyes. "You have nothing to be sorry for. I'm the one who should be sorry, and I am." She bites her lip to stop it from trembling. "You have no idea how sorry I am."

"Don't cry, babe. Please? I can't stand to see you cry."

"I know. I'm sorry."

"We have to stop saying 'sorry'."

"I can't," she whimpers. "I can't get over it. It's all my fault."

"Hey," I put my hand over hers to slow her down. "It's not your fault. I hit him."

"You hit him because of me."

"He's the asshole here. Neither of us should feel sorry for anything."

"Well, I can't turn it off so how about we feel sorry together."

I smile at her warmly. "Yeah, I could do that."

Her face crumbles. Tears well in her eyes, threatening to spill.

"Sutton," I plead, shaking her hand gently. "Don't. It's okay."

"It's not okay. I... I..."

"Take a breath, babe."

"I miss the show," she squeaks out. "I know you have such bigger things to worry about and I feel like a total bitch for thinking about myself, but I can't help it. I'm so damn sad I'm off the show. I loved the show."

"I know you did. And you have every right to be sad. And, hey, who knows? Maybe what McKay wants to show us can help."

Sutton laughs shakily. She pulls her hand free from mine to wipe her face with a napkin. "Whatever it is, it can't get us back on the show. That's over."

"It could get you back next year. We can hope for that."

"I wouldn't. He was really vague when he said he wanted to meet up with us tonight."

"What'd he say exactly?"

"That he had a video we had to see. Knowing him, it's probably an autotuned video of you punching Eric in the face. As much as I'd love to relive that moment, I don't think I can stomach it knowing what it's costing us now."

"We'll have to wait and see," I tell her, but I don't have much more hope than she does.

McKay is an odd dude. He's a great director but he's a little out there. He has a hard time connecting to people directly. He likes them better when he sees them through a camera lens. But what I've heard from everyone on the show is that he's got a sweet spot for Sutton. She says she can't understand why. The only nice thing she's done for him as far as she knows was tell a contestant on the show to go fuck himself when they called McKay retarded a year ago. She said it was nothing, but I don't know. To a guy who struggles with people like McKay does, a moment like that might feel like a lot more than nothing.

"She's rushing it," Sutton comments dryly, staring at the TV. "Did you see that? Her steps are too quick. She's off."

"Yeah, I see it."

"What a mess."

"Brett's doing alright."

"Better than Ana. She's probably drunk."

"That's harsh."

"I know," she replies unapologetically.

Sutton is grumpy. She's bummed she's off the show. She's pissed that her life got me into a scrap with Eric. She's annoyed that I hit him and screwed up my own future, but she's also annoyed with herself for wanting me to hit him even though it screwed up my future, so she's just generally kind of pissed at everything. She feels a lot like the girl I first met two months ago; bitter and so damn angry you can practically see it burning under her skin. But as angry as she is, I know she's still the girl that laid in bed with me for hours talking about everything she loves. Things like New York and a good latte in the morning just as the sun starts to rise. She loves Chinese food even though she rarely lets herself have it. She loves cats even though she's allergic. She loves the color red and the number eight and the sound babies make when they're surprised by something. For an angry woman, she loves a lot of things.

Including me.

I haven't forgotten what she said to me in the studio just before the shit hit the fan. I don't want to forget it. It was one of the best moments of my life. One I haven't addressed with her since it happened because everything we've been dealing with since then has been ugly, and I didn't want her to hear me say those words to her in the middle of a clusterfuck. I want to say it to her when she can enjoy it and be happy about it.

But life is never seamless. There's no perfect time to say or do anything. Sometimes you have to feel what you feel and say it out loud or you could miss your chance. And I don't want to miss anything with Sutton.

"Sutton," I say quietly.

She looks over at me with a scowl on her face. She's

been frowning at the show but when she sees the look in my eyes, her face lightens. It's like she knows what I'm going to say. When I see her lip turn up at the corner in a sort of smile, I know she's as ready to hear it as I am to say it.

"Sutton, I—"

"I have what you need." McKay drops a big, black canvass backpack into the center of our table, jostling our drinks. Ruining the moment.

"Dammnit," I grumble.

McKay frowns down at me. "What's wrong?"

"Nothing, man. Have a seat. How are you doing?" I ask, uninterested.

He sits obediently. "I'm good. How are you?"

"I'm great."

"We're good, McKay," Sutton smiles. "I'm glad to see you."

"Wait a minute." I point at the TV airing the show. The *live* show. "If you're here, who's directing this episode?"

"My assistant director," he replies as though it's obvious. And I guess it should be.

"Why aren't you there?"

"Because I wanted to be here. He could use the practice anyway. He's terrible."

"And you let him have the reins this deep into the season?" Sutton asks incredulously.

"Not on the show anymore," I remind her. "Doesn't matter."

She looks at me indignantly for a second before deflating. "It doesn't mean I don't care about the integrity of the show."

"That show has no integrity," McKay promises her. "That's why I wanted to talk to you. I have what you need.”

“What we need for what?”

“To get Shane off.”

McKay digs into his bag as I cast Sutton a look. “We’re just going to let that slide right through?”

“Shush,” she hisses at me. “He doesn’t mean it like that and you know it.”

“Still funny.”

“Because it sounds like I’m saying I know how to make you orgasm?” McKay asks briskly. He smirks. “I guess it is funny. You’re right, Shane.”

“Thanks, McKay.”

“But, no, that’s not what I mean. I mean this.” He pulls a small laptop out of his bag. It’s covered in stickers for companies I don’t recognize – probably all of them audio/video shit or computer brands – and spins it around to face us. Before opening it, he pauses to wait for our attention. “This isn’t a video of you hitting Eric, Shane. I don’t have footage of that.”

“That’s okay.”

“I did, but I destroyed it.”

“Why?” Sutton asks.

“So it couldn’t be used in court against him,” he says matter-of-fact. “But what I do have could help you out with Eric. I hope it can. I don’t know for sure. That’s why I wanted to show it to you so you could decide what to do with it.”

Sutton shifts anxiously in her seat. “Is it… am I in it?”

“No.”

“Oh. Good.”

“Do you remember Liana?”

“The pop singer that was on three seasons ago?”

“That’s her. She’s in the tape. With Eric.”

“Okay…”

"Do you want to see it?"

Sutton glances at me, shrugging. "I mean, I guess? Yeah?"

I nod to the laptop. "Let's see what you got, man."

McKay pops it open, blindly clicking a button that brings the screen to life. The video is shot from high up like a security camera but the quality is way too good, even for a television studio. This was shot by a very expensive very high resolution camera. It's focused on the stage, though you can see a lot of the rest of the room in the wide-angled lens. There's no one there at first, but after about ten seconds two people walk into view. One is definitely Eric. The other one is a young looking brunette I've never seen before.

"That's Liana," Sutton whispers for my benefit. She frowns at the screen. "McKay, why do you record the studio?"

"Because people are interesting," he answers simply. "And it's a public place. There's no reasonable expectation of privacy there. Legally, I haven't done anything wrong."

"I wasn't thinking you had, I was just curious as to why."

"Because people are interesting," he repeats.

"Have you seen anything *interesting* with me in it?"

"Yes."

"Do those videos still exist?"

"No. I deleted them."

"Do you promise?"

"Do you need me to?"

She smiles at him tenderly. "No. I don't think I do. Thanks, McKay."

"Yes. But watch. This is important."

We watch closely as Liana giggles, stepping up onto

the stage. Eric follows her. He's smiling. Reaching for her. Taking her in his arms. They kiss slowly. He takes off her top even slower. Liana moans, reaching for his pants, and I glance around the room to make sure no one is paying attention to us watching porn in the middle of a bar.

"Are we going to see them have sex?" Sutton asks nervously.

McKay shakes his head. "Not in this version. In the full version you would but I cut it down for time and also necessity. You don't need to see them have sex to get the point."

"What is the point?"

"Listen."

We listen to some hot-and-heavy kissing for about twenty long seconds before Liana finally breaks away. She takes a few steps back from Eric, reaching behind herself to unhook her bra. When she drops it, we get a full HD image of her full silicone injected chest.

"This is a really weird moment for us as a couple," I mutter to Sutton.

"Shhh! Eric is talking. What'd he say?"

"Listen," McKay repeats calmly.

...you okay with that?" Eric asks seductively.

Liana giggles. "That depends. Can you really make it happen?"

"There's not much I can't make happen in this business. If you're serious about it, so am I."

"I am."

"Show me."

"Oh God, no," I breathe tensely. "Don't show him, Liana."

"She does," McKay confirms.

"I figured."

"Shhh!" Sutton hisses.

"How do you do it?" Liana asks as she kicks off her shoes.

"You wanna know all my secrets, huh?"

"All of them. Every last one."

"It's easy. They're just numbers. Numbers can be changed."

Liana laughs. "Kind of like my age, right?"

"I don't know anything about that and don't tell me either," Eric demands quickly. He pulls his shirt off over his head, stalking her back toward the orchestra pit near the staircase. "What I don't know can't hurt me."

"Legally, that's not true," McKay chimes in. "It doesn't matter how old he thinks she is. If he has sex with her when she's underage, it's illegal. Even if she consented."

"Does she?"

"Yes. Several times."

"McKay, when was this video taken?" Sutton asks, getting excited. Not sexually; the video is off-putting in so many ways. She's getting excited about the prospect of nailing Eric's skeevy ass to the wall.

"Two years ago. Almost to the day."

"Is it date stamped?"

"In the coding, yes."

Sutton pulls out her phone, typing frantically.

"What are you doing?" I ask her.

"Looking up Liana's birthday."

"She turns twenty this year," McKay tells her.

Sutton lowers her phone. "When?"

"In October."

"Motherfucker!" she shouts triumphantly.

People in the bar turn to look at us.

I immediately slam the laptop shut before the video

and Eric's sex crime gets any further.

"We have him," she gushes at me. "We can blackmail the hell out of him with this. He'll have to drop the charges against you now."

I smile at her apologetically. "We have to take it to the police."

"What? No way! He'll go to jail too, but he'll never drop the charges against you. Especially when he finds out we turned him in."

"I know and that sucks but it's the right thing to do. Think about it." I gesture to the laptop frozen on an ugly moment in a very young woman's life. "We have him because he actually did statutory rape a girl. She consented, yeah, but the law says she's not mature enough to do that until eighteen."

"She was off by a few months."

"It's still rape, Sutton," I remind her gently.

Her face falls along with her hopes. "Oh my God, you're right. Ugh!" She buries her face in her hands. "I'm a monster."

"No. You're not."

She drops her hands to glare at me. "Yes. I am. I wasn't even thinking of her. I was only thinking about us and how this could help us. Meanwhile she's out there somewhere thinking this was okay when it was so not okay."

"She doesn't care.

We both turn to McKay, surprised.

"What do you mean 'she doesn't care'?" I ask carefully.

"I sent her the video two years ago, right after I found it. I let her know I had it and that what he did was illegal. I sent it to her manager and her mom too. None of them cared. They said I could take it to the cops but they wouldn't press charges. They also said they'd sue my face off if I tried to distribute it."

"Why didn't they want to press charges?"

"Because she loves him."

"Hold up." I put my hands together in a T shape, calling for a time out. "Is she still sleeping with him?"

"Yes."

"What?!" Sutton cries.

I put my hand on her arm. "Baby, you gotta stop shouting. For real. We're in a public place."

"Fuck that. What?!" she repeats loudly. "He's been sleeping with her for the last two years?"

"According to her, yes," McKay confirms.

"Oh. My. God," Sutton chants slowly. She looks at me with so much anger, I feel honestly a little afraid for Eric. "I want you to hit him again, please. And this time, *kill him.*"

"Okay. Again," I say calmly, "public place. Watch what you say. I'm already in legal trouble with this guy. I don't need people standing up as witnesses saying they heard me plotting his murder with you and McKay."

Sutton looks hopefully to McKay. "Do we need Liana to press charges to have him arrested for this?"

"With the video evidence, no. He would be arrested whether she wants him to be or not."

"What's the maximum penalty if he's convicted?"

"If it's a misdemeanor, which it might be considering she was almost eighteen and there was no physical force," McKay explains, "he could get a maximum of a year in prison and/or a thousand dollar fine."

"I'm a little insulted that the fine for punching this asshole in the face and the fine for having sex with an underage girl are the same," I tell them angrily. "I just want that noted."

Sutton runs her cold hand up and down my arm, giving me a sympathetic look. "I know, babe. It's not right."

"None of this is."

"So, what's our next move?" she asks us both. "Do we use it to make him back down or do we turn him in?"

McKay takes his laptop and shoves it back in his bag. "That's up to you. I have to get back to the studio to rescue the show from my assistant. Let me know what you decide."

"McKay, wait." Sutton stands just as he does. She comes around the table, surprising him with a hug. "Thank you for this."

He pats her on the back with one hand, grinning mildly. "Anytime, Sutton."

When she lets him go, I offer him my hand. "Thanks, man."

"Yep."

McKay leaves as abruptly as he showed up. Sutton and I sit down slowly, looking at each other with questioning eyes.

"What do we want to do?" she asks.

I shake my head, unsure. "I don't know. I don't feel right using his crime to negate mine."

"Two wrongs don't make a right? Right?" she laughs weakly.

"No," I chuckle. "And I don't want to be like him. I don't want to use that girl."

"Me neither."

Sutton stares at her drink, frowning sadly. "We're right back where we started, aren't we?"

"Yeah. Looks like it."

"I think we should release the tape," she says

suddenly, her voice rich with conviction. "I think that if you're going to face the consequences of what you did, so should he. I know it won't stop him from pressing charges against you, and yeah, maybe you'll get the max penalty and everything will go to hell, but at least we'll see him burn too. And that has to count for something. At least if he goes down for this, it could stop him from doing it to another girl. He's obviously a predator and a mindfucker. He had me so turned around, I didn't know up from down, and he's definitely got her on the chain too. Who knows, there might be others out there we don't know about."

"You didn't know about Liana," I agree.

"And she probably didn't know about me. She wouldn't have stood for it. Not if she really loves him like she says."

"Okay, but are we doing it for the right reasons or are we doing it for vengeance?"

"Can't it be both?" she asks hopefully.

I smile at her devilish, angelic face. "How about this?" I take her hand firmly in mine. "I'll do it for the right reason. You do it for the wrong reason. And together, we'll have all of our bases covered."

"Like yin and yang."

"Chocolate and vanilla."

"Beef and broccoli."

"I am so hungry," I groan. "Can we get dinner soon? I'm dying here."

"Can we do it *after* we turn in a criminal and crush our enemy like a bug?"

"How about before, but we'll get it to go."

She smiles fondly. "I love the way your mind works."

"And I love you," I tell her seriously. She hesitates, her smile fading into something softer. A gentle gasp between her pink lips that makes me weak in all the right ways. "I love absolutely everything about you, Sutton."

Her smile finds strength again. Her lips find mine, and she sighs against them in a contented whisper that feels like life breathing into my body.

"I love you too, Shane."

EPILOGUE

SUTTON

July 4th
Soldier Stadium
Chicago, IL

It's official. I don't like football.

Seeing Shane getting pummeled over and over by the largest men I've ever seen in my life is not my idea of fun on a sunny Wednesday afternoon. He said it would be fun, but he was wrong. Dead wrong. I worry every time his ass hits the ground. I think this is the time he's not getting up again. They'll wheel him off the field and he'll disappear down the dark tunnel before he comes out dead on the other side. This place is a chocolate factory and Willy Wonka is a psycho. No one gets out alive.

It doesn't help that I'm actually on the field watching. I think the stands would have been better. I wouldn't be so close to the action. I wouldn't hear the smacks and the grunts and the things they say to each other. I'm from New York and some of this shit is new even to me. I'm almost impressed.

"You get used to it," Lilly tells me consolingly.

She's been my rock all afternoon. Normally she sits in the stands with Sloane and the other girlfriends and wives, but Sloane stayed at the hotel with the baby because the heat was just too much for the little guy and I had to be on the field to sing the National Anthem before the game started. Lilly offered to go with me and be my guide, and I couldn't be more grateful to her. She's been really good to me the last few weeks. I've basically been living with Shane in the apartment under her and Colt, and she's become the first girlfriend I've ever had that's my age. Either Lilly is the exception to all the rules or my mother lied to me about what backstabbing bitches women are. Then again, I don't have anything that Lilly wants. If we were in competition together, maybe she'd suck. I guess we'll never know.

It felt good to sing in front of an audience again. I haven't done it in so long, my hands were shaking. I practiced all week until Shane was sick of hearing it and he begged me to stop. He told me I was perfect. I told him to get bent, no one is perfect, and I needed to practice. He politely disappeared upstairs with Colt and Lilly to let me have my meltdown in private. Sometimes a girl needs to freak herself out to calm herself down. It's good that he can accept that.

"I can't imagine ever getting used to this," I tell Lilly doubtfully.

"Just wait until you see a real game."

"What do you mean? This isn't a real game?"

"It's a preseason game. It doesn't count for anything. They do it for practice and to get the legs under the rookies. The guys are going easy on each other because no one wants to get injured for nothing."

"So none of this matters?"

She bobs her head back and forth. "Yes and no. They want the practice. They've been off for months. It's good to get back into the grind and see how the team meshes with it's new players. But if they win or lose, it doesn't count against their regular season record."

"And that record is what gets them to the Super Bowl again?"

"Bowl again?"

She smiles excitedly. "If we play our cards right,

yeah. We're favored to go again."

"How many games do they play in a year?"

"Sixteen."

"And Shane will be in all of them?"

"He's one of our best players. He better be in all of them."

"Wow," I mutter in disbelief. I flinch as the line collides again. Shane shoves a guy back three steps before knocking him straight on his back. "What have I gotten myself into?"

Lilly chuckles lightly. "Like I said. You get used to it."

I guess I should be happy that I'll have to. It's a relief for all of us to see Shane on the field. It was touch and go for a while with the Assault charges from Eric, but once we gave the video of him and Liana to the police, Eric's credibility went out the window. Yes, everyone saw Shane hit him. No one was denying that. But when it came time to go in front of a judge, Eric's testimony that he was the victim was somewhat tainted by the fact that just a week before, he had been convicted of a misdemeanor count of Statutory Rape. It was especially damning when I went on the stand and told the judge the unwilling nature of our relationship. I consented to sex with him, I admitted that, but I made it clear that he was a predator looking for weaknesses in young women. It established a pattern he couldn't talk his way out of.

Eric was fired from *DNA* once the Liana video got out. The day after his replacement took the helm, he offered me my spot back as one of the dancers. I agonized over it for a few days before politely declining. I decided it's time to get back to theater instead. I can't be as big as I once was, but I can be happy. Thanks to Shane, I'm realizing that's worth just a little more than applause. I'm in rehearsals now for a production of *Rear Window* that's looking at a run through the summer. Maybe an extension through the end of the year if it does well. I'm excited every day when I get up to go to work and I can't remember the last time I had that feeling. It's amazing and scary, but I'm leaning into it. I refuse to let fear hold me back anymore. It's an easy stance to take when you have a man like Shane behind you.

The judge gave Shane the maximum fine of a thousand dollars. That was it. The charge is on his record forever now, but he said that's fair. He wasn't innocent. He shouldn't have gotten off free and clear. Shane went ahead and paid his fine, then donated another fifty-thousand dollars to a local women's shelter because he's a good man. He's a unicorn. He's magic in motion.

When the game is over and the Kodiaks have crushed the Bears, we stay for a fireworks show over the stadium. Shane lays out a blanket on the field for us. I eat a hotdog made from real meat, or as real as hotdog meat gets, and I don't throw it up. We share a warm beer. We chat with other players and their girlfriends and wives. We watch kids run around wildly. We laugh when a little boy throws off his diaper and streaks the field in front of everyone. We're a family there under the dusk.

When the show starts, I lay down on my back next to Shane and watch as the sparks fly overhead. Debris rains down on us, making me snuggle harder into his side to avoid being hit as he laughs at me quietly.

"It's not funny," I laugh. "I could lose an eye."

"How is it better if I do?"

"My face is my job, Shane."

"But will you still love me when I'm disfigured from a flaming piece of Chinese plastic?"

"I mean… I'll try," I answer halfheartedly.

He puts his hand under my shirt to tickle my stomach mercilessly.

"Stop!" I laugh, trying to squirm away. It's useless. He's too strong and he has me trapped in his arms. Against his chest. "Stop, stop, stop, stop."

"Say you'll still love me. Say it!"

"I'll love you forever," I giggle breathlessly. "Even if you look like mashed potatoes."

"With gravy?"

"And bacon bits!"

He stops his assault, fully satisfied. "That's all I wanted to hear."

I breathe heavily, still snickering quietly. People are staring. Some are smiling. Some are glaring. I don't care either way. For the first time in my life, I don't give a shit about my audience. All I care about is the thunderous heartbeat in this mountain of a man who holds me tightly, kisses me softly, and loves me absolutely. I've never known comfort like this. I've never laid under the sky with my heart so full it wells up in my eyes and makes me glad to be alive. Knowing Shane is living a whole new life for me. It's one I never dreamed I could have because it looks fake from the outside. Real love is too good to be true so people tell themselves that it's not. You can't understand it until you have it. Until it's in every breath you take.

"I love you, baby," Shane sighs contentedly.

In every song you sing.

"I love you too," I whisper in wonder.

In every step of the dance that is life being lived out loud.

ABOUT THE AUTHOR

Tracey Ward is from Eugene, Oregon where she attended the University of Oregon (Go Ducks!). She published her first book in 2015 and has been adding to her library ever since with books in both the YA and Contemporary Romance genres.

To find more of her work, visit her website – www.traceywardauthor.com

www.ingramcontent.com/pod-product-compliance
Lightning Source LLC
Chambersburg PA
CBHW071537030726
47598CB00001B/136